New York Times & USA Today Bestselling Author

CYNTHIA EDEN

CHAPTER ONE

"There's a killer on the loose."

At that ever-so-dramatic statement, Odin Shaw slowly lifted his head from the comic book that he'd been reading. A gorgeous woman stood in the doorway, one delicate hand clutching the wooden frame, the other pressed to her chest.

He hadn't heard her approach. His bad. Unusual. Normally, he was highly aware of his surroundings. It had been one hell of a slow Friday for him, and he'd just been about to head down to the bar that waited below—

"Did you hear me?" She let go of the doorframe and hurried inside. A couple of fast steps in her canvas shoes that didn't make even a whisper of sound. "There's a killer hunting, and we need to stop him."

He eased the comic book into the top drawer. Squared his shoulders and tipped back his head as he studied her.

His mystery lady had a tumble of thick curls. She'd tried to pin them up, but the dark locks had slid free to frame her face. No makeup was on her face, but she didn't need any. He thought she looked perfect just as she was. Wide, dark eyes. Oval face. Full, unpainted lips.

She was small, maybe around five-foot-four or five-foot-five. Nice curves. Actually, some pretty incredible curves and—

"Hello?" She waved a hand in front of his face. "Are you listening to me at all?"

Right. He should speak. Odin cleared his throat. "I don't believe you have an appointment," he rumbled.

Her pretty mouth parted. "I—" She looked back over her shoulder. "No one was in the lobby. I thought I could come on in. Figured no line meant no wait." Now she peered back at him. "Are you Warren Channing?"

"No."

She blinked. Her eyes weren't just brown. They were golden brown. He liked the gold. Liked the warmth in her gaze and he liked the long, long dark lashes that framed her eyes.

"If you're not Warren, then who are you?" She took another step forward. This step brought her to his desk. Her hands—small, with short nails painted a soft pink—pressed to the wood.

"Odin." His name came out sounding like a growl.

Her eyebrows rose. "Battle god."

He stiffened.

"Responsible for the creation—and also the destruction—of the world. At least according to Norse myth." Her smile was quick, and, holy fuck, she had dimples. Sweet dimples that winked at him before she confessed, "I'm a mythology buff. I actually teach history at the college down the road and I—I am rambling." She blew out a breath. "Odin."

He nodded. *That's me.*

Her head tilted. "I talk a lot when I'm nervous. You should know that I am very, very nervous right now."

He thought she was very, very gorgeous.

"Since you are sitting in the office at Trouble for Hire, I take it to mean that you're a PI?"

"I am." His license was all new and shiny.

"You...work with Warren?"

"Honeymoon."

A furrow appeared between those pretty eyes of hers. Hell. Had he just given her a one-word answer? He needed to do better than this.

Odin rose.

And those eyes of hers—they widened.

Damn. He'd forgotten. He'd been sitting. When he stood, he clocked in at past six-foot-four. And with his muscled weight, he could be intimidating.

She backed up a step.

No *could be* about it. He was scaring the pretty lady. "War is on his honeymoon."

"War?" She was almost gaping up at him.

"Warren—War. He's on his honeymoon. I'm running things."

She licked her lips.

His body instantly jolted. A rather over-the-top reaction to such a simple motion, but it *had* been a long time since he'd—

"I want you," she said.

Well, that was blunt. And surprising. But he nodded and figured if his luck was about to turn around this way, then who the hell was he to argue? After the clusterfuck of the last year, maybe he deserved something good.

The lady in front of him definitely qualified as *good*.

She shoved her hand into the oversized bag that was flung over her left shoulder. When her hand came back up, she tossed a thick—very thick—wad of cash on his desk. "Will that cover it?"

He looked at the cash. Then at her. "What all do you want me doing?"

"I want you to help me stop the killer!" Her breath huffed out. "I need to hire you. That should cover your fee, right?"

He suspected that hunk of cash would cover a dozen PI fees. He pushed the cash back toward her. "Why don't we start at the beginning?" Because he wasn't going to take advantage of her. That wasn't how he'd been raised. The woman was obviously upset about something. He would figure out what it was and try to help.

"The beginning? That's kinda far back. How about we cut to the current situation?" She squared her delicate shoulders. "I saw on the news that your office stopped that killer a few weeks ago. The man who was strangling those women in Florida."

Yes, they had stopped him. Odin waited.

"You don't talk a lot, do you?" She nibbled on her lower lip.

Odin shrugged. When he talked, he had a tendency to sometimes say the wrong shit. Especially where women were concerned. This woman was fucking *beautiful,* and he was trying to not open his mouth and say something like—

"And you're really big. Like, scary big."

He glowered. Then realized his glower probably just made him look even scarier.

"I mean that in the best possible way, of course," she continued quickly. Perkily. "I bet the bad guys see you and immediately start running." She nodded and now seemed thrilled. "If they're smart, they'd run."

His gaze swept over her. She wasn't running. Didn't seem at all put off by him. And damn it all, but he was finding her...intriguing.

The evening was definitely looking up. "Who are you?" He wanted her name.

Her golden brown eyes gleamed even more. "I didn't tell you? I am so sorry!" She offered her hand to him. Silver rings were on two of her fingers, and a little bracelet jingled around her wrist. "I'm Maisey. Maisey Bright." Her dimples winked. "And you are the answer to my dreams."

I would love to hear all about your dreams, lady. He took her hand in his. Made sure to keep his grip easy because his bear-like hand easily swallowed hers. The moment he touched her, a surge of heat zipped through his fingers, down his arm, and straight to his core. Her skin was soft, silky, and her scent reached out to wrap around him. A creamy, decadent scent. Like strawberries and cream. Or strawberries and—

He was leaning toward her. Closing in and his gaze had dropped to her mouth. Okay, sure, it had been a while, but he needed to get himself under control. Odin forced his hand to let her go. "Why don't you sit down?"

"Okay." She hopped onto the edge of his desk.

He frowned.

"Oh. You didn't mean here, did you? But the couch is way over there." She motioned vaguely as one shoe swung in a quick rhythm. "Look, let's cut to the chase."

That sounded like a great idea. He slowly lowered back into his chair. He couldn't take his gaze off her.

"You stopped a killer before. You and your partner, I guess? War? I like that name way better than Warren, by the way. Sounds a lot tougher."

He just waited.

She sucked in a breath. "I'm desperate, you see. That's why I pulled all of that money out of my savings and I came here." She lowered her voice. "I know some PIs like to deal only in cash."

They did? Since when?

"If you don't take the case, I will go to someone else. But after I saw your agency on the news, and since you have such great experience in my particular area of concern, I thought you'd be the best fit for me."

He would *not* imagine how they would fit together. He could be professional. He normally *was* professional.

His gaze dipped over to her swinging foot.

"You stopped one serial killer, so I know you will be able to stop another."

His gaze flew back to her face. "What?"

She gave an encouraging nod of her head. "You can stop this guy, too. With my help, we can get him locked away in no time. The streets—and my neighborhood—will be safe again."

He was trying to follow along. Odin hadn't had a drop to drink from the bar downstairs. Totally sober, but...still confused. "You have a serial killer in your neighborhood?" Was that what Maisey was trying to tell him?

She leaned closer. Her hands flattened on the desk. "Yes."

He shook his head.

She nodded. "Not just in my neighborhood." Her voice dropped as if to reveal a secret. "He lives right next door to me."

Odin stared into her gleaming eyes. Let his gaze sweep over her beautiful face. A few more tendrils of hair had escaped to slide around her cheekbones. "Look," he began gruffly. "I'm sure you got scared after all the news stories started circulating, but there aren't serial killers clustering in the streets. You are perfectly fine and—"

"I'm not crazy."

He didn't remember using the c-word. He'd carefully avoided that word. War had told him it was bad for business and to not use it, no matter what clients might say when they strode through his office door.

"Is that what you think?" Maisey's voice notched up. "That I saw what happened to those other women and I got scared and started imagining things? That I am imagining a serial killer next door?"

He had considered that option, yes.

Her eyes narrowed. "You're just like the cops."

No, he wasn't. He didn't have a badge. He had a PI license. "You, ah, went to the cops with this story?"

She jumped off the desk. Began to pace. "They didn't believe me, either. Why not?" She swung back toward him. "Do I give off some vibe that says I'm delusional? Because I am not delusional, I assure you of that. I know what is happening. I *know* I am on to something dangerous, and I just need concrete proof." She pointed at him. "That is where you come in."

"Me?"

"You." She nodded. "You'll help me find irrefutable evidence that the cops can't deny." She started pacing again. Fast, determined strides.

"Irrefutable evidence...that your neighbor is a serial killer." His head tilted as he studied her. She was quite fascinating to watch. The faded jeans she wore clung lovingly to a truly world-class ass.

Not that he was supposed to be noticing things like that. *Don't focus on a client's ass.* He was sure that was probably one of War's rules for the office.

"Exactly! Undeniable proof that he is guilty!" She spun and beamed at him. "So we have an agreement? You'll take my case?"

He offered her a strained smile in return but said, "No."

The wattage on her killer grin dimmed. "Excuse me?"

"Do you watch true crime movies?" His fingers began to tap against the edge of the desk.

"Well, sure, who doesn't?"

"And let me guess…whodunits, are those your favorite books?" More tapping.

"I love Agatha Christie. Is that some kind of sin?"

Nope. No sin. His fingers kept tapping. "Do you listen to murder podcasts?"

Her chin jerked up. "I might have my own podcast. So what if I do?"

He nodded and his fingers stilled. "I get it. That's popular these days. And with the shows and podcasts saying killers are everywhere…you started seeing them…everywhere."

Her jaw hardened. "I'm not seeing them everywhere." She stalked back toward him. "I'm seeing one killer—one particular killer—right next door. I want you to help me prove that he's guilty."

"Yeah, that's the part I'm getting stuck on."

"Stuck?"

He tried to be delicate. Not really his strong suit, but he made an effort. "I can't take your money for something I might not be able to do. Just wouldn't be right. Not ethical, you get me?"

"Come again?" Judging by her expression, she obviously did not get him.

"Say I take the case. I start investigating. Only I discover that your neighbor is just some normal Joe and not a secret killer who is hacking up people in his basement."

"He doesn't have a basement," she mumbled.

Not the point. "If I find out you don't have Dexter next door, then you'll have lost your savings." His gaze darted to the wad of money still on his desk. "I wouldn't feel good about that."

"Why not? I'd feel great."

She...what? He narrowed his eyes as he studied her. He could not figure out this woman. *So much for tact.*

"If you can prove I'm wrong, that's fabulous. Wonderful." She skirted around his desk. He turned to face her, and the legs of his chair squeaked. "I will be able to sleep at night," Maisey continued as she came to a halt inches from him. "I'll stop feeling like I might be next on his hit list. Take the case. Guilt or innocence—that's what we're proving. You have real experience at this—"

Not so much. He'd handled *one* serial killer case, and he'd primarily worked in the background on it. She was under the way wrong impression. He tried to correct the situation. "I, uh—"

"Your agency stopped the last killer that terrorized this state." She was directly in front of him. Her delectable scent surrounded Odin. "With your experience and my enthusiasm—"

The lady had plenty of enthusiasm, all right. He'd definitely give her points for that.

She leaned forward and put her hands down on the arms of his chair. "We can do this!"

He knew what he wanted to do. It involved leaning forward and kissing that delectable mouth of hers.

Not what she was trying to hire him to do.

"Help me," Maisey entreated. Her voice was husky and her gaze was so deep and Odin didn't want to look away. He *couldn't* look away. "What do you have to lose? I am paying you, *and* you just might bag a killer. Double win."

He searched her eyes. Considered the situation. "If I tell you no, what will you do?"

Her lips pressed together. Then, "Don't tell me no." Almost a plea.

"What will you do?" Odin pushed.

She swallowed. Straightened. "I will find another PI. I told you that already. I won't give up. You might think I'm being overzealous..."

A bit. Yes. Nice word to describe her. *Overzealous.*

"The cops might think I'm imagining things, but I know what's happening. I won't stop. I will keep going until I can get someone who will help me."

Odin frowned. "There are some seriously shady PIs out there." Understatement. One she should have already realized. "You can't just trust anyone you meet."

"That's why I came here. I came to the best. At least, that's what the reporter on the news said about Trouble for Hire." A pause. "What if I show you the perp? Will you at least come with me and check things out to see what you think of him before you turn me down?"

He thought it was a bad idea. A waste of time. Odin wasn't going to look at some random guy and magically change his mind. This was a BS case.

"I'll pay you to come with me. Please. Come to my house. See the evidence I have. It's circumstantial—thus the need for the whole *concrete, irrefutable* evidence hunt—but it still makes for a compelling argument. Come and just consider it, will you? After that, if you still want to tell me no, then fine, do it."

He intended to do just that. He intended to tell her that this was not going to work. He didn't need to go to her house. He didn't need to see her evidence or meet the neighbor. He didn't need to do any of that stuff. There was no way this woman's neighbor was a serial killer. It wasn't like serial killers were thick on the ground. One of them had just been apprehended in the area, and the chances of another being on the loose in Pensacola, Florida, at the same time? Astronomically unlikely. Things like that didn't happen.

He should give the pretty lady back her money. Tell her a polite—but firm—no and send Maisey on her way. That was absolutely what he should do. But Odin stared into those incredible eyes of hers and heard himself say, "What the hell? Nothing else is on my schedule for the night."

Her face lit up.

Absolutely fucking gorgeous.

Odin knew that he had probably just crossed some serious PI line. He was sure there was a rule about not taking a case just because you thought the client was mega hot. But...

It was a slow evening.

And he'd never really enjoyed following *all* the rules. In fact, if his buddy War wasn't currently sunning it up on a honeymoon in the Keys, War would probably tell him...some rules were made to be broken.

***

He was perfect.

Better than any dream she'd had. As Maisey Bright stood beside her car and waited for Odin Shaw to park his black Jeep, she tried not to jump with absolute joy.

He was big, he was muscled, and he was *fierce*. One look into those glittering blue eyes of his, and every drop of moisture had dried from her mouth. She'd stood in the doorway of that PI office, stared at a face that was all hard lines and planes, and she'd barely been able to catch her breath.

Odin looked tough. The sexy kind of tough that said he could take care of business without breaking a sweat. He could kick ass, solve crimes, and get the bad guys tossed in a jail cell in no time. She bet fear wasn't part of his vocabulary. She bet that he knew a dozen ways to disable an attacker. She bet that he—

"Are we just going to stand here all night?"

He was right in front of her and she'd been daydreaming again. It was just hard not to fantasize when someone like Odin appeared. She wondered how long he'd been standing there on the sidewalk. For the sake of her pride, she really hoped it hadn't been longer than a minute...or three.

"Our suspect lives next door." She turned and pointed to the right—

He grabbed her hand. His hold was incredibly gentle, but she could feel the calluses on his fingers. *Probably from his workout regimen.*

"Don't point," he rasped as he pulled her a little closer to him. "Not like we want to give the guy a head's up that we're talking about him. You never know if he's watching."

Wait, did Odin believe her? It sounded as if he might. Joy had her nearly shaking. *Finally*.

She tilted her head back and peered up at him. Next to Odin, she felt small. *Delicate*. The man had muscles and strength pouring from him.

Try not to drool.

"Is it just the two of you on this street?" His gaze swept the area even as he kept a hold on her hand. "I thought you said you wanted to keep the neighborhood safe."

"Yes, well, it *will* be a neighborhood. But for now, we're the only two with completed houses." Thick woods surrounded their street. Beyond the woods, a swamp waited. She'd heard the croaks from the gators out there plenty of times.

The woods and the swamp—they were perfect for anyone who wanted to hide a body.

Like my neighbor...

Maisey suspected Clay had bought his house just for the location. It was a serial killer's dream.

"Come inside," she told Odin quickly. "I have a murder board set up in the guest room."

"A murder board?"

She pulled her hand from his grip and tried to ignore the way her fingers were doing a weird little tingle. "Yes, you know, a board where I put up all of my evidence so I can keep track of all the players and events." She hurried toward her front door. "Detectives use them quite frequently in homicide investigations."

"Do they now."

It didn't exactly sound like a question. She slanted him a suspicious glance over her shoulder before hurriedly unlocking her door. The alarm began to beep, so Maisey hustled forward and shut it off.

Odin closed the door behind them. "You've made several mistakes so far."

She paused on her way to the hall.

"Mistake one." His voice was grim. "Don't invite a strange man into your home and then let him watch you type in your alarm code. If I come back when you aren't here, I'll know the code. I'll have access to you."

Her heart lurched in her chest. But she shook her head. "You aren't a strange man. You're—*we're* working together." They were partners. A crime-solving team. "The cops and the press both endorsed your agency. I did research on Warren—War—before I stepped foot in that office. He's a decorated war hero." Hardly some dangerous criminal.

"I'm not War. You don't know me."

Her shoulders stiffened. His voice was deep and dark. It was a voice that seemed to rumble right through her. Maisey forced herself to turn and glance back at him. "Should I be afraid of you?"

"Yes." An immediate reply.

Her breath left her in a startled rush. "That wasn't the answer I expected! I *hired* you!" Why was he now trying to scare her? Shouldn't he be reassuring her that she'd made a great investment?

"I warned you..." He closed in with slow, deliberate steps. "You can't trust every PI you meet. You can't trust *anyone* you meet. If I've learned anything from my time with War, it's that people are never who you think they are. Evil hides in plain sight."

He was *trying* to scare her. Looking all big and intimidating and keeping his expression extra fierce. But the man didn't understand who he was dealing with. "I know evil hides everywhere. How do you think I realized what my neighbor was? I've learned to look beneath the surface." She'd *had* to look beneath the surface. Growing up as she had, there hadn't exactly been a lot of options for her.

If you wanted to find the truth, you had to dig it up for yourself. Often...literally.

"Mistake two..."

Her spine snapped even straighter. As if that small movement would miraculously give her more height so Odin didn't loom over her with his immense form.

"No weapon." His lips thinned. "You're alone with me, and you're completely defenseless."

She was most certainly not defenseless. "There's a lamp two feet away. I could always grab it and slam it into your head." If he tried anything funny with her, she'd jump up and ram that baby at him.

His gaze darted to the lamp, then back to her. "Try it," Odin dared. "Let's see what happens."

Was he serious? "You want me to slam a lamp into your head?"

"I want you to realize that what you're doing isn't a game! You can't just go up to some strange man and invite him in your place—"

"Oh, is that what this is about?" Relief rushed through her. "If it makes you feel better, I don't invite strange men home. Not my style. So you don't have to worry about me heading out to the bar scene and picking up a random guy." She gave him a reassuring pat on the chest. "Thanks for worrying about me, though. It's sweet." Maisey turned away. "Now let me show you the murder—"

"I am *not* sweet."

He sounded offended. Men. "Fine. You're salty. Better?" Her steps quickened as she passed her bedroom and turned for the door on the right. She swung it open and—

Stopped. Stared in shock.

The board was...empty.

She felt Odin move in behind her. Actually felt the air shift as he drew closer. "Huh," he said. "That your evidence? Because it's a little...not there."

Maisey couldn't move. "There were pictures. Maps. Printed copies of old newspapers and victim statements." This couldn't be happening. "He *took* it all." Anger poured through her as Maisey took three frantic steps forward.

Odin's hand closed around her shoulder. "You're saying someone broke in?"

"I'm saying all my evidence is gone!" Wait—maybe not all. She whirled back toward him. Shot *past* him and ran for her bedroom. Her laptop was in there. She had backup files on the laptop. She could show that info to Odin.

"If someone broke into your house, we should call the cops."

The cops. They should definitely talk about the cops and contacting them. But first—her laptop.

She raced into her bedroom. Odin's steps followed slowly behind her. Maisey headed straight for her favorite reading chair. She'd left the laptop there and it was—

Gone.

Her breath shuddered in and out. "He took it all."

"Um...Maisey?"

She jerked her gaze off the chair. Forced herself to turn toward him. "My laptop is gone. The evidence on my murder board is gone. He took everything."

Odin didn't speak. Just stared at her with inscrutable blue eyes, and she realized—

Maisey stumbled back a step. "You don't believe me?"

"Don't believe that your next door neighbor is a killer? Or don't believe that he broke in here— disabled your alarm, stole your murder board info and your laptop before *resetting* your alarm and slipping out? You're gonna need to be specific about what you think I *don't* believe."

"All of the above," she whispered. She had to blink because the room had just gone blurry. Blurry because she had tears of frustration and fear filling her eyes. No one believed her. Not even Odin. "I had all the material here," she told him.

Her voice trembled. So did her hands. Maisey balled them into fists. "Everything was here." She knew what had happened. "He must have realized I was on to him. He slipped inside and took it all." Now, without the promised information, she looked even crazier. Dammit.

"Do you have security cameras?" Odin asked her, voice expressionless.

"No."

"Any sort of tracking device on your laptop?"

She shook her head. Swiped away a tear. "I am not lying. All of this is real."

"If you've had a home invasion, we should call the cops."

"They aren't going to believe me." Frustration burned through her. "You're my PI, and you don't even believe me!"

He edged closer to her. Studied her with those bright blue eyes of his. His hand rose, and the back of his knuckles carefully skimmed her cheek.

He's wiping away my tears.

That just made everything worse. Made her feel even more miserable because on top of everything else, hot and sexy Odin *pitied* her. "Don't," she bit out.

He stiffened.

"Maybe you should just go," Maisey mumbled. Because there was no way she could prove her story at this point. Everything was gone. She'd have to start over at square one. *This time, I'll have a backup for my backup.* Keeping the info on her computer hadn't been good enough.

"You need to call the cops," Odin insisted.

He didn't get it. "They won't believe me."

"Doesn't matter if they do or not. They'll dust for fingerprints. Maybe find some evidence. You have to report your laptop as missing."

"No." A rough exhalation of air. "I had a break-in here a month ago, and they didn't find any evidence. They don't routinely look for prints, just so you know." That was a big misconception, one she'd had, too. "The cop who came told me this wasn't *CSI*."

His eyebrows lifted.

"Prints can't be pulled from all surfaces. And the cop told me they usually only dust if they have someone that they can compare the prints to." *Hello, like my neighbor*. But the cop hadn't listened to that explanation from her.

"Back up. You've had *two* break-ins recently?"

She nodded. This one made two.

Odin's jaw hardened. "We're calling the cops. They're checking the scene."

"But—"

"I'm *your* PI, remember? Isn't that what you just said?"

She had said that, yes. Maisey sniffed.

"Then do what I tell you. Call the cops. First order of business is to get the theft on record. Then we go from there."

Her breath caught. "Wait. Do you believe me?" Hope was struggling to flare to life again.

His gaze drifted over her face. "I'm your PI," he said slowly, voice growling. "And we're going to figure this shit out."

That was not a resounding, *oh, hell, yes, I believe you*. But she'd still take it. Gladly take it.

Without another thought, Maisey threw her body against Odin. Her arms wrapped around him—tried to, anyway. "Thank you," she whispered.

He was tense and felt rather like a muscled wall against her.

But...

His hand awkwardly patted her shoulder. "You're welcome."

He'd given her hope. Did Odin get how important that was? She had her own PI now. And together, they *were* going to stop the serial killer next door.

CHAPTER TWO

The swirl of blue lights lit up the exterior of Maisey's house. The two uniformed cops had finished their search, and just as Maisey had predicted, they hadn't turned up much. They'd been helpful enough. Even promised to patrol more in the area.

One guy had even said he'd try to get a crime scene tech out the next day...

But neither fellow had seemed to think the crime would be solved. They'd asked for the serial number of her laptop. Told her that they'd check the local pawn shops. Then they'd gotten a call to another scene.

That call had led to the currently flashing lights as they prepared to rush away.

A twig snapped behind Odin. He didn't move.

"Is everything all right?" A male voice called as Maisey's neighbor closed in. "I saw the police lights, and I was afraid something had happened to Maisey!"

Slowly, Odin turned his head to look at the man. Tall, leanly muscled. Dressed in khaki pants and a white, dress shirt, with the sleeves rolled up to his elbows. Clean-cut. Sounding appropriately concerned. Looking it, too, as the blue lights darted over his face.

"She's fine," Odin assured him. "Just had a break-in."

"A break-in?" The man took a lurching step toward Maisey's house. "I should go check on her!"

Odin moved into his path. "Yeah...no." He crossed his arms over his chest.

The guy jerked to a halt. "Who are you?"

I'm her PI. "Maisey's special friend."

"What?"

"I'll be helping her out tonight." A pause. "Don't think I caught your name." His gaze scanned over the neighbor. A thorough scan from the guy's head to his slightly dirty dress shoes.

The neighbor craned to peer around Odin. "Didn't catch yours, either."

"Odin." A pause. "Did you catch it?" He pushed a hint of steel into his voice. A hint of...*stop looking at her and deal with me, asshole.*

The man's head turned back to him. "I did." Flat. "And I'm Clay. Clay Prescott."

"Were you home tonight, Clay?"

"Why?" Suspicious. Guarded.

Odin shrugged. "Because I thought you might have seen the jerk who broke into Maisey's home."

Clay glanced back over his shoulder, toward his place. "I wasn't home."

"Huh. Too bad. If you'd been here, you might have been able to spot the intruder."

Clay's attention shifted back to him. "I didn't see anything. I just got back a few minutes ago. I didn't—*Maisey!*"

Now he did lunge around Odin and rush toward Maisey. Clay sure seemed eager to get close to her. As he approached, Odin saw Maisey stiffen.

Clay lifted his hands, as if he'd touch her—*hell, no, don't you dare*—but he froze awkwardly before actually making contact. "Uh, are you ok?"

Maisey's gaze flew toward Odin. Then back to Clay. "Fine."

She sounded anything but fine.

"Your friend..." Clay jerked his thumb toward Odin. "He said you had a break-in."

"Yes." Soft.

Odin sidled away from them, but he kept his eyes on Maisey. It only took him a moment to push through the bushes, to get next to the car parked in Clay's drive, and to touch the hood...

Ice cold.

No way the guy had *just* gotten home. That made lie number one for Clay Prescott.

"What was taken?" Clay demanded to know.

Well, well. Clay was certainly the curious-slash-nosey neighbor.

The police cruiser pulled away. The lights were still flashing as the cops raced to the next scene.

Odin sidled back toward Maisey.

"My laptop," he heard her say. "A few other things." A nice, vague reply, Odin thought. Better than her saying, *"My murder board."* A sigh escaped Maisey's lips as she added, "But the laptop was the most important thing."

Clay curled his hand around her shoulder. Gave her a seemingly reassuring squeeze.

Odin's eyes narrowed. *You need to stop that shit.* A growl rumbled in his throat.

Clay's gaze immediately jumped to him.

"Don't," Odin told him flatly.

"Don't...what?"

"Don't touch what isn't yours."

Clay's eyes seemed to bulge. "Excuse me?"

"No." Odin closed in. He lifted Clay's hand *off* a visibly uncomfortable Maisey. "She doesn't want you touching her. So you *don't*."

Maisey crept closer to Odin.

Clay's gaze drifted between them. "Special friend," he muttered.

Odin inclined his head. "*Very* special. The kind of friend who gets seriously pissed when anything or anyone upsets Maisey." And he was staring straight at someone who upset her very, very much. It was time for Clay to exit the scene. But first, "Where did you say you were tonight?"

"I didn't." Clay's attention shifted back to Maisey.

The man sure seemed to enjoy staring at her. *Too much.*

Maisey's arm brushed against Odin. She was almost standing on top of his feet. She'd also gotten very quiet. When she'd come to his office, she'd been a bundle of energy and words. She'd told him that she talked a lot when she was nervous.

Apparently, when she was scared, she went dead silent. Odin made a mental note to never forget that about her.

Actually, he made a mental note to remember *everything* about her.

"Where were you?" Odin asked as he sized up Maisey's suspect.

"Why the hell do you want to know?" Clay's focus was still on Maisey.

He needed to stop that shit.

"Because you're her only neighbor," Odin replied.

Maisey caught his arm. Put it around her shoulders.

Odin stiffened. But if she wanted him holding her...

He pulled her closer.

Clay's stare finally rose to lock with his. Unfortunately, there wasn't enough light for Odin to clearly make out the guy's expression.

But I'm betting he's pissed.

"You're her only neighbor," Odin repeated smoothly. "So I thought you might have seen something useful. Coming or going from your destination, that is."

"I was out walking along the beach. Watching the sunset then taking in the stars. Like I said, I only just returned home. Didn't see anything useful." A long exhale. "I'm sorry this happened, Maisey. I keep meaning to get one of those security doorbell cameras. If I'd had one, at least I could have seen the people driving by on the street."

"Maisey will have one of those cameras installed first thing tomorrow," Odin assured him. "In fact, her whole house will be equipped with cameras. She's getting a long overdue security upgrade." His voice lowered. "This will *not* happen again."

"I'm getting an upgrade?" Maisey asked as her head turned toward him.

"Yes." He felt her stare, but his focus was on his target. "Thanks for being neighborly," he said to Clay. "But I've got Maisey from here on out."

Clay didn't take the hint. In fact, he leaned toward Maisey, even as she stood in Odin's arms. "If you need me, remember, I'm right next door." His voice deepened as Clay added, "I can come to you anytime, day or night."

For some reason, those last few words...

I can come to you anytime, day or night.

They felt like a threat.

They even *sounded* like one.

So Odin responded as if they *were* one. "The hell you will."

Clay jerked back. "What?"

"I'll be with Maisey, day or night. So don't worry. I've got her covered." *From here on out.*

Maisey was stiff against him.

Clay slowly backed away.

Odin waited until Clay turned for his house and then—

"It's a good thing you had all the files from your laptop backed up on your computer at work," he told Maisey, making sure his voice was loud enough to carry. "That will sure help you out."

Clay paused. A barely-there pause. A barely-there stumble of his feet. Then he was hurrying for his house. Almost double-timing it to get inside.

Oh, no. Not suspicious. At all.

"Odin." Maisey's voice. Whispery. Husky. *Sensual.* "Odin, I don't have—"

He turned her in his arms. "Don't worry, baby, I'll stay the night." Again, his voice was nice and loud. He knew they had an avid audience.

Maisey gave a little start of surprise.

Odin lowered his head so that his lips were near her ear. Her delectable scent teased him. "Inside," he barely breathed the word.

She shivered.

"We'll talk...inside," he promised. His lips were so close to her that they brushed over the shell of her ear.

Another shiver shook her. But she gave a quick nod and pulled from him. Maisey nearly ran back to her house.

Odin took his time following her. Nice and slow. He let his gaze sweep over the area, and when he reached her porch, he turned toward Clay's house.

Clay was watching him. His porch light fell on Clay as he stared straight over at Odin.

Odin tossed him a wave. Then he stalked inside Maisey's home. He kicked the door shut behind him.

"OhmyGod," Maisey's voice was cracking. "What was all of that about?"

He crossed his arms over his chest. Put his back against the door. Considered his options.

Decided to go with the truth. "Your neighbor is a liar. The hood of his car was ice cold. No way he *just* arrived home."

Her eyes flared.

"He's hiding something." No, Odin wasn't jumping on the serial killer theory, but he was worried. Clay had stared at Maisey like she was a freaking bowl of sweet, warm milk, and he was a thirsty cat.

"Why did you tell him I had a backup? I don't have a backup! There is no backup for the material on my laptop!"

"He doesn't know that. And now, if he *is* our guy, he'll go after what he thinks is on the computer at your office. When he makes his move..." *If* he made a move. "We'll have him."

Her breath shuddered out. She inched toward him. "So you really believe me?" Hope glinted in her eyes.

"I believe something is happening here." Two break-ins? That was bad. No way was he leaving Maisey on her own until he sorted out what was going on with her. "Guess you convinced me, after all." Even without her murder board. He stuck out his hand. "Maisey Bright, you just hired yourself a PI."

She looked at his hand. Then at him. Even before she launched forward, Odin knew she was going to hug him again.

He didn't hate the idea. In fact, when Maisey happily launched her body at him and gave him a surprisingly strong squeeze, warmth poured through him.

Sometimes, you didn't realize quite how cold you were, not until someone offered you a little fire.

"Thank you!" Maisey exclaimed. Her head pressed to his chest. "You will not regret this, I swear it!"

His hand lifted. He'd been intending to give her a reassuring pat on the shoulder, just as he'd done before. But...

Instead...

Both of his hands moved to curl around her. To hold her. He was way bigger than her. So much stronger. But damn if he didn't feel like they fit together. Like she felt right.

"Odin?" Her head lifted. She didn't let him go. Just kept herself crushed against him. "You won't regret taking the case."

Part of him already did. Because being this close to Maisey...

Hello, torture.

And Odin knew a thing or twenty about torture.

He forced his hands to release her, but she didn't let him go. Just kept beaming up at him.

"You're a hugger," he finally said. "Got it."

Surprise flashed on her face. "Actually, I'm not." A laugh tumbled from her as Maisey's dimples peeked at him. The laugh was light and sweet and exactly what he would expect from her. All infectious and cutely disarming. "I guess I just like hugging you."

Dangerous.

That's what she was. Sweetly disarming and incredibly dangerous. Because the woman should not go around dropping bombshell statements like that to him.

"This is probably the wrong time to ask." Maisey licked her lips.

Do not react. Do not—

"But do you have a girlfriend? Wife? Any sort of significant other who would—"

"No."

Her smile expanded. "That's fabulous. Wonderful to know."

It was? Wait. Did she feel the same hot surge of attraction that he—

"This way, no one will get upset when you spend the night with me."

He focused on breathing. But her scent just got sucked into his nostrils.

"That is what you said you'd do, wasn't it? Spend the night with me?" Now she *did* let him go, and he immediately missed her warmth as he went back to being in the cold.

Her eyebrows did a fast wiggle. "I'm assuming you said that statement all extra loud so Clay would know I'd have protection tonight."

"Yes." A rasp.

"And maybe you were just bullshitting but if you could actually stay, I would feel a million times better. At least, until I get the upgraded alarm system you were talking about. Wait, was that for real, too?" Now worry flashed across her face. "But if I'm giving you all of my savings to cover the costs of the case, I won't have enough money to pay for the new alarm, too, and—"

"I'm not a bastard."

"I never thought you were." An immediate reply.

"Not some dick who takes advantage of desperate, really attractive women."

Her eyebrows didn't wiggle, but they did fly up. "Did you just call me desperate?"

Shit. He had. War would say it had been a typical Odin move. *Open mouth, insert big-ass foot.*

"And...really attractive?" She bit her lower lip. "Did you call me that, too?"

Because he didn't want to risk saying something else wrong, Odin gave a curt nod.

"That is—no man has ever told me that before."

"That you're desperate?" No, he was sure the fools hadn't. It was a dumbass thing to say. "Yeah, about that. I'm—"

"Really attractive." She gave him a quick, nervous smile. "You're the first man to tell me that."

"You're shitting me."

"Uh, no?" Her nose wrinkled. "I'm not."

He backed up a step. Took her in. Every inch of her. "You're telling me...no guy has ever said you were beautiful?"

That quick laugh came from her again. "Actually, I have been told that, but the men in question were both at bars and drinking was involved so..." Her words trailed away. "It's not like it's something that is just dropped into a casual conversation."

She'd been surrounded by idiots. Obviously. "Consider this a casual conversation."

"It...doesn't feel casual."

"Whatever." He stared straight into her eyes. "You are beautiful."

Her smile stretched.

"Probably the most gorgeous woman I've ever seen."

Now her eyes were sparkling.

"And I would love to fuck you all night long."

Her lips parted. A faint squeak emerged from her mouth.

Sonofabitch. "I should have held that last part back. I can see that now." He scraped a hand over his jaw. "My bad. Won't happen again."

Her lips were still parted. Her eyes were huge.

"Yeah, so, my conversational skills? Not always the best." Far from it. "You don't have to worry," Odin tried to reassure her. "I was just—uh, stating a fact. Kind of was on a roll and I went a little too far." He held his hands up, palms out, toward her. "You have nothing to worry about. I'm not planning to touch you, and there is zero fucking pressure."

A blink. Then another one. Her head slid to the left. "Do you mean...there is zero pressure for me while I am around you—as in, no pressure in general—or that there is zero pressure to fuck you?"

Now he raked his hand through his hair. "Both?"

More laughter.

Well, at least she was having a good time. "I'll keep my hands far away from you," he growled as both of his hands dropped to his sides. "I was just putting the truth out there. You're an attractive woman. Fucking you would be great and—dammit, I need to just stop while I am only about a mile behind." He squared his shoulders. "I'll bunk on your couch tonight. Tomorrow, I *will* get you a new alarm system installed." Time to get this runaway train back on the tracks. Time to stop talking about how much he'd love fucking her. Even though…yes, he would love it one hell of a lot. "And, no, you are not paying me separately for the upgrade. We'll sort out the bill later. The priority now is to get you safe. If the perp has been in here twice already, we don't want him going for a third shot." Because maybe on that third time when he came inside, he'd find Maisey.

Odin waited for her response.

Her warm gaze slowly drifted from the top of his head all the way down to his freaking football-field-like shoes. She shook her head. "No."

"No?" Was she calling off their partnership? Already? Just because he'd confessed that—

"You are entirely too big to ever fit on my couch. That will not happen."

His gaze cut to the couch. Oh, hell, no, not happening. "I'll take the floor."

"That will be horribly uncomfortable!"

"Trust me, I've slept on worse. Like a thousand times worse when I was in the field. Give me a pillow, and I'll think I'm in paradise."

She inched closer to him. "The field? Were you in the military like Warren—ah, War?"

Different branch from War. "I served."

She stared at him, all expectant-like. Oh. Maybe he was supposed to share more?

Maisey motioned toward him.

"I can't talk about most of it," he mumbled. "Classified."

"What were you, some super-secret black ops guy?" she teased back.

"Exactly." He wasn't teasing.

Based on the swift inhale she gave, he realized that she knew that fact, too. "SEAL?" she whispered.

"No." That had been War. A fish from day one.

She tapped her chin. Assessed him again. Nodded. "The unit."

His shoulders stiffened.

"You're Delta, aren't you? I mean, you *were*?"

He didn't reply. Neither confirmed nor denied.

"That's the army's elite group. Delta and the SEALs are the most highly trained special ops groups that Uncle Sam has. First established in 1977 by Colonel Charlie Beckwith, the ops are usually secret." She swallowed. "Supposed to be around 1200 Delta Force ops out there. The Unit. Task Force Green. They're called both and even though the US military won't officially admit that—"

"How do you know so much about Delta?"

"I'm good with research. Didn't I mention that before? I'm working to get my Ph.D., and it's not like you can get one of those without knowing how to research your ass off." Her gaze flickered away from his. "It's the research that got me into my current situation. I started on a missing person case. A personal case. Went down the rabbit hole. Couldn't find my way out." She turned away from him. Made her way to what turned out to be a closet. As he watched, she rustled around inside and pulled out a pillow and some blankets.

He didn't move as she shuffled back to him. But her gaze dipped to the items she held, and Maisey shook her head. "I can't let you sleep on the floor. Not after you've been nice enough to help me."

Nice? She had not called him that. "First sweet, now nice." Hell. "Lady, you could not be more wrong about me." Did they need to revisit the whole "fucking" part of their conversation?

"Oh, that's right." Maisey rocked back on her heels. "You like to be salty."

His eyes narrowed on her. "Are you teasing me?"

"Sorry. Yes. But it's been a crazy day and I'm kind of all over the place right now." She blew out a breath. "Why don't you take my bed? I'll take the couch."

He shook his head. "My mom raised me better than that." He tugged the pillow and blankets from her. His fingers brushed against hers.

Maisey gave a startled jerk.

Interesting. "You should check my references."

"Excuse me?"

"You're making another mistake. Just letting me stay tonight without any worries. I could be waiting until you go to sleep and then I will—"

She retreated a step. "You're back to trying to scare me."

He was back to trying to get Maisey to take precautions. "Want some references? You mentioned the news station earlier. After the serial case, War and I became friends with the station manager. You can call Simone Davis, and she can vouch for me."

Maisey pulled out her phone. Dialed the number he gave her, and after a brief talk with Simone, she nodded. Then she curled her hand around the phone as she lowered it back to her side. "I met her once. She came to an event at the college." More hair escaped to join the curls around her face. "Simone just said you can watch her ass anytime."

His lips twitched.

"But, just so you know—just so you get that I am not taking unnecessary risks—the cops on scene recognized you earlier. And I asked one for more information about you. He said you had a good reputation, that you and War were creating something strong down here. You have the endorsement of the PD. Figured that meant I could feel safe around you."

She was one hundred percent safe with him. Odin dropped the blankets and pillow onto the floor. "I'm gonna want to hear about all the information you had on your neighbor."

"Hearing isn't the same as seeing the material with your own eyes. You might just think I'm making it up as I go along."

Maybe. Maybe not. "Tell me what you've got."

"*A History of Bloody Murder and Madness.*"

"Uh, okay." Where was he supposed to go with that?

"It's the name of my podcast. I research famous unsolved crimes and talk about who I think the actual killers were. You know, like say…Jack the Ripper. No one ever actually uncovered his real identity, but in my podcast, I spent four episodes talking about who I thought he was. And, of course, there is the Lizzie Borden case. Most people just take for granted that Lizzie picked up an ax and killed her parents back in the late 1800s, but what if she didn't do it? What if someone else was behind the attack and Lizzie took the fall?"

He tried to follow along. Failed. "What do Jack the Ripper and Lizzie Borden have to do with your neighbor?"

"Nothing." Her hands twisted in front of her. "Everything."

Super clear answer. He frowned at her.

"Research. That's how I got the details about Jack and Lizzie. How I found new pieces in the puzzles. When something doesn't feel right, I can't stop. I have to keep digging and digging. Clay—he didn't *feel* right. Not from day one."

So she thought her next door neighbor was a killer because of a *feeling*?

"He got the job he has after my friend Whitney Augustine vanished. She was the head of the psych department, and one day, she just didn't show up for work. Her car was found in her driveway. Her personal belongings were still in the house, and Whitney was just…gone."

Now he held up a hand. "Back up."

She stared at him expectantly.

"You didn't mention that you *work* with Clay Prescott."

"Technically, I don't. He's psychology. I'm history. Our paths hardly ever cross but..." She shrugged. "Yes, we are at the same college."

"And you became suspicious of him after Whitney Augustine vanished."

"I was looking for her. Like I told you, she was my friend." Her lips pressed together. Then... "She wouldn't have just vanished without telling me. I mean, it's like she just fell off the face of the earth. That doesn't happen."

Sometimes it did. When you were running from someone. Or something.

"There was a packed bag found in her den. A suitcase that she used for travel. Because of that bag, the cops just assumed she'd left on her own, so they didn't spend a lot of resources looking for her." Frustration boiled in her voice. "That made zero sense! If she was leaving, she would have taken the bag. Not left it. But they said there were no signs of foul play. The trail got cold. And everyone else seemed to move on and forget about her."

Obviously, Maisey hadn't forgotten. Pain was in her voice as she spoke of her friend.

"I couldn't let it go. I started looking at her life. Trying to see if I could help her. If Whitney was in trouble, I *needed* to help her. And that's when I found him."

"Prescott?"

A quick nod. "He'd started at Dunson a few months before Whitney's disappearance. She was the one who brought him here. They had worked together at another college before Whitney moved to this area. Only...when I looked at that other school—Plymouth South, it's also located here in Florida—do you know what I found?"

He had no idea.

"The professor that Clay replaced there—Jenny Lynch—she also vanished."

His shoulders stiffened. "You have my attention."

"Right?" she exclaimed. "Because that is too big of a coincidence. This guy gets two desirable jobs because the women who'd been in those spots just vanished? Like that just randomly happens?"

Statistically, yes, that shit didn't just happen. Not twice.

"Then I looked deeper."

Of course, she had.

"When Clay was eighteen, he was dating a girl named Hannah Martinez. They'd been high school sweethearts. Until...a few days before graduation, Hannah disappeared."

Fuck.

"She was never found. Just as Jenny Lynch was never found. And my friend Whitney? It's been two months, and there has been no sign of her. I filed a missing person's report, but I swear, I don't think it's gone anywhere since the first week." Her hands had fisted. "Then Clay was promoted to Whitney's position at the college, and he moved into the neighborhood. Right next to me. And I had the first break-in. And everything just feels...*off.*"

Because everything damn well was off. Three women missing, and the common denominator was Clay? Suspicious as hell.

"I know it's circumstantial. But he has ties to the missing women. He is the only link I've found between them all. The cops said it wasn't enough. I get that I need more. But you—" She inched closer. "I have you now. You can help me to find more." Her shoulders rolled back. "Or, if I'm totally wrong, you can help me to figure that out, too. But Whitney was good to me. I can't just forget about her. I have to try. And if he is hurting women, k-killing them," she stammered a bit on that word, "then we have to stop him."

Odin stared into her eyes. What was a man supposed to do when a woman looked at him with eyes like hers? All soulful, deep? Hopeful? She was staring at him like he was some kind of damn hero, when he'd been feeling like the walking dead for months.

"I'm so glad I have you." She gave him a quick smile, one that packed the double wallop of her dimples.

Uh, yeah, when exactly was the last time someone had told him *that?*

"We'll get the truth," Odin promised. The words sounded like a vow because they were. She had faith in him. She was staring at him like he was the good guy. Asking him to save the freaking day and shit.

He'd do his best. For her.

For the friend that was missing. He'd figure out what was happening with Clay Prescott. Sure, Odin's tactics might not be the best—he might have to twist and break more rules in order to get to the truth. But, no matter what, he *would* get the job done.

Maisey rocked forward onto the balls of her feet. Judging by her expression and body language, he really, really felt like another hug was coming on. That hug would be wrong for a thousand different reasons. The main reason? If she touched him again, he'd hold on—too tightly—to her.

So Odin stepped back. Tried to remove himself from temptation.

Her long eyelashes flickered at his movement.

"Get some sleep," he ordered gruffly. "Tomorrow, we start this case."

She swallowed. "Right. Ah...thanks, again." She turned away. Hurried in those cute canvas sneakers toward her bedroom. When the door shut behind her with a soft click, Odin realized he'd been holding his breath.

He released it in a slow rush.

What in the hell am I doing?

***

She wasn't sure what woke her. One minute, Maisey had been in a deep sleep. *Maybe* having a slightly sexual dream about a big, blond Viking type who stared at her with smoldering blue eyes as he pulled her close—

But then she was jerking awake and her heart was about to burst from her chest and Maisey opened her mouth to scream because something was wrong and her instincts were going crazy and—

"Don't make a sound."

Her head whipped to the right.

A big, menacing shadow loomed beside her bed.

Screw not making a sound. She sucked in a breath and prepared to give the biggest scream of her life.

CHAPTER THREE

"Maisey. It's me." He sat on the edge of the bed.

Odin.

The big, menacing shadow was Odin. Of course, it was. And those were Odin's slightly callused fingertips closing around her wrist.

But why was Odin in her bedroom? *On* her bed?

"We've got a situation."

They did? She focused on breathing. Big, heaving breaths as her heart galloped in her chest.

"Our perp is on the move."

Her gaze cut to the bedside table. The glowing numbers on her clock told her it was 1:47 a.m. An odd time for her neighbor to be taking a drive.

"He just loaded up the back of his car with one big-ass duffel bag."

"OhmyGod." Now her hand twisted so that she was the one holding onto him. "The kind of bag that you use to hide a body?" she whispered.

"Okay, so, when I said don't make a sound, I really just meant don't scream. You don't have to whisper. It's just us."

Maisey cleared her throat and repeated, "The kind of bag that you use to hide a body?"

"Or the kind of bag you use when you've just packed up all of your shit because you know that you're suspected of a serious crime and you want to make a run for it."

Yes, fine, that, too.

"I'm going over there," Odin announced. He stood. Pulled his hand from hers. "I just didn't want you to wake up and find me gone. Didn't want you, ah, worrying or something."

She jumped out of bed, too. "You mean *we're* going over there." Her t-shirt brushed over her thighs. "Just let me get some pants." Pants. Shoes. Maybe a weapon. No, definitely a weapon. She tried to spring past him and rush toward her closet. She kept a baseball bat at the ready in there.

His arm curled around her and pulled her back against him. "Oh, fuck." He let her go as if he'd been burned. "You're not wearing a bra."

"No, I'm not. I'm wearing a t-shirt and panties because I was sleeping and I like to be comfortable while I sleep and—"

"*Fuck,*" he said again.

"Give me two minutes, and I'll be dressed." Once more, she sprang for the closet.

"You're staying *here*. If he's a killer, then I don't want you in his line of sight. I just wanted you to know where I was going."

He was benching her? She'd just flipped on the light in her closet.

"Turn the light off," Odin ordered. "We don't want him knowing we're awake over here."

She flipped the light right back off.

"Lock the front door behind me. I have to go, *now*. He went back into his house, probably to grab more belongings, and I need to get over there before our guy races away."

Odin's shadowy form was moving for her bedroom door. Maisey bounded after him. She bounded so fast that she bumped into his back.

"Panties," he growled.

"Um, what about them?" She *was* wearing them. She'd assured him of that already.

He didn't speak. Just stalked through her house in the darkness and didn't even stumble. Meanwhile, she was clinging tightly to the back of his t-shirt and trying not to trip with every step.

"Bet they are sexy as fuck," Odin finally muttered.

Her cheeks flushed. Her panties were so not. They were white and plain, but she made a mental note to purchase some sexy underwear. Especially if Odin was going to be all curious about them.

She heard the faint sound of an engine. "He's trying to get away!"

"The hell he is." Odin yanked open the front door and rushed into the night.

***

The car had just whipped into the road. A sporty red Mustang. Odin realized the headlights were off. Just another mark against old Clay Prescott. Because who the hell drove away in the middle of the night with the headlights *off*?

The bad guy, that was who.

Odin thought he'd have to give chase, and he was already preparing to hop in his Jeep—a recent purchase that he'd gotten for a steal after the big case with War's lady—but then Clay braked his car. He jumped out. Ran back to the house.

Seriously? He'd forgotten something else?

And the dick had just left his car idling in the street.

Fine. If he wanted to make things easy on Odin, that was cool.

Odin hurried toward the vehicle. The dumbass had left the keys in the ignition. Odin glanced toward the front of Clay's house, then helped himself to those keys. The car's engine fell silent, and the quiet on the street felt deafening.

Odin took the keys around to the trunk. Pushed the trunk release lever and had the back swinging up. He stared at the giant duffel bag and remembered Maisey's words.

The kind of bag that you use to hide a body?

The bag was certainly lumpy in the way that could indicate a body was inside. The left side even appeared to be round like...like maybe with the shape of a head. Hell, he really did not want to find a dead body in that bag.

But he had to look and see.

He leaned forward and tugged down the zipper. The round object rolled right out—

"What in the hell are you doing?" Clay Prescott called.

More round objects rolled out and slid around the trunk. Basketballs. The duffel bag had been full of freaking basketballs.

"You left your car running in the middle of the night." Odin's fingers curled around the keys he held. "I was worried. Especially when I saw the trunk was open and you were nowhere to be seen."

"The trunk was open?" Clay ducked his head to peer inside. "Dammit, the balls fell out again." He scrambled to push them back into the bag.

Odin slid to the right. He saw that Clay had what looked like whistles hanging out of the right pocket of his jogging pants. "Going to coach a game?" he asked, voice mild. *At almost two a.m.?*

"I volunteer at the community center. The kids have a practice at seven in the morning, but I have a flight I have to catch at four. The assistant coach is going to cover for me." He zipped up the bag. "I realized I had all the equipment, so I was going to drop it off." Clay shoved back from the vehicle. "Are those my keys you're holding?"

"Took them out when I realized the car was on, but no one was inside." Odin tossed the key fob back to Clay. "Going out of town, huh? Where are you heading?"

Clay slammed the trunk. "Why the hell are you out here at this time of night?"

"Because my girlfriend had a break-in at her place hours ago." *And you're my fucking chief suspect.* Instead of saying that, Odin added, "I woke up to the sound of an engine running only there were no headlights turned on for the vehicle. Seemed like someone was trying to be sneaky outside. So I investigated."

"Ah...girlfriend, huh? No more 'special friend' BS?" Clay blew out a hard breath. "Figured she'd be with someone." He cast a fast glance toward Maisey's place. "And look, I wasn't trying to be sneaky. Okay, I mean...I kinda was. I didn't want to wake her or anything so I was keeping the lights off so they wouldn't shine through her window."

Clay still hadn't told Odin where he was heading. Odin had seen a small, overnight bag in the rear seat, so it obviously wasn't a big trip.

"It's a memorial service," Clay muttered. "An old friend of mine...it's been ten years since Hannah...um, since her death. I'm flying up to Tennessee to pay my respects, then coming back late Sunday night."

Ten years? Exactly? Maisey hadn't mentioned that. Anniversaries were often very significant for perps.

"Now, if you don't mind..." Clay moved toward the driver's side. "I need to get going. Lots to do before my flight."

"Sure thing." He took up a position on the sidewalk. "Have a good trip. Oh, and Clay?"

Clay had just started to slide into the vehicle. At Odin's words, he paused.

"My condolences on your friend. Even after ten years, I'm sure it still hurts."

"Not as much as you might think." Clay slid inside. Slammed the door.

Drove away.

Not as much as you might think. That was one cold-ass thing to say. But then, Odin was starting to think that Clay Prescott was one cold-ass man. Odin stood there until the vehicle left the street. He saw Clay turn on his lights just as he turned right.

When he was sure the other man was gone, Odin slowly pulled his hand from his pocket. Before he'd tossed the keys back to Clay, he'd taken the liberty of keeping one key for himself.

The key to Clay's house.

He heard footsteps rustling behind him. At least Maisey had waited until Clay left before making an appearance. *And, please, be wearing pants.* Because the mental image of Maisey just in her t-shirt and panties was more than enough to have his over-eager dick springing to attention.

"Since you let him go, I'm guessing there wasn't a body in the trunk?" Her low voice teased his ears.

He turned toward her. "Basketballs. Your serial killer next door volunteers at the community center and coaches basketball."

"I knew that. He also works in a soup kitchen once a month and has a free tutoring program at the college." She inched closer. "So either the man is a saint or he is really good at hiding his true self. Ted Bundy was good at fooling people, too, you know." She put her hands on her hips. Jean-clad hips, thank Christ. She was dressed.

And he was...mostly glad.

A horny-as-hell part of him was sad.

"Why was he taking basketballs out in the middle of the night?"

"Because your killer has a four a.m. flight. He's dropping them off at the community center on his way to the airport." A pause. "Turns out, it's the tenth anniversary of his...friend's death. He's heading back to Tennessee to pay his respects."

"Hannah," she breathed the name. "It *has* been ten years."

"He won't be back until Sunday night, so that gives us plenty of time..." He lifted his hand. The moonlight and starlight overhead would provide just enough light for her to see what he held. "To search his house."

"How did you get the key?" Maisey definitely sounded impressed.

Good. "I'm a professional." Though, stealing from suspects was probably not what most professional PIs did. Oh, well. He was still new to the biz. "You want to take a look inside?"

"*Yes. Absolutely one hundred percent, yes.*"

He headed for Clay's house.

She grabbed his arm. Pressed her body against his. "But is this legal?"

"Of course, not."

"Odin..."

Now she seemed all nervous. "You don't have to come in with me. I can do a sweep on my own."

"No, I am definitely coming in with you. But if we get caught, I'm taking the fall, got it? This is all happening because of me. So if we set off some sort of alarm or if the cops catch us—or anything like that, I'll take full responsibility. I will not drag you down with me."

Cute. He lightly ran the back of his knuckles over her face. As if she'd have to drag him anywhere.

She leaned toward him. "I've never committed a B&E before."

Hardly surprising. The woman screamed sunshine and baked cookies and innocence.

Meanwhile, hell, he'd had all too much experience with the darker side of life. "Just stay close to me. I'll take care of you."

She did stay close. Stuck to him like glue as they slipped inside. There was no security system at Clay's house. No exterior cameras. There had only been two keys on the fob—the key to the car and the key to the house. Taking it had been easy. Everything about the set-up was easy, and that very easiness sent off warnings in Odin's head.

Did he want me inside? Had everything been a set-up?

A quick search was showing no obvious clues that could help them. Not like Odin expected a giant red sign that would shout EVIDENCE, but it would have been nice. Instead, the man's house was stocked with only the smallest bit of furniture. His clothes were haphazardly tossed into his closet and onto the floor of his bedroom. Odin turned up no weapons. No body disposal items, nothing that would—

He heard an engine.

"Uh, Odin?" Maisey bumped into him. "Did you hear that?"

He'd heard that and he was peeking through the blinds to see— "He's back."

"No."

"Yes." Back and heading toward the house and dammit, maybe this had been a clever set-up. The guy was rushing back to catch them in the act. But...

No time to get out. Just protect Maisey. He grabbed her hand and pushed her toward the open closet.

He also deliberately dropped the key to the house. Let it fall to the floor, *after* he did a quick wipe with his shirt to smudge any would-be prints.

"Wait!" Maisey cried. "We need to get—"

He slid into the closet with her. Pulled the door shut.

"Oh, this is tiny," Maisey murmured. "Or maybe you're just really big. Yes, that's it, of course. You're super big, so you make small spaces seem even smaller and—"

Maisey talked when she was nervous. She was obviously super nervous and her talking was going to be a problem because they'd left the front door unlocked and now Clay was back inside. The hardwood floors were groaning beneath his feet.

"He's going to find us. I'll take the blame, just like I said, but, if he's the killer, he will—"

Odin kissed her.

CHAPTER FOUR

Odin's mouth was against hers. His lips were warm and firm and his hands had curled around her hips as he brought her closer to him. Maisey's heart pounded so loudly in her ears that she couldn't hear anything but the mad drumming. Her lips were slightly parted, and her tongue slipped forward to tease Odin as—

What in the hell am I doing?

Her body jolted. She tried to jerk back, but even though Odin's mouth lifted from hers, he didn't let her go.

"Not yet." His voice was barely a breath.

Not yet? Why not—

Then she heard the slam.

"Now," he said. Again, his voice was still low. "He got the key and left."

He'd left? But they'd only been kissing for a few seconds and— "This is one hell of a place for a first kiss."

"Sorry." A rasp. "You talk when you're nervous, so I was trying to help settle you down."

Settle her down? "Excuse me?"

"That was...not the right thing to say." Another rasp. "We should get out of here. Before your neighbor decides to come back again for shits and giggles."

His hold fell away. She shivered. Odin had been warm. Wonderfully warm. And now she felt a chill even as he inched open the closet door.

"He realized he was missing his key. Came racing back for it. I'd deliberately dropped it on the floor, just in case that was the reason why he was charging back."

She latched onto his arm, stopping him before Odin could leave the closet. "How do you know that was why he came back?"

"Because he came in the bedroom cursing about the key."

He had? Maisey didn't admit to not hearing that part. Telling Odin that she'd been so stunned by his kiss that she hadn't heard anything but the frantic beating of her own heart wouldn't come off as all cool and collected.

Then again, she'd never, ever been the cool and collected type.

Odin, obviously, was. Ice cold. The kiss had been nothing for him. Only a way for him to settle her down.

"Are you all right?" he asked quietly.

Dandy. "Why?" she choked out.

"Because you just growled."

She barely stopped herself from growling again. Settle down, her ass. She'd show him some settling down—once they were out of Clay's place. The search had been a bust, and the sooner they got out of there, the better.

***

Maisey didn't speak as they made their way back to her house. Odin checked, but there was no sign of Clay or his red Mustang. The road was dead quiet.

Once they were inside her home, he figured she'd head for her bedroom. Maybe crash. He'd go back to his uncomfortable position on the floor. Stare up at the ceiling. Think about her mouth.

"You could try saying…'Be quiet.'"

He'd just secured her door. Odin turned around, pressed his back against the wood, and studied her.

"You could have put a finger to my lips. That's like, a universal signal for being quiet. And, yes, I talk when I'm nervous. That's why I am talking like crazy right now." She huffed out a breath. "You don't *settle someone down* by putting your mouth on said person. You don't—"

"I lied."

She took a fast step toward him. "You did what?"

"I could have handled it better. Should have. If you want the full truth, I actually thought Clay was going to bust into the closet and catch us."

"Wait…what?" Another fast step.

"And if he came in and found us making out, I thought it would catch him off guard. Confuse the hell out of him. Whatever. You don't expect intruders to stop for a make-out session."

"No, you don't." Maisey shook her head. "What is happening right now?"

He was trying to explain the situation to her. Wasn't that what she wanted? "While he was caught off-guard, I would have attacked."

"*That* was your strategy?" Once more, she shook her head. "It sucks. Terrible strategy."

A shrug. "I'll remember that for next time."

But her eyes narrowed on him. Her delicate nostrils flared. And she stalked toward him. "Liar."

Hadn't he just admitted—

Her hand lifted, and her index finger jabbed him in the chest. "You kissed me...because you wanted to kiss me."

He didn't remember denying that point. He'd wondered how she'd taste ever since they first met.

"You acted on instinct. I was talking. You were thinking about my mouth. Then bam, you kissed me. And it didn't settle down either one of us."

She'd flipped on the lights as soon as they'd entered her place, so Odin could see her features perfectly.

She waited. Lifted a brow.

Was he supposed to say something? There hadn't been a question in her words. With his track record, keeping silent was probably the best course of action.

"Are you denying it?" Maisey demanded.

Ah, now there *was* a question. His lips parted.

"Or are you going to act like you don't feel this attraction between us?" Then she seemed to hold her breath.

Her gaze darted down to her poking finger. Her eyes flared as she yanked the finger back.

But he caught her hand. Closed his fingers around hers. "I deny nothing."

Her stare slowly rose until her incredible gaze was on his.

"I want you." Maybe it would be better to just get it out in the open. So he didn't hold back. He let the words tumble forth. *Screw it*. He held back with everyone else. Always watched his words as carefully as he could, but with her...

Maybe he'd try something new. Maybe she'd run from him as fast as she could. Then again, maybe she wouldn't.

"I wanted you from the first moment I saw you in my office. You were standing in the doorway, one hand pressed to the frame. And I thought you were the most gorgeous woman I'd ever seen."

Her tongue swiped across her lower lip.

"You wanted to hire me as your PI. I wanted to get you naked."

A swift inhale. "Is that why you took the case? Because you want to...have sex with me?"

"I took the case because you need help. Because when we got to your place, someone had broken in. Me wanting you—that's something I have to deal with. I can keep my control. Don't worry about that." He'd learned early in life how important—how necessary—control could be. When you were bigger than everyone else, stronger, when one punch from you could send an enemy—or a friend—staggering to the ground, you learned that you didn't get to be wild. That acting on impulse wasn't for you.

His life was ordered. Regimented. That was how he made sure no one ever got hurt. That *he* didn't hurt anyone.

"You can keep your control. That's just wonderful to know." She shivered.

Odin realized that he was stroking the delicate skin along her inner wrist. He stopped. Let her hand go. For a moment, her hand just lingered in the air, then Maisey slowly lowered it back to her side.

"I did kiss you because I was trying to come up with a distraction—both in case Clay entered the closet and because you were...stressed." He'd wanted her focus on something other than her fear. "I shouldn't have done it. Next time, I'll try something else." He hoped that reassured her. "You can get some sleep." His voice turned gruff. "No one will come inside tonight. And I'll get the new security upgrades started ASAP." There were some folks in the area who owed him favors. He'd call in those favors.

She turned away.

His breath eased out.

She took a few steps toward her bedroom door. Stopped.

Every muscle in his body seemed to tighten. *Go to bed, Maisey. Keep moving. One foot in front of the other. One foot—*

She whirled back toward him. "My turn."

What was her turn?

But she was striding back his way and his muscles just went tighter as she drew closer.

When she finally came to a stop, she was right in front of him once again. "I want to try again."

"Try...what?"

"I was scared and the bad guy was right on the other side of the door and my heart was beating like a million miles an hour." Her shoulders squared. "I want to try the kiss again."

Bad idea. So very bad.

"You're Mr. Control, aren't you? So it's not like it should be a big thing. And you just established that anything personal between us has nothing to do with the case."

He'd established that? Odin tried to mentally run back through his words. He didn't really remember—

"You kissed me before. I think, in the interest of fairness, I should get to kiss you now. Then we'll be all even, and we can go to bed." Her cheeks sucked in. "Separately. I mean for us to go to bed *separately*. Me in my room. You in your—um, spot on the floor."

She was nervous again.

She was also inching ever so much closer. Her hands moved to press to his chest. She rose onto her tiptoes.

She wants to kiss me. And he damn well wanted her mouth. "If you really want to make this work, how about I give you a hand?" Odin closed his hands over her hips, lifted her up with zero effort, and turned to press her back against the nearby wall. Now they were on perfect level. She'd give him a quick kiss. He would not lose his control. Then they'd go to bed.

Separately.

But he didn't anticipate that she'd curl her arms around his neck. Didn't anticipate that she'd curl her legs around his hips.

"I do like this position," Maisey whispered.

Fuck, so do I.

And Odin definitely didn't anticipate that when she put those silky, soft lips of hers against his, when she dipped her tongue into his mouth—

I want to devour her.

He didn't anticipate the rush of frantic, consuming desire that swept through him. Because, hell, yes, he'd enjoyed the kiss with her before. But he'd also been worried about the creep on the other side of the door and how to deal with him. This time, the only thing he thought about was her.

Maisey and her sweet mouth. Maisey and her wicked little tongue. Maisey and the way she pressed her body against his.

Her curves. Her scent.

Her.

His mouth opened wider. The hands on her waist tightened. His cock shoved hard against the front of his jeans as he pushed against the juncture of her thighs.

Maisey moaned again, and he greedily swallowed the sound. His tongue slid against hers. Took. Tasted. And with every second that passed, he just wanted more. *More.*

Everything.

His heart thundered. Heat and lust burned through him. His fingers shoved underneath the t-shirt she wore, and he touched her smooth, warm skin. He wanted her clothes gone. He wanted to strip her. To fuck her right there against the door. He wanted—

What in the hell?

Odin wrenched his mouth away from hers. His breath sawed out, heavy and hard. Hers did the same as she stared back at him. Her lips were red, still parted, and he found himself starting to dip back toward her for another taste—

No. Stop. Red flags were flying. Because this situation—fuck, he *wanted* her. He wanted to sink as deeply into her as he could go. He wanted Maisey's soft pink nails to rake down his back. He wanted to make her scream for him. He wanted—

Control.

"Wow," she whispered.

Wow, indeed. Same damn thought he had. Kissing her had been *incredible*. He wanted her mouth again. Wanted that t-shirt of hers to get tossed across the room.

"You really do have impressive control." Her lashes flickered.

A pang of unease stirred within him. Had that been a hint of pain in her voice?

"Guess you can turn things on and off easily, huh? Good to know." She gave him a quick smile. Her dimples didn't even flash because the smile barely curved her lips. But her hands did push against his arms. "You can put me down now. I'd say we're e-even."

Was that what they were?

But she'd asked to be put down, so he slowly lowered her until her feet touched the floor. As soon as his hands lifted from her, Maisey bolted away from him.

He took a quick, instinctive step after her, but then stopped.

She'd wanted to be even.

I just want her.

She didn't look back, so she didn't see that his hands had clenched into fists at his sides. She didn't see that his gaze was locked on her. That his jaw was clenched. That his cock shoved hard against the front of his jeans. She didn't see that he was freaking practically drooling after her.

Her bedroom door closed behind her with a soft click.

***

Her eyes squeezed shut as Maisey's back pressed to the bedroom door. She could still feel his mouth against hers. Could still feel the hot strength of his body against hers. She'd been rubbing and arching against him, lost to every single thing but the way Odin made her feel.

Then he'd pulled back.

Stared at her with a hard gaze and expressionless face.

She'd been about to go up in flames, and he'd been pulling away. Not like she'd ever been the type to inspire a guy to go crazy with lust, but...

I think I went crazy with lust. A first for her. She'd been ready to crawl all over him. Wait. Okay. Fine. She *had* been crawling all over him.

Her PI. Her partner. The man she'd be seeing again first thing in the morning.

Her eyes cracked open. She stumbled for the bed. Kicked off her shoes. Then just kinda fell face-first onto the bed. The pillow muffled her embarrassed groan. Maybe by tomorrow, she'd be able to look at Odin without fantasizing about ripping off his clothes.

Maybe. Maybe not.

***

The bedroom light at 104 Azalea Lane flickered off first. Five minutes later, the light in the den turned off.

Interesting.

A big shadow had been moving in the den before the light died away.

Maisey's new friend.

Had he returned to the bedroom with her? Or was he sleeping in the den? Just how close of a friend was he?

And would he be a problem?

The house near Maisey's was quiet. Completely dark. 106 Azalea Lane waited in the darkness. Maisey had been in that house. So had her friend. What had she been searching for? And, more alarming...had she found it?

CHAPTER FIVE

The rest of the weekend had been dead quiet. True to his word, Odin had gotten a top-of-the-line alarm system installed for Maisey. He'd gone over all the bells and whistles for her. Ever-so-professionally. Not even mentioning the kiss—the *two* kisses—they'd shared. Then he'd told her that he had some digging to do on her neighbor. He'd promised to let her know as soon as he had any updates.

And she hadn't heard from him since then. It was Monday evening. *Monday*. Maisey had tried being patient. She got that *maybe* Odin had weekend plans. And, sure, he'd given up his Friday night and a big chunk of the day Saturday to do her alarm system. She was appreciative. She was grateful.

But...

But—what? Why was she having this issue? Intellectually, Maisey knew she couldn't be his only client. Not like she expected him to give her some magical twenty-four, seven attention. Though, sure, that would be awesome.

Maisey stared at her phone as it sat on her desk. Then, heaving a sigh, she snagged the phone and called Odin. Only she got his voicemail, not the man himself. Maisey cleared her throat. "So, hi, it's me." Would he recognize her voice? *If not, he would have zero idea who me is.* "Maisey," she rushed to say. "I wanted to check in about the case." Her desk chair's wheels rolled back across the floor. "See if you had any news and...um, honestly, I was hoping I could *help* you with the case." That had been her grand plan when she first went to his office. "I thought we could work together like partners." She stood and slung her bag over shoulder. Her empty laptop bag.

Odin had hinted to Clay that Maisey had backed up all of the information from her stolen laptop—that she'd saved that data to her computer at work. Technically, she supposed it hadn't been a hint. He'd just come out and said she had the files at the college. But there had been no attempts on her office. No determined thief who wanted to see if she had more evidence. And she was only hauling around the empty bag now because she *did* plan to go and buy a new laptop that evening.

She'd also let the silence trail too long on her phone. "Call me when you have a chance, would you?" Maisey rattled off her number. "Thanks, and I—"

His voicemail hung up on her.

Wonderful. She was sure that her rambling message sounded awesome. Or not.

She was about to drop her phone into the bag when it vibrated in her hand. She'd programmed Odin's number in already, and when she saw it light up the screen, her finger immediately swiped to take the call. "Odin! You got my message?" And he'd responded so very quickly. That seemed like a good sign.

"Your what?"

"My voicemail?" She cleared her throat. "You got the message I left for you?"

"No."

"Uh..."

"We need to talk."

Weren't they talking? She headed down the corridor. The Humanities building was empty. Her last class had been an hour ago, and she'd only stayed because she needed to get lessons set up for the next session later in the week. "I'm leaving campus now," she told him. "Maybe we could meet up?"

"I'm here."

He was? Her steps quickened.

"I'm waiting in the parking lot." His voice hardened. "It's deserted. Why the hell are you staying here alone? No other vehicles are around."

Her shoulders stiffened as she grabbed for the stairwell door. She could have waited for the elevator but the thing was seriously slower than Christmas. And she was only on the third floor—she loved sneaking in some cardio. "There's a security guard who patrols the area every fifteen minutes. I'm safe. I'm—" The line went dead. She heard the flash of static. *Dang it!* Dead zone. For some reason, that always happened on these stairs. But as soon as she got to the first floor, reception would return. Maisey kept the phone to her ear as she hurried down the steps.

She was on the fifth step down when she realized something was wrong.

The stairwell door hadn't swung shut behind her.

She paused just for a moment, the phone still at her ear, and she started to turn around and see what was—

Something—someone—slammed into her. The phone flew from Maisey's fingers and tumbled down the stairs. *She* tumbled down the stairs right after it.

***

"Maisey?" Odin's grip on his phone tightened. "*Maisey!*" She'd just been telling him that she was safe and then—nothing.

The line had disconnected, and Odin automatically called her again even as he took off at a run for the Humanities building. It was a towering, brick building. The bricks had been painted white, and the windows gleamed in the setting sun. He knew she had an office on the third floor. The history department was on the west end of the third floor. He'd done recon work on Maisey and her creepy neighbor. Maisey was on the third floor, while Clay and the rest of the psych department were on the fourth.

Odin rushed into the Humanities building—

"Hey!" A sharp voice called, "Stop!"

He didn't want to stop. Maisey still wasn't picking up the phone, and adrenaline pounded through him.

"Campus security!" The voice barked, "Spin toward me."

Dammit. Odin spun toward him. "I'm worried about my friend. I was just going to meet her." Then he got a good look at the guard.

Seriously? The man appeared to be pushing ninety. His body curved forward as he studied Odin, and the man's white hair shot from beneath his gray hat.

His grizzled jaw tightened as the man snapped, "Classes are over. No students are in the building now."

"She's not a student." He still had the phone in his hand. "She's a professor. Maisey Bright. She's—"

"Maisey!" A delighted smile stretched the guard's face. "Plays a great game of poker, that woman does."

He filed that away for later. "Listen, Maisey was just talking to me, but then we got disconnected. I'm worried something happened to her." *And talking to you is stopping me from finding her so...*

The guard waved at him. "She's probably in the stairwell. Signal is crap there."

The stairwell.

"Give her a minute," the guard assured him. His gold name tag identified the guard as Sandy. "She'll be along soon enough. She always takes the stairs. Says it gives her extra steps and cardio time."

Odin did some quick calculations. If she'd been on the stairs when her phone went out, she should have already been on the ground level. He'd had to run across the parking lot and dodge across about fifty yards in a common area before he'd burst into the Humanities building.

An *unlocked* building. Maybe the guard said students shouldn't be there, but there had been nothing to keep them—or anyone else—out.

He shot for the stairwell. Threw open the door. Took a fast step inside and—*crunch.*

"Do you see her?" Sandy called out. "Told you," he said, before Odin could answer. "She likes her cardio."

Odin lifted his shoe. Stared down at the cracked screen of a phone. *Fuck.* "Maisey!" he roared.

"Damn, man. Calm down." Sandy had sidled into the stairwell. "Why she—oh, that's her phone. She has that cute dragon phone case. Told her I wanted one for myself—"

Odin had just lunged up three steps when he stopped. He looked back. Looked down. He'd come in on the first floor, and he could see stairs leading even lower. There was some kind of bag on those stairs. A laptop bag? "Where do those go?" Odin pointed.

Sandy followed his pointing finger. "The basement. That's where we get our deliveries. There's a big garage area that opens and the trucks can come right in and—"

The trucks could come in down there. If they could come in, that meant someone else could get out.

With Maisey?

He bounded down the stairs and straight for the basement.

"I'll keep the phone for her!" Sandy promised. "Maisey will not like that the screen is broken, that's for sure."

Odin shoved open the basement door. *"Maisey!"*

The scene before him had rage exploding within Odin.

A black pickup truck had been backed into the garage. The passenger door hung open, and some prick in a ski mask was trying to haul Maisey—an unconscious Maisey—toward that open door. *"Let her go!"* Odin roared.

The guy's ski-mask-covered head jerked.

A weak moan slid from Maisey. Blood dripped from a scratch on her cheek.

The sonofabitch had hurt her. An inhuman snarl broke from Odin, and he launched forward.

"Crazy bastard!" The ski-mask-wearing man yelled. "Want her? Then take her!" He shoved Maisey toward Odin. Or rather—just *shoved her.* Because Odin was rushing as fast as he could, but he wasn't close enough, and Maisey was hurtling straight for the cement.

"No!" he thundered and leapt for her. He caught her inches from the cement and spun so that his arm scraped over the rough floor of the garage. His hold tightened around her. *I've got you, it's okay.* She was safe. Safe, but barely moving. "Baby?" he brushed back her hair.

He heard the slam of a door. His head whipped up. The SOB who'd tried to take Maisey was in the truck and preparing to rush away. *The hell you will.*

Odin carefully lowered Maisey to the cement. He saw a long, black pole propped near the wall. He grabbed that pole even as he flew toward the driver's side of the truck. The wheels squealed. Odin slammed the pole into the door. Into the window.

The truck lunged past him.

He slammed his pole into the left taillight. The light shattered. The truck fish-tailed as it roared away.

"What in the world is going on down here?" Sandy's voice boomed. "This is a private area, and you don't get to just run in here whenever you—wait...Maisey? What did you do to Maisey?"

Odin glared after the truck. *I will find you, asshole.*

A radio crackled. "I need backup!" Sandy ordered. "Humanities building. We've got an employee down and—"

Odin grabbed the radio from him. "A black Chevy pick-up truck just left the scene. He's got a busted left taillight, a cracked driver's side window, and a dent in the driver's door. That perp just tried to abduct Maisey Bright, and whatever the hell you do, do *not* let him leave this campus, do you understand me? *Do not.*"

"Oh, my." Sandy gulped. "Oh. My."

Odin shoved the radio back at Sandy. "Get the cops here." Not just the campus guards. Then he dropped beside Maisey.

Her eyes were cracking open. A groan slipped from her lips.

Carefully, he smoothed his hand over her cheek. "Baby?" The endearment spilled out. He cleared his throat. "Maisey? You back with me?"

Her lashes fluttered a little more. "Odin?"

His heart shoved into his chest. "I'm here. You're safe."

"I...fell down the stairs."

Sandy sidled closer. "Hate to tell you, but you broke your phone."

If she'd tumbled down the stairs, she was lucky she hadn't broken a leg. An arm.

Her neck.

His back teeth clenched. *I am going to find that bastard, and he will pay.* Quickly, but thoroughly, he did a scan of her body as he searched for injuries.

"Odin? Why are you poking at me?" Maisey asked, all fretful.

"How is your head?" he returned, instead of answering. "You seeing anything odd? Your vision good?"

Her eyes narrowed. "I was...on the stairs."

"And your phone broke," Sandy supplied.

Not helping.

"Now I'm in the garage." Maisey's head turned to the left. To the right. "How did I get down here?" Her voice rose a notch.

Carefully, Odin curled his hand under her chin. "You are safe. I have you. Everything is going to be okay."

Her hand flew up and her fingers locked around his wrist. "I...I don't think I was alone on the stairs," she whispered. Fear filled her gaze.

"No." He could hear a siren coming closer. Help was on the way. "You weren't."

CHAPTER SIX

"Someone tried to kidnap me." Maisey was having trouble wrapping her head around that whole horrifying situation. "*Me*. Someone actually tried to kidnap *me*."

Her memories were sketchy. She remembered something being off in the stairwell. *The door didn't close. It always clangs closed behind me.*

It hadn't closed because someone had followed her into the stairwell. She'd realized that, then she'd fallen.

Or been pushed? Her money was on being pushed. She took a swift left turn at the edge of her sofa and paced back toward a watchful Odin.

"If you hadn't been there..." She seriously owed him. "Where would I be right now?" She stumbled. Stopped. "What would be happening to me?" And had this same thing happened to Whitney? When she'd vanished, had she been taken by someone, swiped right from campus only to never be seen again?

Maisey's hands wrapped around her stomach. An EMT had checked her out. Except for a few bruises and scrapes, he'd said she was good. He'd called her lucky.

Only luck didn't have a whole lot to do with the matter. She was alive, standing in her house—because Odin had saved her.

"Don't." The word was low. Rough. His expression was all dark and broody. Come to think of it, he'd had that same dark and broody expression ever since she'd opened her eyes and seen him in the garage. "Don't think about what could have happened. That path won't do you any good."

Yes, well, she knew the path was a nightmare, but she couldn't stop her overactive imagination from tumbling right down it. Once she'd been taken away from campus, her abductor could have tied her up. Tortured her. Used a knife or a—

"Maisey." Odin was right in front of her. She didn't remember him rising from the chair. Probably because she'd been imagining her own death scene. "You are safe. I'm here. Nothing is going to happen to you while I am—"

She heard a quick jingle. Knew it was the sound of her new motion sensor alerting her to someone at her front door even before the doorbell rang.

Odin's lips tightened.

"It could be the cops again," Maisey murmured. They'd said they would follow up after taking her statement on the campus. The black truck had been found—abandoned—in the Engineering parking lot. Campus security had tracked down the student who owned the truck, but she'd been stunned to discover what had happened. Turned out, she'd reported the truck missing a day ago.

The perp had vanished. Switched vehicles, then driven away. Or, heck, maybe even walked away once he'd ditched the ski mask.

"Maybe they have more questions," she continued as she tried to steady her still racing heartbeat. "Or maybe..." If you wanted to be really positive... "Maybe they caught the guy!"

His expression told her that he doubted that particular turn of events. Odin pulled up his phone. He'd linked her security system both to her phone and his. Since her phone was broken, it was good that he had the setup still accessible on his device. He stared at the screen, and if possible, his expression grew ever darker as he saw the person waiting on her doorstep.

"Odin?"

"It's your neighbor. Guess he came to pay you another late-night visit."

It was nine. Hardly super late but...

"I'll deal with him," Odin promised. "Just...rest or something, would you?"

No, she would not. Resting was the last thing she felt like doing. Maisey was pretty sure she would be jumping out of her skin any moment. She sidled along behind Odin, and he tossed her a frown.

The doorbell rang again.

Odin flipped the lock and wrenched open the door. "Now is not a good time for us," he snapped.

The porch light fell on Clay's face. "I heard about Maisey's attack!" He craned his body and head to see around Odin's massive form. "Maisey! Are you all right? What can I do? How can I help?"

Those hardly sounded like the words of a cold-blooded killer. Then again, if he *was* a cold-blooded killer, wouldn't he be trying to throw them off the scent? Wouldn't he be *acting* concerned?

"Maisey has all the help she needs, but thanks for stopping by," Odin assured him. He started to slam the door shut on Clay.

"Wait!" Maisey jumped forward. What was Odin doing? This was an opportunity for them to question their suspect. "Thank you for checking on me, Clay."

Swearing under his breath, Odin eased back.

"Of course! Word is spreading through the staff like wildfire." Clay stepped over the threshold and into her house.

Odin's body stiffened.

She put her hand on his arm. *Easy.* "How was your trip?"

"My trip?" His brow wrinkled. "You can't want to talk about that!"

Yes, she did want to talk about that trip. Very much. She wanted to hear about it and Hannah Martinez.

"Forget my trip. You were attacked! Judith from the English Department said that you were nearly killed!"

"Kidnapped," Odin corrected in that deep, rumbling voice of his. A voice that sent shivers sliding over Maisey's skin. "She was nearly kidnapped."

Clay's mouth opened and closed as he struggled for words. Finally, he burst out, "But why would someone want to kidnap Maisey?"

"Why would someone want to break into her house?" Odin threw the question back at him. "Because my instincts say the break-ins and the abduction attempt are related."

"Your instincts?" Clay gave a nervous laugh. "What are you, a cop or something?"

"Something," Odin replied flatly.

His body was practically vibrating with fury. She could feel it. "Odin is a PI," she mumbled.

Clay backed. "You...you're dating a PI?"

Odin's arm lifted and wrapped around her shoulders. He pulled her closer to him. "Damn straight she is. And this PI is gonna make absolutely certain that *no one* hurts her." She looked at his face and saw that Odin's bright stare was locked on Clay with laser-like focus as he continued, "I will find the person who tried to take her. I will make him suffer."

Another nervous laugh came from Clay. "Don't you mean...the cops will find him? Not so sure that's what you should be doing by yourself—"

"This is personal. I'll find the bastard who is after Maisey." The air thickened with dangerous intensity. "He will be stopped."

Clay gulped. Sweat dotted his brow. "Got a lot of practice tracking down criminals, huh?"

"Enough."

Clay's gaze darted to Maisey. "Can we...can we talk alone?"

Why? But before she could reply—

"No." Odin's voice was clipped. "Now back up or lose the foot."

The foot? Maisey looked down. Saw that Clay's foot was still over the threshold.

Odin was moving to slam the door.

With a yelp, Clay yanked his foot back.

Bam. She stared at the closed door. Odin flipped the locks.

"I think I should have talked more to him." Her head tilted as she nibbled on her lower lip. "I wanted to grill him about his trip and that would have given me a chance to—"

"You need to stop playing." He took her arm. Pulled her back to the den. It was a gentle pull, sure, but still most definitely a pull.

At the couch, she yanked her arm free of his hold. "I'm not playing at anything."

"No?" Again, his voice was a dangerous rumble. "You want to go off and have a private chat with our lead suspect."

Yes, so she—

"Worst fucking idea ever."

Anger hummed through her. "No, really, tell me what you truly think."

"It's the worst fucking idea ever," he snapped again.

Her eyes narrowed. "At least I am trying to get more information. I hired you on Friday, and we have not made any progress on the case!"

"Are you kidding me right now?"

She honestly didn't even know what she was doing. All of the tension inside of her was erupting and words were just sort of tumbling out of her mouth. "You ghosted me." There. She'd said it. What pissed her off. "I thought we were working on this together."

"From here on out, we fucking are." A muscle flexed along his jaw. "I'm sticking to you like glue. No more stake-outs down the street. I'll be here."

She was lost. "What stake-out down the street?"

"Did you truly think I was just gonna abandon you after the break-in on Friday?"

Yes, she had certainly considered that possibility. That went back to the whole "ghosted" bit that she'd just mentioned.

"I didn't think you'd like me cramping your style, so I stayed a safe distance back. I wanted to watch to make sure you weren't having any unwanted guests."

Maisey needed to be sure she was understanding. "Saturday night...you were watching my house?"

A hard nod.

"Sunday night...you were watching my house."

"Didn't I just say as damn much?"

"Why didn't you come inside?"

His eyes *blazed*. "Thought it would be better...to have space."

What did that mean?

"Also, if the perp didn't think I was here, figured he'd be more likely to make a move." He heaved out a breath. "Even had eyes on you at the campus. After all, we'd told Clay that you had a backup on your computer there. I wanted to see if he tried to access it."

"Is that why you were in the parking lot?"

"Clay wasn't on campus. I'd seen him leave earlier. I thought you were *safe*. When he left, I went to do some recon work. When I got back, the parking lot was empty, but you were still there. Shit. Do you know how scared I was when I lost contact with you?"

Big, bad Odin had been scared? She found that hard to believe. "I am not a mind reader."

"What the hell are you talking about?"

"Do you know what it means to keep someone in the loop?"

A muscle jerked along his jaw.

"This…" She motioned between them. Her bracelets jingled on her left wrist. "This is the loop. You and me. You're supposed to keep me in the loop. That means you are supposed to tell me what's happening. I can't work with you if I don't know what the heck you are doing!"

His nostrils flared. "You smell fucking delicious."

"I—" Maisey shook her head. "What does that have to do with anything?"

"Hell of a lot. *Space*. I was trying to give you space by staying outside but that shit is over. I won't make the same mistake again." His eyes glittered. He stepped closer. "Like *glue*."

Her throat was very dry.

"You want the full loop details?"

"Yes, I would like that very much."

"During the day, I was following up leads. Working the case. At night, I was making sure you were safe."

She could not look away from his stare.

"I screwed up earlier. That is on me. I underestimated the danger. If I'd been a few minutes slower in that garage, you'd be gone." His hands lifted and closed around her shoulders. *"You would be gone."*

He pulled her closer. His grip was strong, but he wasn't hurting her. He was very careful. There was a heat, an intensity, in his touch that swept through her. Maisey couldn't look away from him. The air was tight and thick. She was dimly aware of her own thudding heart beats. Mostly, though, she was aware of Odin. He pretty much overpowered everything else.

Maisey knew this was not the time to tell Odin that he was hot. That he was so gorgeous that she was having trouble breathing. She knew she was obviously going through some sort of emotional meltdown because of the attack. Anything she said or did would be influenced by her ricocheting emotions. But—

"You are so sexy," she whispered.

His eyebrows shot down. "What?"

"Thank you for saving me today."

"It's my freaking job to protect you."

No, it wasn't. She'd hired him to find proof of Clay's guilt or innocence. Odin staking out her place... Odin saving her from an attacker...that was beyond the scope of their initial deal.

"You shouldn't have been in that situation. That's on me."

"Why are you blaming yourself? You're not the one who tried to take me." Had he missed her thank-you moment? She was grateful—beyond grateful—because he had saved her ass.

"You're my client. I will keep you safe, I will— *fuck*." He hauled her against him. "You scared the hell out of me."

This was the second time he'd mentioned being afraid. Before she could press him about that...

His mouth took hers.

Surprise held her immobile—for like, all of two seconds. Then she was throwing her hands around his shoulders and holding on tightly even as she pressed up to get even closer to him.

Odin.

He lifted her up. She loved it when he did that. Lifted her up and held her against his body and made her feel all delicate and feminine against him while he was hard strength and power. His tongue thrust into her mouth, and she didn't even try to hold back her moan. This, *this* was what she wanted. This surge of desire that made her feel reckless, wild. Alive.

Her nails bit into his shoulders. Her mouth met his in a greedy explosion of need and hunger. This reaction didn't normally happen to her. When she kissed a man, she didn't go from a peck on the lips to wanting to tear the clothes off the guy's body within about a minute.

Not normal. At all.

Maisey had always thought normal was way over-rated.

One of his big hands was sliding under her shirt. She loved the feel of his fingers on her skin, and if she and Odin could get more of the clothing out of the way, that would be great.

Vaguely, she became aware that he was moving. Turning his body, turning them, and heading maybe...to her bedroom?

Her legs wrapped around his hips. The better to hold on. She didn't stop kissing him though. She caught his lower lip, gave it a sensual tug.

"*Maisey...*"

She had never particularly liked her name. But when Odin said it...all deep and gravelly and hungry-like...

She rubbed against him.

He lowered her onto the bed.

Wait, the bed?

He caught her hands. Pressed them against the mattress. Loomed over her. The trip from the den to the bedroom was kind of vague for her. Her heart thundered, and her gaze locked on his.

He wasn't kissing her any longer. Just staring at her with eyes gone stormy from need.

She licked her lips.

"That...wasn't supposed to happen," Odin said.

What wasn't? Him kissing her? Or them winding up in her bedroom?

"You need to sleep."

Sleeping was the last thing she felt like doing. Her body was screaming with energy. "No."

His hands were still around her wrists. Her legs weren't around his hips any longer. They dangled over the side of the bed. Actually, they dangled and spread and he was between them. His hips were lodged between her open legs, and there was no way on earth that she could miss the heavy arousal pressing against her.

"I don't want to sleep," Maisey told him. She was afraid that if she slept, she'd have a nightmare. A flashback to the stairwell and garage. Doing podcasts about historical crimes was different from actually being a victim in a *current* crime. Being a victim made *everything* different.

"I want you," Odin gritted out.

She sucked in a breath.

"But not like this. Not when you're scared and you're looking for an outlet."

Still reeling, Maisey gazed up at him.

"And not when I'm so pissed I can barely think," he added gruffly. "Not when I keep thinking about how I want to find that sonofabitch and rip him apart."

Her heart jolted. "You saved me." Her hand lifted and touched his jaw. She could feel the stubble beneath her fingertips. "I don't...do this."

He tensed. "Do what?"

"I don't meet a guy then stumble into bed with him the next day."

"It's not the next day. It's been several days."

Her heart slammed into her chest. "I just...I don't want you to think this is normal for me. I-I feel..."

"Adrenaline. Fear. An emotional tornado that's about to blow you apart." His jaw flexed. "Got it." He let her hands go. Shoved up.

She scampered up, too. She pushed to her knees and grabbed his arm. "Stop. You don't know what I feel." She barely knew herself. "Every time that you kiss me, I get so turned on that even breathing seems hard."

He didn't move.

"I don't react that way to most guys." How about...to any other guy? "I'm not one for pretending or being coy…" She wouldn't know how to be coy to save her life. "I say what I think. I want you to know—" *Deep breath*. "The way I'm reacting with you, this isn't normally me."

A hard nod. His eyes glittered.

"You are not understanding me at all." Her hold tightened on him. "It's not adrenaline. It's not because I had a terror-filled attack. It's because I want you. And you want me. We're two adults. We're not seeing anyone else." She hadn't dated in months. She'd pulled back because she was too over the scene of people being fake. Fake social media. Fake smiles. Over people acting like their worlds were perfect when they weren't. "I get that you're my PI." Had that *my* sounded a little possessive? Maisey thought that it might have. She found that she felt a little possessive toward him. "But who says we can't be more?"

There. She'd done it. Put herself out there. More than she ever had before. Because Odin—he was different. Real. Nothing fake about him. What you saw was what you got. And what she saw…

Hero.

He'd saved her. He was working with her to unmask a killer. In a world that was too often filled with darkness, she had stumbled onto a real, true-blue, good guy. What were the odds of that?

"Oh, Maisey…" A sad shake of his head. "You don't want to go down this path with me."

She did. Hadn't she just said as much?

His fingers curled around her wrist. Slowly lowered her arm.

"You don't know who I am."

"You're Odin. Former Delta. PI. Hero. You're—"

"I'm a man who has done plenty of bad things in my life. Things that you don't want to ever touch you." He glanced at his fingers around her wrist. "I'm not good for you."

Bull. She thought he was exactly what she needed.

"I shouldn't be touching you," Odin muttered.

"I like it when you touch me." A low, husky confession.

A shudder worked over him. "You shouldn't say things like that."

Yes, she should. "I'm not into lying."

His gaze held hers. "Neither am I, so believe me when I say...*I am not good for you.*"

CHAPTER SEVEN

The bedroom door creaked open. Odin saw the small sliver of light trickle into the den. He was on the floor, turned toward her door, and, hell, no, he hadn't been sleeping. It was hard for a man to sleep when his dick was at full attention and he kept thinking about what a straight-up fool he'd been.

She wanted you. She'd stared into his eyes, looking at him like he'd just saved the fucking day, and said that she wanted him.

She was trying to put him in the role of the hero. That wasn't who he was. He had blood on his hands. Scars on his soul. She didn't get it. Didn't understand that he'd joined the military not to save the world but because he'd needed someone—something—to control him. He'd needed—

Maisey was tiptoeing across the floor.

"Where are you going?" Odin growled.

She yelped. Jumped a good foot.

He hadn't meant to scare her. Story of his life, though. Sooner or later, he wound up scaring most people. His buddy War was probably the one exception to that rule. Then again, nothing had ever scared War.

Correction. Rose scared him. The woman who'd stolen War's heart.

"I was coming to check on you," Maisey admitted.

He sat up. He'd taken off his shirt, stripped down to just his boxers, and the blanket she gave him was shoved over his hips. "Why?"

"Because I wanted to make sure you were still here." She crept closer. She wore jogging shorts. Loose and sliding around her hips. A thin t-shirt.

No bra. Odin swallowed. He could see her tight nipples poking against the front of her shirt.

Breathe, man. Breathe and get your eyes off her chest!

"I was scared," Maisey added in a quick rush. "I couldn't go to sleep."

He'd been horny as hell and not able to sleep. Three hours had passed since the scene in her bedroom, and he'd been sure Maisey had slipped off to dream land.

"Every time I close my eyes, I think about the things that could have happened."

"Told you, don't do—"

"Yes, well, it's easier said than done." She rocked forward onto the balls of her feet. "I've done reports on some of the worst crimes in history. I watch every kind of crime show I can find but...it's different, when it happens to you."

Yes, it was.

"This might sound crazy but is it okay if I leave my bedroom door open? That way, if I get scared, I can just sit up and see you and I can—"

He stood up.

Her gaze immediately dropped to his chest. "What..." A fast expulsion of air. "What happened to you?"

The scars. Hell. He raked a hand over them. "Gunshots."

She hurried forward. Her hand lifted and pressed to his chest. "That's a lot of gunshots."

Yes, it had been. If War hadn't dragged his ass out of that firefight, Odin would be dead. "Always thought I was stronger than him." It still stunned him that War had hauled him so far. "But no matter how many times I told him to leave me, War wouldn't let go."

Her fingertips traced lightly over one of the scars.

A surge of heat lanced right through Odin.

"War saved you?"

"Yeah, and he never lets me forget it." Odin knew he should have stopped fighting after that scene from hell, but he hadn't. He'd gone back into the field, despite War's protests. He'd gone back because he'd wanted to prove that he still had what it took to get the job done.

But I just found more death.

He'd found that it was too easy to get lost in battles. For that brutal return, he hadn't still been Delta. He'd been working with a different unit. Even bloodier and more dangerous and so far removed from the official books that no one ever heard a whisper about them.

"Sounds like War is a good friend."

She was still touching him, and her touch was making him crave her even more. "You should stop." Rough.

Maisey's eyes widened. "I just—oh. Didn't realize I was, uh, doing that." She snatched her hand back.

"War's not my friend."

She cleared her throat. "When a man saves your life, I'd count him as a friend."

"He's family. My brother. Not blood, but who cares about that?" Not Odin. Every time he'd wanted to sink into the dark and get lost—when he'd wanted to give in to the bloodlust that always seemed to call to him, War had been there, pulling him back. Control had always been so easy for War. He didn't have to fight like Odin did in order to keep it in place.

With Maisey, Odin found that he had to fight twice as hard.

Never wanted someone so badly. Want to take and take and let the rest of the world burn away.

She'd backed away. Two quick steps that put space between them. Only her delectable scent lingered in the air around Odin. She put her hands behind her back. "The door," Maisey said, absolutely confusing him because he'd gotten lost staring at her. "Is it okay with you if I leave it open?"

Her fear. She'd come out because she was afraid. "No."

"Oh. Okay." A jerky nod. "It's ridiculous to be afraid of being alone. I'll just—I'll let you get back to sleep. Sorry for bothering you."

He was an asshole. Why did things always come out wrong when he spoke?

Maisey spun away and practically ran for her bedroom.

He grabbed the blankets and the pillow.

***

Her body was completely straight and stiff in the bed, and her heart was racing so hard that every thunderous boom filled Maisey's ears. The booms were so loud that she almost didn't hear her bedroom door squeak open.

Almost.

Maisey bolted upright in bed. "Odin!"

"Yes?" Calm. Quiet. The total opposite of her cry.

Her chest heaved. "What...what are you doing?"

"Going to bed."

She'd left her bedside lamp on, and she could see him clearly as he stalked across the room—with the blankets and pillow curled under one arm—and he settled down on the floor near her bed. Maisey blinked, then immediately grabbed the side of the mattress and lowered her head so she was peering down at him. The angle put her almost right on top of him. "Why are you in here?"

"Because you're afraid."

"I..." She was afraid, yes. But... "You said no."

"I meant..." His words were halting. "No, you didn't need to leave the door open. If you didn't want to be alone, then I would just come in here with you."

She stared at him.

He smiled at her.

Hold up. Had he smiled before? She couldn't remember, but his smile had some of the tension sliding from her shoulders. "That's really sweet of you."

His smile slipped.

Right. He *hated* being called sweet. *Salty.* "I appreciate it," she quickly corrected.

"Try to sleep."

Her hair was hanging forward and she was half-off the bed. She pushed back. Settled against her pillows. Her hands slid over the sheets. Smoothed them unnecessarily.

"I'm glad you're...okay." Again, his voice was halting. "I would never want anything bad to happen to you."

That made two of them. Not like she wanted something horrible to happen, either. Not to her. Not to any of the people she cared about. *Like Whitney.* "Do you think..." She licked dry lips. "Is this what happened to Whitney? She was taken. Maybe tossed into a car. Driven away." *Killed?*

"Your friend Whitney..." He stopped.

She rolled toward him. "My friend Whitney—what?"

"How well did you really know her?"

The question caught her off-guard. "As well as you can know someone, I suppose. I mean, we all have secrets." Wasn't that the way of things?

"What secrets do you have?"

"Tell me yours," she heard herself say, "and maybe I'll tell you a few of mine."

Silence.

Fine. She took that as a *no.* It was not secret-sharing time.

"Whitney frequented a bar about thirty miles away. It's a hangout for criminals and people looking to hire criminals for dirty jobs." A pause. "Since you hired me, I've spent some time looking into her life. Tracing her last steps. Got a few acquaintances who knew some info about her—like that she visited Ramsey's every Friday. Just like clockwork."

Ramsey's. The name clicked. Relief filled her. "That wasn't something shady. That was just research."

"What?"

"Research. She told me that she wanted to get more field work under her belt. She'd been going to Ramsey's to observe—"

"Ramsey's isn't a place where you go to have a damn tea party," he rumbled.

"Whitney didn't go there for tea. She had an interest in criminal psychology." Once more, her fingers slid over the sheets.

"You get that her *interest* might have led to her disappearance?"

No, because she'd been so sure that Clay—

Maisey stopped the thought. She'd wanted to find proof of Clay's guilt or innocence. Odin was telling her there might be other suspects. "We'll go to Ramsey's?"

"I was planning to go tomorrow—"

"We'll go," she said definitely. "Because you said you were going to be staying extra close to me, remember? What better way than to take me with you?" Maisey held her breath.

"Tricky," Odin finally said. "Fine. You go with me. But you do not leave my sight, not even for a second, got it?"

"Got it." She slid onto her back and smiled up at the ceiling. All too quickly, her smile fled. The moments seemed to slowly tick past. Maisey strained but she couldn't even hear the sound of Odin breathing. Carefully, she inched over to the side of the bed and cast a quick glance down at—

He was staring right up at her. His hands were behind his head. The blanket fell around his hips.

"Hi," Odin told her softly.

Her stomach did a little quiver. "Hi."

"Still can't sleep?"

She was wired. Her fingers kept wanting to tremble. "I've never been nearly abducted before."

"You'll crash and when you do, it will be hard." A pause. "You know I won't let this happen again?"

Because he was staying close. Her fingers tightened around the edge of the mattress. "I don't want to let this happen again. I need to learn how to protect myself." She would be enrolling in a self-defense class, ASAP. She should also buy some mace. Maybe a knife that she could hide in her bag or even a taser. There were even taser-like guns, weren't there?

"I'll teach you. I can show you moves that will make a man twice your size cry like a baby."

That sounded promising.

"War taught Rose, and the tricks he showed her damn well came in handy."

Rose. The name was familiar. Rose Shadow had been the reporter who'd first led Maisey to

Odin—or rather, to Trouble for Hire Investigations.

"The trick is that you can't be afraid of hurting your opponent. You can't hold back." A pause. "Though it's always the fucking opposite for me."

"I don't understand." She was still peering down at him.

One hand moved from behind his head. He held his hand up to her. Stretched out his fingers. "Put yours against mine."

She did. A shiver darted through her.

"I've always been bigger. Stronger. Holding back is the *only* way I don't hurt people. That's why I made my rules."

Her fingers slid over a little. Curled with his. She wasn't even sure why she'd done that, but now they were holding hands. She expected him to pull away.

He didn't.

"What are your rules?" Maisey asked, curious. A heavy lethargy pulled at her, and she yawned.

"Don't ever hit first. One hit from me can be enough to knock someone out. So I make sure the person I'm fighting has it coming."

That seemed like a good rule. "What else?"

"Finish the fight. Never walk away when your opponent can still attack." A beat of silence. "If you show mercy to the wrong person, it can come back to bite you in the ass."

She thought of the scars on his chest. "Is that what happened to you? Did you show the wrong person mercy?"

His hand pulled away from hers. "If we keep talking, you won't ever get to sleep."

She'd liked holding his hand. But he didn't want to talk anymore, she got that. Maybe she'd pushed too hard. She'd been getting him to reveal personal information, but she hadn't told him much about herself. "I like solving mysteries," Maisey admitted. She let her eyes drift closed.

"I did notice that about you," he murmured.

"Want to know why?" Another yawn. Hmmm. Maybe Odin had been right. Maybe she was about to crash.

"Why?"

"Because I'm a mystery." Her breath rustled out. "Don't know where I came from. Just appeared at the hospital. Left right outside the emergency room doors." She'd always wanted to find her birth parents. She never had. "The local sheriff and his wife raised me. Pop sure loved solving mysteries, too." But he was gone now. So was her mom. Some days she missed them so much it just physically hurt.

"Maisey?"

"Thank you for making sure I'm not alone." Sleep pulled at her. "Night, Odin."

Silence. So much silence that she was drifting off just as—

"Good night, sweetheart."

***

"*Odin!*" The scream tore from her.

"Right here." His hand closed over hers.

Her heart stuttered. "He was coming for me again."

"Only a dream. A bad dream." His hold tightened. "I'm right here. No one is taking you. I swear it."

She drifted back to sleep.

***

Sunlight trickled through the blinds. Maisey rolled over and slowly stretched. Then she carefully peeked over the edge of the bed.

No Odin.

Her gaze darted around the room. The blankets had been neatly folded and placed on her reading chair, with the pillow stacked on top. But there was no sign of her PI. "Odin?" She slipped from the bed. Shoved her hair out of her eyes and headed for the bathroom. Maybe he was in the kitchen, getting some breakfast.

She swung open the bathroom door. It took her sleep-fuzzed mind a moment too long to process the scene before her.

The blurry form of a man behind her foggy shower door...

Steam drifted in the air around her. Steam, but there was no water because he'd just turned off the shower and he was—

Opening the glass shower door.

"Odin!" Her cry of alarm came too late. Maisey got a full-frontal view. Full, frontal, and fabulous because obviously that had *not* been a cold shower. Oh, no, mega hot. Not just because of the steam in the air but because of—

"Wanna hand me a towel?"

She grabbed a nearby towel and threw it at him. She didn't even wait to see if he caught it. Maisey had already spun around. "I am so sorry! I had no idea you were in here. I—" *I should go. I should definitely go.*

"I'm covered."

Immediately, she looked back.

Gah. Why had she looked back? Now the towel was draped over his hips, but beads of moisture darted their way over that amazing muscled chest of his and down his abs. *Abs for days and days…*

"Feel free to have your turn." He motioned for the shower. "And since I know how much you like for things to be…*even*…" He winked at her. "Maybe I'll get my turn, too."

What was he talking about—oh, right. Their first kiss. Then their second. And her saying they needed to be even and… "Are you asking to see me naked?" Her mind was not functioning properly. She hadn't gotten even a sip of coffee yet. It was too early for this.

Or…maybe not early enough?

He closed in on her. "Why?" His hand curled under her chin. A careful, tender touch. "Are you offering?"

CHAPTER EIGHT

She was beautiful first thing in the morning. Maisey's thick hair tumbled around her shoulders, gently tousled. Her eyes were wide, her plump lips parted, and all Odin wanted to do was lean forward and pull her against him.

"Are you teasing me right now?"

He straightened. He *had* been leaning forward. "I don't tease. Ask any of my friends." They'd laugh their asses off at the very idea.

"I haven't met any of your friends. So it's hard for me to ask them." Her gaze dipped down his body. Lingered. Warmed. The gold in her eyes seemed to burn brighter.

Well, well... "Like what you see?"

"Very much," she replied instantly even as she did a quick, fanning motion with her hand. "But I'm sure you get compliments from women all the time. I'm sure they tell you how much they'd love to lick the water off your abs and—"

A laugh sputtered out of him.

Her eyes closed.

His hand rose and pressed to her cheek. "Can't say anyone has ever told me that before." He couldn't recall the last time he'd laughed, either. He brushed his lips over her forehead. The caress seemed to be the most natural thing in the world. But his laughter faded as he eased back. Because suddenly, he did have an image of Maisey licking the water off his abs. Only in that image, her mouth dipped lower and lower. She tugged the towel from his hips and her mouth went right to his—

"I should shower. Get dressed," Maisey blurted.

Ah, so she *hadn't* been offering to get naked for him. Too bad. His hand slid away from her silken skin. "When you change your mind, you let me know." He brushed past her. His body had to press against hers. The bathroom was small. He was big.

She was perfect.

"Change my mind—about what?"

He looked back at her. "Letting me see you naked."

Maisey gulped. "You…were serious."

Had she doubted that? Maybe he should make certain they were crystal clear. "We've been dancing around things so far. A few kisses."

Her nose scrunched. "I thought they were pretty good kisses."

Damn fantastic. "Those are the preliminaries. But if I get you naked, if you're standing in front of me and I get to see every single inch of you, I'm gonna want to touch."

She swallowed.

"Then taste. Lick and kiss." His voice roughened. "Then I'll want to fuck."

"That's, um, quite the order of operations you have going there."

What was it about her that made him feel so good? His dick was shoving against the towel, making a freaking tent that she *had* to see, and even though he wanted her like mad, her words still made him want to smile.

She didn't get it. He wasn't the smiling type. Odin wasn't the guy who did the easy jokes and laughed all the time. He had a buddy who covered that bill. Odin was the serious one. The too-intense one. The one who never seemed to fit so well with crowds and who always said stupid shit to women.

Except…

Maisey makes everything feel different.

He released a breath. Ignored his aching dick, for the moment. "If you're standing before me, naked, offering your body to me, I will fucking take it." Bald. Flat. A warning. "I won't pull back the way I've done after a few kisses. You cross that line, you take that step, and I will devour you."

She didn't move.

He did. It was either get the hell out of there or pounce on her. He stalked from the bathroom. Shut the door. Then glared down at his eager dick.

***

Maisey stared at the door.

I will devour you. Before he'd left, she'd had to clamp her lips together to hold back her instinctive response of, *Promises, promises.*

Now she focused on breathing. Nice, slow breaths. Steam still drifted in the air around her. Oh, no. That would not do. She didn't need anything to make her hotter. She was feeling more than hot and bothered enough, thanks.

Maisey spun and marched for the shower. She yanked on the water. The very, very cold water.

I will devour you.

***

"This place doesn't look so bad." Nightfall had just swept over the area. The day had passed in a whirlwind of activity. Odin had gone with her to get a new laptop. He'd trailed her back to campus where they'd reviewed security footage and found absolutely nothing useful. They'd followed Clay for a while. Again, they'd turned up nothing overly useful.

And now it was time for the big event. A trip to Ramsey's. The graveled parking lot was filled with a variety of vehicles. Sports cars, trucks, motorcycles. Some extremely high end. Some looking as if they'd fall apart if you blew on them too hard. Thick woods surrounded the long, flat building. No other businesses were nearby. As she slowly approached the entrance—and the two bouncers who sat on tall, black stools—the loud scream of music blasted from inside of Ramsey's.

Maisey hadn't exactly been sure how to dress for this occasion. She'd fretted over the outfit for a good thirty minutes because she had wanted to be certain she blended. After three changes, she'd finally settled for a pair of old jeans, ripped on the left thigh, and a form-fitting, black top. She'd gone with red high heels, too, because she needed to sex it up a bit, didn't she?

Maybe?

Odin had looked at her outfit and just grunted.

He hadn't seemed to care what he wore. Jeans. T-shirt. Boots. Done. She'd discovered that was just his typical outfit. Maisey had to admit, it worked for him. *Sexy.* Kind of an effortless sexiness.

He was at her side as they headed for the bouncers. She offered them a big, friendly smile.

"Dim it," Odin muttered as he bent his head and wrapped his arm around her shoulders. He hauled her up against him.

Dim it? Her smile slipped.

The bouncers were sweeping their gazes over her.

"Haven't seen you here before," one said.

"That's because I haven't come here before," Odin snapped back.

"Wasn't talking to you," the guy fired. He had a smirk on his face as he let his gaze dart over Maisey. Looked like he was in his early twenties, with bright blond, almost white hair. He wore a thick, leather coat even though it was helluva hot and, as always, the humidity in the area was killer.

Odin moved in front of her. Positioned himself so that he loomed over the bouncer on his stool. "I'm talking to *you*, asshole," Odin told him.

Oh. So he was going to play the scene aggressively? Fair enough. The people in the club would probably respect that kind of approach. She tried to realign her posture so she looked tougher, too.

"She's with me." Odin's voice rang out. "*Me*. Got it? So if I'm not here, she's not here. Now open the fucking door and let us in."

Odin was way bigger than the white-haired bouncer.

The other bouncer laughed at the exchange. "Dumbass," he said, not to Odin, but to the shriveled-up guy in the coat. "Never pick on someone three times your size." He hopped off his stool and opened the door for Odin. "Sorry, man. He's still new. Thinks he has something to prove."

Odin didn't move. "Don't screw with me again," he ordered the blond.

Since the door was open, Maisey crept over to slip inside—

Odin's arm came around her shoulders again. He brushed his mouth over her cheek then whispered in her ear, "Did we forget the plan?"

The plan...for her to stick close to him. She *was* close to him so Maisey fired him a disgruntled look. But then they were heading inside, and she was so busy taking everything in that she stopped worrying about Odin and just studied the scene.

Wow. No wonder Whitney had been coming there for research. The place was packed. Money was exchanging hands—she could see the sly trade-offs beneath the tables. And the guys on the right, the ones over there playing pool and drinking beers from long-necked bottles—she recognized some of their tats. They were part of a local motorcycle group that—

"Don't stare too long. They'll think you're interested. They'll come over. I'll have to correct their wrong assumptions. That correction will involve ass kicking."

Now he had her attention once more. Maisey's head whipped back toward him. "What about rule one?"

He curled his hands around her hips. They'd just reached the bar, and he lifted her up and put her on the nearby stool. His fingers lingered around her. "Warned you already," he said, as his head dipped toward her throat.

To be a helpful, team player, Maisey tipped back her head so he'd have better access.

His lips feathered over her skin.

Hello. Her breath shuddered out. Since when was her neck *that* sensitive? Her nipples hardened and her body pulsed.

"Rules don't apply tonight."

They didn't?

"I have to play this scene a certain way. You won't like what you see me do." His head lifted. He stared straight into her eyes.

Her hands rose and pressed to his chest. "I like everything I see about you."

"You won't like what's coming next."

Maisey highly doubted that. To date, she'd pretty much liked everything about Odin. To be safe, though… "Before you get all big and bad, how about we just try *asking* for the info?" Seemed like a grand idea to her.

"Uh, Maisey…" He shook his head. "In a place like this, you don't just sashay up and *ask* for intel."

"I'm not so sure about that." You never knew until you asked. She spun around on her stool.

"Hi, bartender!" Her voice was friendly and warm. In her experience, if you were nice to people, then generally, people were nice back.

Behind her, Odin swore.

The bartender peered at her and ambled closer.

"I'm looking for my friend." Maisey's hand shoved into the cute little bag she'd brought along. Odin had given her mace to put inside the bag. She was working on getting her taser. Maisey hauled up her new phone—they'd picked it up today and gotten it synced with her account. She scrolled until she had a picture of Whitney. She flipped the phone around toward the bartender. "By any chance, have you seen her?"

The bartender—a grizzled guy with a, well, she supposed Odin might describe it as a fuck-you face—looked at the picture for all of two seconds, then glared at Maisey. "You're a cop."

"What? No, absolutely not." She smiled brighter.

The bartender's beady stare darted to Odin. He pointed. "Cop."

"This is going about how I expected...once you started talking," Odin groused.

"No," Maisey tried to explain to the confused bartender. "My friend is missing, and we're just trying to find her. If you'd look at the picture again, I think you might remember her. She was—"

"I remember her," he gritted back. Then, "*Cop!*" he yelled.

That yell cut over the screaming music.

"If you know her," Maisey continued doggedly because she was sure she'd seen a flicker of recognition in the man's eyes, "then I would appreciate it if you would tell me what you know. I can pay you."

"Don't move," Odin told Maisey.

She threw a disgruntled look over her shoulder. "Why would I move? I am making headway here. And we didn't have to get physical. I didn't have to see that dark, dangerous side that you—" She broke off because she'd just caught sight of the movement happening behind him. A bearded man was rushing up with a chair held high above his head. "Odin!"

Odin's body tensed.

The chair slammed into him. The wooden legs broke and rained down to the floor.

Maisey's jaw dropped. "He hit you!" *With a chair*. Oh. My. God.

"I let him hit first," Odin said as he rolled back his shoulders. "Did that for you. See, I followed the rule—"

"Odin! He's getting another chair!"

Odin spun around.

And the crazy attacker was coming at Odin with another chair. He'd lifted it high over his shoulders—probably because he thought that would give the blow more force. But Maisey realized the movement had just exposed the guy. Odin simply lifted his foot and shoved his boot hard into the man's paunchy stomach.

The air left the attacker with a *whoosh* of sound, and he staggered back. He bumped into a table, fell, and the chair he'd held slammed down on top of him.

The band hadn't stopped playing. In this kind of place, Maisey figured you didn't stop when one little fight broke out. Though, honestly, this did not strike her as a *little* fight. Especially not when—

"To the left!" Maisey yelled. "I think he has friends!"

Odin's gaze swung to the left.

A table of men had gotten to their feet. One slammed his beer bottle onto the edge of the table, breaking it, and then he charged at Odin with the weapon.

"Don't you dare!" Maisey shouted. "Don't you even think of cutting him!" This was madness!

And why was Odin just standing there? He should be jumping for cover! "Odin!"

Odin didn't seem particularly worried. When the attacker launched toward him, Odin just side stepped, and he let the man's own momentum propel him a bit too far past Odin. As soon as the man—and his weapon—slipped by Odin, then Odin's arm flew out. He locked his forearm around the attacker's throat and jerked him back. Back—then Odin slammed him *down* onto the floor.

A groan burst from the man even as the broken beer bottle rolled away.

Maisey couldn't even breathe a sigh of relief because two more men were coming at Odin. Two others from that table.

The band kept playing. If anything, they got louder.

Maisey stared around in growing horror.
"Stay back," Odin told her. "I've got this."
His attackers closed in.

CHAPTER NINE

Maisey gaped at the scene before her. Odin was being attacked by multiple strangers, and he just kept taking them down like it was *nothing*. He wasn't just brute strength pummeling them, either. No, he was moving with a lethal grace that almost seemed mesmerizing as he—

Three more men went for him.

"Hell, no." Maisey's hand shoved into her bag and came back up with the mace he'd given her. She and Odin hadn't gone over any fighting techniques that day—they would be correcting that, ASAP—but in the meantime, she was not just going to sit there and watch him get attacked by a gang of men. Yes, Odin was impressive, certainly. But he couldn't last forever as more enemies seemed to spring from every corner of the dark club.

She leveled a furious glance at the bartender. "This is your fault."

He backed up a step. "Don't spray that shit in my eyes!"

"*Don't tempt me.*" But her target wasn't the bartender—and to think, she'd intended to give him a twenty in exchange for information. *You just lost your payday, my friend.* Maisey dismissed him from her thoughts because her goal was the men attacking Odin. She jumped off the barstool and launched toward the fray.

And a wall stepped in front of her. "Sorry, but he won't like that."

The wall wasn't quite as big as Odin. Broad shoulders. Built chest. Her gaze lifted. Dark hair. Bright eyes—eyes a very similar shade of blue to Odin's. And he was grinning. Grinning as if he'd just been told the very best joke in the entire world. "Get out of my way," Maisey ordered him. Her hand tightened around the mace.

"Wouldn't recommend using that in here." He pointed up. "The ceiling fans are blowing for all they are worth, and you'll probably get kickback in your eyes. Plus, when you do manage to spray some jackasses, they'll just get mad and charge at you, and that will make Odin lose his ever-loving-mind. Man always has a thing for protecting the ladies. Or, hell, protecting anyone he thinks might be weaker than he is."

She shot around the stranger.

He curled his arm around her stomach and yanked her right back. Furious, she slammed her elbow into his midsection—she knew that move from her crime shows. Then she stomped down with her foot, aiming for his fancy tennis shoes. He swore, but didn't let her go and, in fact, his grip tightened. She was getting ready to head-butt him—another move from her crime shows—when a detail clicked for her. *He called Odin by name.* "Wait, you *know* Odin?"

At that moment, Odin looked up. He saw her—saw her struggling—and let out what could only be termed a roar.

"Uh, oh." The man holding her didn't seem particularly concerned. "Now he's pissed. Look what you did."

What *she'd* done? And now—Odin was pissed *now*? As in, he hadn't been pissed before? He'd certainly looked pissed to her.

Odin threw off the men who'd been on him. Threw them so hard one man stumbled about four feet before crashing into the floor.

"Got to admire Odin's style." The man's grip finally loosened on her. "When he works, it is a thing of beauty."

She jerked free and spun toward him. She had her mace up and pointed toward his eyes.

He smiled at her. His bright blue eyes gleamed. "Hello. I should have introduced myself before. I'm a friend of Odin's. Looked like he was in trouble, so I thought I'd help out."

She heard a crash behind her. Maisey winced. "You aren't helping. You're holding me up and stopping me from—"

"Potentially getting hurt?" he cut in to finish. "Absolutely. You're welcome. If you get hurt, I have a feeling Odin will burn this place to the ground."

He didn't mean that, of course. Or did he?

But she didn't want to find out. The whole scene was insane and she had to take control. She leapt up on the nearest table. Some people were still dancing. The band kept playing and— "I just want to find my friend!" Maisey shouted. A few heads turned her way. "We are *not* cops." Though, jeez, she would sure love it if some cops could come to help out. "I'm a history teacher and a podcaster. He's my partner." She pointed to Odin. He wasn't looking at her. "My friend is Whitney Augustine. She used to come here, but she's been missing, and I just wanted a lead. I wanted something or someone to help me find her."

The men at the pool table had stopped playing. Actually, it was three men and two women. One guy from that group turned toward her. Jet black hair. Dark eyes. Tattoos on his fisted hands. He began striding toward her, and Maisey tensed.

"You just had to attract attention." It was the fellow who'd claimed to be Odin's friend. He huffed out a breath. "Here we go," he muttered as he placed himself in front of her and her table. "I knew this wasn't going to be a lucky night."

But the man with the tats was focused completely on her. "I know Whitney."

He did?

He raised a fist into the air, and the fighting just...stopped. Or rather, the men fighting Odin stopped. Odin continued right on as he plowed a fist into one guy's jaw.

Down he went.

The man with the tats opened his raised hand. She realized that he had a red rose tattooed inside one palm. Her gaze was caught by that tattoo. Maisey remembered that before she'd vanished, Whitney had suddenly taken a keen interest in roses. She'd had a fresh red rose in her office every single day.

"Who are you?" Maisey asked. She started to leap off the table.

Odin appeared. He reached for her. Lifted her down. "Raising some hell?"

No, she absolutely had not been. Why would he suggest that? "I was getting intel." And doing a pretty fine job of it. "You were the one raising hell." As evidenced by the wreckage and the injured people scattered around Ramsey's.

Odin's jaw firmed, but he glanced toward the man who'd admitted to knowing Whitney.

"Let's take this into the back," the man with the tats said. He'd dropped his hand. Fisted the rose once again. "No one else needs to hear this." With those words, he spun on his heel and began walking toward a red door on the right.

Maisey took a quick step to follow him.

"Seriously?" It was the so-called "friend" of Odin's. "Your girlfriend has like, zero self-preservation skills, man. It is a good thing I was here to help you out. Must've been fate."

Odin's head swung toward him. "Jinx." He shook his head, as if he couldn't quite believe what—who—he was seeing. "What in the hell are you doing in this place?"

"Oh, you know." A shrug. "Looking for a good time. A bad time. Anything in between." He scraped a hand over his stubbled jaw and pointed to Maisey. "That one was ready to jump into the fray with you. I held her back, like the amazing friend that I am."

Odin's attention shifted to her. Then fell to her hand. The one that still gripped her mace.

"Could we move this along?" Maisey urged. She noticed that there didn't appear to be even a scratch on Odin. Considering he'd been hit with multiple chairs, she figured that was a miracle. "The man with intel is waiting on us."

Odin looked around the bar. She knew by the stubborn set of his jaw that he was not happy.

She was hardly thrilled herself. *Odin could have been seriously hurt*. And she suspected his next plan without him having to say a word. "Don't even think it," Maisey warned him. "I'm supposed to stay with you, Odin. You aren't having a chat without me."

"Not like I'd leave you out here." His fingers threaded with hers. "Jinx, you'll watch the door?"

"On it," Jinx said instantly.

Okay, so, they *were* friends. Especially if Odin trusted the guy to guard their backs. Odin kept a tight grip on her right hand. With her left, she tucked her mace back into her bag. For the moment, it seemed she wouldn't be needing it. There was some sort of temporary truce happening in the bar. "Sorry I almost maced you," Maisey told Jinx.

"Think nothing of it," he assured her with a wink. "Happens all the time."

Did it? How unfortunate. And what did he do to provoke mace attacks?

"Don't believe anything he says," Odin told her gruffly as he steered her toward the red door. Everyone seemed to be giving them a wide berth. Everyone but Jinx. He ambled behind them. "The man is never serious."

"Life is too short for that," Jinx called, obviously overhearing. "Besides, you're serious enough for both of us."

She frowned back at him. "I do not like the tone. Odin has a wonderful laugh and a great sense of humor."

"Oh." Jinx nodded. "You're drunk. I didn't realize that. It would explain why you were dancing on the table."

Her mouth dropped open. "I absolutely was not dancing—"

Odin kicked open the red door. "Guard it," he snapped to Jinx.

Jinx saluted him.

Odin pulled her inside.

When the door shut, it was like stepping into another world. *Silence.* Immediate and intense. The blasting music vanished as if it had never existed.

"Soundproof." Odin nodded. He still held her hand in his. "Perfect place for you to do business, huh, Ramsey?"

He knew this guy, too? And, wait—Ramsey? As in, this man owned the place?

"Ah, my reputation proceeds me." The man he'd called Ramsey gave a half-smile that never reached his eyes. "Sorry, but I don't know *you.*"

"He's Odin," Maisey supplied, and her voice sounded too high to her own ears. "I'm Maisey. I'm—"

"Maisey Bright." Ramsey took two steps toward her. Studied her with that faint smile still on his face and not in his eyes. "Now, you, I do know. Whitney mentioned you a time or two."

Oh? Maisey didn't trust this man. Not for a second. "Funny, she never mentioned you."

His smile disappeared. "That's because our relationship was private."

Relationship? "You were involved with her?" Ramsey was attractive in a dangerous and deadly sort of way. If you went for that. But...

"We were fucking," Ramsey told her.

Okay. That cut to the chase. *Blunt.*

"You realize you just jumped to the top of our suspect list," Odin said. He let go of Maisey's hand. He angled his body so it was in front of hers, but if she inched to the side, she could still see Ramsey.

She inched.

"I didn't hurt Whitney. I'd never hurt her." Ramsey's voice was flat.

"Ramsey..." Odin sighed. "You have a record a mile long."

Ramsey shrugged. "So? You tell me once when I have ever hurt a woman." His gaze slid to Maisey once more. "I've been looking for Whitney, too. The night she vanished, she was supposed to come and meet me. Here, at the bar. Only I waited and she never showed." His eyelids flickered. "Thought maybe she'd changed her mind."

"Changed her mind?" Maisey latched onto that. "About what?"

Another shrug. "Does it matter?"

"Yes, it does." How could he think it didn't? "Everything matters. She's missing. She's the third woman to go missing like this and—"

"Third?" Ramsey's voice dropped. Became lethal. "What in the hell are you talking about?"

Maisey wet dry lips. "I've been researching. There were two other cases like this before Whitney was taken. Two other women who just vanished, leaving all of their belongings behind."

"You're saying she was *taken*." His eyes had turned to slits.

"Well, yes, that's why we're here. We wanted to see if anyone here knew what had happened." She brushed back a lock of her hair.

"What Maisey means..." Odin said. "Is we are looking for other suspects. And you just conveniently jumped into our path. You were fucking Whitney. Did you get mad when she rejected you? Did you make Whitney Augustine disappear?"

Silence.

"That wasn't very tactful," Maisey whispered to Odin.

"Screw tact." Not a whisper.

Okay. If they were going down that path, then she'd be blunt, too. "You gave her the roses," she told Ramsey. "The ones that kept appearing in her office each day."

Ramsey jerked.

She took that response as a yes. And if he'd been giving Whitney the roses that made her smile so often... "It wasn't just about fucking."

Ramsey's lips pressed into a thin line.

"Her face lit up when she showed me her roses. She cared about you." Maisey scooted around Odin's formidable frame so she could better face-off with Ramsey. "You were going off together, weren't you? Running away?"

His gaze cut from hers. "My life isn't the kind of life a woman like her could fit in."

Maisey nodded. This was making sense to her. "So you were going to leave that life. Together. Both of you. But then she didn't show. *She* vanished. You thought she'd rejected you."

His Adam's apple bobbed.

"You were looking for her, thinking she'd gone somewhere to...what? Hide from you?"

A shrug of one shoulder. "Not like it's the first time people have run from me."

He wasn't looking at her. She couldn't read his expression, his feelings, if he didn't look her way. She needed to see his eyes. "Whitney could see the good in people."

His head swung toward her.

"If she was with you, it wasn't because she had a thing for bad boys. She was with you because she saw something good." She held his gaze. "A packed bag was found in her home. She intended to leave with you. But something stopped her." Something...someone. "If you weren't involved in what happened..." And her instincts said that he wasn't. She could *see* his pain as she stared into his dark eyes. "Then help us to figure out who was. Did Whitney mention anything about someone following her? Or someone who made her nervous? Or anything that might have happened—"

"He's dead," Ramsey said simply.

"Excuse me?" She must have misheard.

Odin swore.

"Whoever took my Whitney—he's a fucking dead man. I'm putting out the word as soon as we leave this room. Offering fifty Gs for info. Then I'll find him, and I'll kill him. By the time I am done with him, the bastard will be begging me to end him."

This was *not* the way she'd expected the conversation to go. "The police—"

"Time for you to leave the bar. I don't think it's in your best interest to come back." His stare shifted between them. "Either of you."

This guy was gonna go all rogue and get his own justice? Super bad plan. Amazingly bad. "What if you kill the wrong person?" Maisey asked. Had he considered that possibility?

Another shrug.

Dammit, he shrugged too much.

"Odin is a PI!" She slapped her hand against his chest. "He works with Trouble for Hire. You know they stopped that last serial killer—"

Ramsey took a lurching step back. "You're telling me a *serial killer* took my Whitney?"

Her lips clamped together before she could tell him that, yes, she very much feared that—

"We don't know," Odin rumbled. "That's what we're investigating."

"Who are your suspects? Other than me."

Odin shook his head. "I give you a name, and you'll kill the person, guilty or innocent."

Ramsey surged forward. He was smaller than Odin, but his rage was clear. "What the hell would you do?" He jerked his thumb toward Maisey. "Someone takes your girl—someone *steals* her— and you find out it might be a freaking serial. You gonna stand there and tell me you wouldn't rip apart every fucker you found?"

Odin's face changed. A subtle change, but, suddenly, he looked just as dangerous and deadly as Ramsey. "Someone comes after *my* girl, someone tries to take *her* from me, and I will crucify the motherfucker."

Goosebumps rose on her arms.

"She *was* almost taken last night," Odin added grimly. "Right on the campus of Dunson College. Got there just in time to pull her away from the bastard. He escaped, but I *will* find him."

"You think it was the same person?" Ramsey's body rocked forward. "Whoever took my Whitney is now after her?" Another thumb jerk to Maisey.

"We're asking questions people don't like," Odin replied. "We're making someone nervous."

Yes, they were making the perp nervous. The creep they were hunting.

Ramsey smiled again. An ice-cold smile that *did* reach his eyes. It lit his stare with lethal promise. "Then it's gonna be a race."

Maisey didn't see a race...

"You two find him first...or I do," Ramsey murmured. "And you already know what will happen when I get my hands on him."

He was gonna kill the guy.

"Now, get the hell out of my way. The talk is over."

Maisey didn't move. No, she *did* move. After about ten seconds had passed of Odin and Ramsey having a stare-off, she jumped between them. "Two other women are missing. This isn't just about Whitney. It's about all of them. Their families deserve to know what happened. You can't just take the killer and make him vanish. You can't torture him—"

"Sure, I can. It's the same thing your man would do for you."

He thought Odin would torture for her? And Odin wasn't exactly denying the charge. For the moment, she blazed on and said, "You get a lead, give it to us. Let us try to help those other victims and their families. *Then* you can have him." Actually, she intended to call the cops, but this didn't seem like the moment to tell Ramsey that plan. "Deal?" She held her breath.

He grunted. Walked around her and Odin. Yanked open the door.

Does that mean no deal? Maisey was afraid that was precisely what his exit meant. Her breath slowly eased out. "That was intense." Maisey turned toward Odin. "I guess we should go—" She broke off. Odin still appeared way dangerous. Way scary.

Way...out of control?

It was in the bright gleam of his eyes. The hard set of his jaw. In the fierce glare that he was leveling on her. "Wh-what?" A little stutter that she couldn't help.

"Do you know how dangerous this shit is?"

"How is it dangerous?" They'd just been having a private conversation. Granted, that conversation had been with one seriously intense and possibly homicidal guy. "I have you. My own personal PI. My—"

He yanked her into his arms. Hauled her up against him. Took her mouth. The kiss was angry and rough and she had not expected him to be kissing her in this place. Not when it looked like he was so angry he wanted to thunder and rage.

But he was kissing her with a frantic need, a need that she couldn't deny, and Maisey found her nails sinking into his powerful arms as she arched ever closer. Every time they kissed, she could swear the passion just got hotter and hotter and...oh, wow, his tongue...

Stop. Not the place. Tell him this is—

"Jeez, man," Jinx's wry voice announced. "This is not the place for that shit. Half the bar wants to kick your ass. The other half wants you to become their new gang leader or something. Save the make-out session for later."

Odin's body stiffened. His hold on her tightened, but he lifted his head.

"Don't shoot the messenger," Jinx drawled as he stood in the open doorway. "Not like I said don't ever have fun. Just don't do it here. We need to clear our asses out of this place, stat. As soon as Ramsey marched out, he immediately called a meeting with all his top people. That's bad news, in case you didn't know."

Ramsey was calling a meeting—because he wanted to hunt Whitney's killer. Hunt him. Torture him. Kill him. "This was not part of the plan," Maisey whispered.

Odin's eyes glittered down at her.

"Whatever the plan was," Jinx said, "it's gone to shit. And I say again—we need to clear out. *Now.* I rather like my face—the ladies do, too—so I am not in the mood to have it hammered in tonight."

Odin's head moved in a jerky nod. His eyes never left Maisey. "Don't talk to anyone. Don't look at them."

What in the world was he going on about now—

"The situation is gonna be delicate as fuck. We'll handle it with kid gloves."

Still in the doorway, Jinx cleared his throat. "Hate to break it to you, O, but you are so not the delicate type. You're more of a sledgehammer."

A growl was Odin's response.

"Right." Jinx coughed. "So I'll go first. We'll put the lovely lady in the middle..."

Another growl.

"And you'll be the caboose on this party train," Jinx finished. "That way, if things go to hell faster than I think, I can get your girl out, you can kick some ass, then I'll come back in to help. Plan?"

"I don't like that plan," Maisey said immediately. "Leaving Odin behind is not an option for me." Why would they run to safety and leave Odin behind?

"OhmyGod. Did you really say that?" Jinx snagged her hand. Curled his fingers with hers. "That is some precious shit right there. Like, *precious*. But we're moving now." With that, he hauled her out of the door.

She dug in her heels. Because, seriously, what part of *leaving Odin behind is not an option for me* had he not understood? But then she felt Odin's massive hands clamp around her hips as he urged her forward.

As soon as they stepped out...

Silence. A silence that was the total opposite of the way the bar had been moments before. A silence that almost matched the sound-proof room.

The band wasn't playing any longer. All eyes were immediately on them. She stumbled, but Odin's grip made sure she didn't fall. Maisey kept going forward, and her eyes darted toward the pool table. Sure enough, Ramsey was huddled tight with a group of grizzled guys and the two ladies who'd been with them earlier. One of the women casually twirled a knife in her hand.

Ramsey looked up. Nodded to Maisey.

She nodded back. Was that even the right response? She wasn't sure. But the exit was close. The bouncer even had it open for them. The same bouncer who'd given her and Odin the hard time when they first went in. Now, his eyes were huge, and he seemed pale.

Jinx hauled her over the threshold. "Great service," he said loudly, seemingly directing his words at the blond bouncer. "Fabulous band. I will leave a five-star review online for you, and I will definitely be back to—"

"You *won't* be back." Ramsey's hard voice boomed out.

"I will not be back," Jinx immediately said. "And I will not tell my friends to visit. Horrible, disgusting hole in the wall. Why would anyone ever want to come here?"

The bouncer glared. But he also still looked afraid.

Jinx finally let go of Maisey's hand—so he could slap the bouncer on the shoulder. "No offense," he told the bouncer. "As far as holes-in-the-wall go, it's a grand one."

Odin hadn't let her go. He hadn't—

"Not done with the big one," someone snarled from behind them. "Bastard broke my nose—"

Odin heaved her forward. "Get her to safety," he barked at Jinx.

All the humor had fled Jinx's face. He suddenly looked almost as intense and deadly as Odin. "Roger that." He grabbed for Maisey.

But she wasn't in the mood to be grabbed again, thank you very much. She whirled back for Odin and yanked out her mace to—

Odin downed his lunging attacker with one blow. A fast snap that sent the man slamming into the dirty floor. A few others began to rise from their chairs.

"No!" Maisey leapt in front of Odin. "We're leaving." *As fast as we can.* "Ramsey!" She focused on him. "*We are leaving.*" Which was code for—*tell these people to stop!*

"What. The. Fuck?" Odin rumbled behind her.

"Back up," she told Odin.

Ramsey had waved his hand toward her. "No one touches the woman."

Okay. That was something. If no one was touching her, then they couldn't get to Odin since she was currently in front of them. Maisey thought there were far too many bleeding, bruised people in the bar who seemed eager for another shot at Odin. Honestly, she was surprised they hadn't learned their lesson the first time they'd tangled with him.

She inched back. She'd get Odin through the door. They'd jump in the Jeep. Get the heck out of Dodge. Good plan. Winning plan. It was—

Odin lifted her up. Just scooped her right into those massive arms of his. Then he stalked out of the club. The bouncer slammed the door closed behind them.

Odin didn't speak. He didn't let her go. Just kept angry stomping with her toward their ride. She realized that Jinx was shadowing their movements. Maisey strained to see if anyone was following their little group out of the club.

Luckily, the door to Ramsey's stayed closed. She could hear the shriek of music again. The band had resumed playing.

Odin plunked her down in the passenger seat of the Jeep. Even though it was dark, she could feel the heat of what she knew was his glare. "What the fuck was that?" Odin snarled.

"It was sweetness," Jinx replied. "Pure, perfect sweetness. I swear, if you aren't dating her, I will volunteer to do the deed. I will—"

In a flash, Odin had whirled and grabbed Jinx. Shoved the other man against the Jeep.

But Jinx simply held up his hands. "That was a test. Happy to say you passed with flying colors, you high achiever you."

"Not the time," Odin gritted out.

"I agree." Jinx glanced toward the bar. "How about you take the pretty lady home, then you and I can meet up to talk about what the hell is going on?"

"No," Maisey said instantly.

Both men's heads swung toward her.

"We will *all* talk about what's happening. It's my case. I hired Odin. No one is cutting me out." They could just stop that plan right then and there.

"War's cabin." Banked rage filled Odin's voice. "Meet us there. Make sure you're not followed."

"No one follows me. I'm a master at evasive action." With that, Jinx sidled away and vanished into the shadows.

Odin hurried around the Jeep. Jumped inside. Had them out of the parking lot and roaring down the road. He took a series of twists and turns, and even though Maisey was familiar with the area, he had her lost in moments. He was also driving helluva fast. "Uh, Odin..."

He took a hard left.

She grabbed the dashboard. "I think we should slow down."

"I have to make sure we're not tailed." A quick right.

Her eyes closed. Motion sickness was not her friend. "We should also make sure that we arrive alive." That was important, too.

The Jeep hurtled forward. Her breath blew out. At least they were done with the turns. The Jeep's top was off, and the wind whipped her hair, tossing it around her face. Was it her imagination, or had he slowed, just a bit?

Her eyes cracked open. She could smell the ocean. She took a deep, steadying gulp of air. "We should...talk about what happened."

"Oh, we'll fucking talk about it, all right."

She turned toward him. "Are you mad at me?" After she'd tried to help him? Multiple times?

"Mad isn't the right word."

"Then what is the right word?" Her own anger stirred.

"You'll find out." A grim warning. "As soon as we get to War's cabin."

She didn't like his tone. "Odin?"

"I don't recommend pushing me right now, Maisey."

"Oh, really? I don't recommend that you push *me* either. In case you missed it, I saved your ass back there!" Where was the gratitude?

"What?"

"I saved your ass. Yours. Your hot, sexy ass. I saved it. I got us out of there without more fighting."

He shook his head. "Not believing this."

He'd better believe it. "You had some crazy plan about staying behind and fighting alone. Not happening." That very idea still had her seeing red. "In case you missed it, you aren't a one-man show any longer. You and I? We're partners. That means I don't leave you. It means—"

"*Don't push, Maisey.* You won't like what happens next..."

"I don't like anything that has happened so far this night!" This night had not been her idea of a good time. "You took on a bar full of criminals all by yourself! You were some kind of crazy fighting machine and I was terrified that you were going to get hurt!" The truth burst from her. "I don't want you hurt! You *can't* be hurt because—" She stopped. Just in the nick of time. Just before she'd said something she couldn't take back. Something along the lines of...

You can't be hurt because...I am starting to care too much about you.

Maisey didn't say another word.

CHAPTER TEN

He whipped off the road. The Jeep bounced, dipped. *Gah!* She held onto the seat for dear life but they were actually...on some kind of road? Possibly a driveway?

Just how long had they been driving? Everything had passed in a blur of fear, nausea, and anger for her, but as he sped ahead, she realized that she could now hear the crash of waves. They were thundering against the shore. He'd taken her to the beach? "Uh, Odin?"

He braked the Jeep in front of a beach house, one that stood high on wooden stilts that would protect it from storm surges. He killed the engine and leapt from the Jeep.

Slowly, she unhooked her seat belt. "I take it that this place is War's cabin?" Her voice was a little more subdued now. Her racing heartbeat had calmed down, and as she'd been reassured that they hadn't been followed, some of her fear had receded.

"Yes." Nothing else. Just that fast, rough response. He glanced around. "We need to get inside."

"But we weren't followed." What was the rush? She'd like to take a minute and just breathe.

"I'll feel better when we're inside."

By all means, she wanted him to feel better. Maisey stomped her way to the cabin. Up the stairs. The salty air wrapped around her, and the waves kept pounding as he unlocked the front door and ushered her onto a screened porch. She barely glanced at her surroundings before he was swinging open another door. This one led to the main portion of the house and—

"What in the hell were you thinking?"

She spun toward him. Maisey had to suck in a sharp breath at the look on his face. When he'd been driving, she'd known that he was mad. But...

The expression on his face was absolutely savage.

"You put yourself in front of me." A hard step toward her. "Don't ever do that shit again."

Her shoulders squared. "You put yourself in front of me all the time. It's kinda been your thing since we met."

Another hard step. "Damn straight it's my thing." He towered over her. "In case you missed it, I'm bigger than you, stronger than you, and a million times meaner than you. I can take a threat. I can take an attack..."

Okay, he was deliberately trying to be all intimidating and tough and he had no idea just how mean she could be when the situation called for it—

"But I cannot fucking take anything happening to you," he added, voice thickening even more. "I'm not *worth* something happening to you. Got it? I can take the hits. I've always taken them. I *will* always take them. But you are different. *Never put yourself in danger for me.*"

Her chin lifted. "That's just not a promise I'm willing to make."

"*What?*" Veins seemed to bulge in his neck.

"I'm not going to say that I'll hide and let danger take you. Not happening. If I can help you, I'm gonna do it!"

He grabbed her. Hauled her into his arms. Crushed his mouth against hers. The kiss was unlike the others they'd shared. Absolutely consuming. Crazed. Desperate.

She kissed him back the same way. Her mouth opened wider. Her tongue met his in a hungry dance. His taste had lust exploding through her.

The storm of emotions she'd felt on the drive there had transformed in an instant—became greedy, consuming lust. She yanked at his shirt. Shoved it out of her way. Then her hands were touching hot, hard skin. Lickable, sexy skin. He was so strong. So gorgeous.

Her hands slid down. She grabbed the front of his jeans. Yanked at the button. Distantly, she was aware that this was very much not the way she usually acted. She didn't rip off men's clothes. Didn't haul down their zippers—as she was doing. He wasn't wearing underwear—such a typical, macho Odin thing, she wasn't even a little surprised—and his heavy cock sprang toward her. She put one of her hands on him. Squeezed him with her fingers. Like everything else about Odin, his cock was built on the same massive scale and she wasn't sure—

"Fucking *need* you." His hands were on the snap of *her* jeans now. He yanked at the button, hauled down that zipper.

She kicked off her heels. Shimmied out of the jeans. Let go of him just long enough so that she could completely ditch her jeans.

Odin lifted her and carried her a few feet. Dazed, she glanced around. Had the vague thought of...*Please, do not let anyone else be here!* But he'd said War was on his honeymoon so that meant the place was empty, didn't it?

He lowered her onto the edge of a tall table. Pushed her legs apart. She still had on her panties, so those were—

Ripped away. Maisey gasped at the sound of the fabric tearing. "Odin?"

He put his mouth on her. Pressed his mouth right against her sex, and Maisey choked out a moan as she arched against him. He wasn't doing some careful foreplay. Not some getting-to-know-you move. His mouth took her like he'd tasted her a thousand times before. Like he knew exactly what she wanted.

And he did.

His tongue licked her clit. His lips feathered over her. His finger slid into her. One, then he worked in a second as she gasped and arched. He was lashing her clit with the fast licks of his tongue, and it was incredible. She tried to say his name, but she couldn't. His fingers were stretching her. His mouth was making her insane, and her whole body was tightening as the lust and hunger she felt amped up to a fever pitch.

A hard banging echoed through the cabin. "*Odin!*" A bellow.

Odin didn't stop. His mouth became even rougher. His fingers slid out of her, then his tongue thrust inside.

Maisey lost it. She came on a wave of release so powerful that she couldn't even squeak out a breath. She could only feel pleasure so intense that she shuddered and her sex quivered and her heart thundered. Nothing had ever felt this good. Sex *wasn't* supposed to be this good. If it was, then, God, she'd been doing it wrong for years. Because this was a whole new insane level of *amazing*.

More banging. "Odin! You told me to meet you! Open the damn door!"

Her eyes opened. She looked down. Odin was still between her legs.

Odin is between my legs.

She still had on her shirt. Her bra. His hands were on her thighs—her very spread thighs—and as she gaped at him, his head slowly lifted. When she saw his eyes, the burning, primitive heat in his possessive stare, Maisey couldn't look away.

That had been...wow.

She swallowed. Licked her lips. "I think..." Her voice was too husky. She cleared her throat and tried again. "Your friend wants inside."

His gaze dropped to her sex. "So the fuck do I."

She did not have a comeback for that one. Except...*I want you in, too.*

Odin stared at her exposed body. Then his fingers slid up her thigh. Slid to her quivering core...

"Odin," she whispered.

"Odin!" Jinx thundered. "I am about to pick this lock! You know I'll do it!"

Odin's fingers brushed over her sex. His breath panted out, and she could see him fighting for his self-control.

Maisey was afraid to move.

But with his fingers teasing her...

Pleasure built again. She was so primed. So tuned to him—

Odin shuddered and moved back. His fingers slid away from her. "There's a guest bath down the hallway." His voice rasped. "You can straighten up in there." His hands slid to his open jeans. His cock—very heavy and big—thrust toward her. He pushed it back into his jeans. With an effort and a curse, he zipped and buttoned up. "I'll deal with Jinx."

Her heart hammered as she sat up on that table. She finally became aware that it was—"Oh, no. Is this a kitchen table?" Heat burned her cheeks. "I can never come here and have a meal with your friend War. Never. Ever. This is so embarrassing."

Odin caught her hand. Stared into her eyes.

Her tumble of words stopped.

"When Jinx is gone, I'm having you. Don't fucking care if it's on a table, on the floor, in a bed, or up against a wall. I'm getting in you as deep as I can go..."

Her mouth was dry.

"And I am not stopping until I come in you at least four times."

What? Four?

And who said stuff like that?

Obviously...Odin.

"Don't worry." His fingers skimmed her cheeks. "You'll come first, every single time."

That was good to know.

"Odin!" Jinx's annoyed voice. "Just so you're aware, I've picked the lock. Did it in like five seconds. I am coming in! This is a warning so everyone had sure as hell better be decent in there! But I'm getting worried, so I am coming—"

Odin stepped back. "Guest bath," he said. "Go. Because if he sees you like this..." A ragged breath. *"Go."*

Right, yes, going was on her agenda. Provided that she could get off the table and her legs would not crumple beneath her. She tried to give him a smile.

A furrow appeared between his brows.

She wondered how uncertain her smile looked. Probably as uncertain as she felt. Everything in her world was suddenly way off-balance, seeming to sway and shift, and, sure enough, as soon as her feet touched the floor, her knees did a little shimmy and her body was swaying, too, as she prepared for a fast fall.

Odin curled one hand under her arm. "You okay?"

She steadied. "F-fine." Far, far from it. Maisey honestly wasn't sure if she would ever be fine again. "You can let go."

"But I don't want to. Not ever."

She stared into his eyes.

And heard the squeak of the door opening. *Not* the door that led to the screen porch. The door that led directly into the cabin. She realized that Jinx had been on the porch the whole time, and now he was about to see her—

Bare from the waist down. Oh, no. Red stained her cheeks. She wrenched away from Odin, grabbed her jeans, and rushed down the hallway. She flew into the guest bathroom—or what she hoped was the guest bath—and slammed the door shut behind her.

***

He's a friend. You don't attack a friend. Odin mentally repeated his mantra four times as he tried to get himself back under control. *But I can still taste her.*

"Well," Jinx sighed. "You seem to be unharmed. When you didn't answer the door—or respond to my many calls—I was afraid the bad guys had beat me here. That they'd incapacitated you, and you were unable to call out for help in your poor, pitiful, weakened state."

Odin could feel a faint tremble in his fingers. *Because I want her so fucking much.* It had taken all of his strength not to drive into her. He'd tasted her. He'd felt her come against his mouth. She'd been gorgeous when the pleasure hit her. He'd lapped her up, and he wanted *more*. He wanted his dick buried in her. He wanted to feel the contractions of her release around his cock. He wanted—

"Yo. Earth to Odin. Hate to ask but, are those panties next to your boot?"

His gaze shot to the floor. Sure the hell enough, he saw the delicate panties—panties he'd torn in his haste to touch Maisey—on the floor. He scooped them up, swallowed them in one big fist, and whirled to face Jinx. "Not a word to her," he warned.

Jinx blinked, striving to look innocent. Failing because Jinx had never been innocent. "A word? About what? Whatever would I say? I mean, would I ask the lovely lady if she was currently running around all commando because—"

Odin surged toward him.

Jinx jumped back. Only to trip on high heels. Maisey's high heels. He righted himself quickly before he could fall on his ass. "Oh, look at that." More fake innocence. "So weird, but I think your girlfriend lost both her panties and her shoes. Now, wonder what made her do that?"

"*Jinx...*"

"Guess you weren't under attack in here, huh?" A fast grin. A saucy wink.

Odin did not smile back. He leveled a killing glare at Jinx. "You make her feel uncomfortable, and I will make you sorry."

The grin faded, a little. "Just a joke, man. I mean, hey, good for you on finding a girlfriend who can put up with you and your scary-ass, serious self. Not like you—"

"She's not my girlfriend. She's a client." The words felt hollow.

"You're holding her panties in your hand. Pretty sure that means she's your girlfriend."

And I can still taste her on my tongue. Does that mean she's mine? He wanted her to be his.

No, screw that…she is. She was *his*. She just might not know it yet.

"How about you give me an update on what the hell is going on—not your sexual shit, but why you just had half the criminals in the area coming at you—and then I will let you get back to your, ah, personal business, okay?" Jinx's blue eyes glinted. "Does that sound like a deal?"

"What the hell are you even doing down here?" Odin rolled back his shoulders—and shoved Maisey's panties in his pocket. "You went off the radar. Haven't seen you or heard from you in months."

Jinx's stare darted away.

On the surface, Jinx was always all smiles and laughter. But that was just surface. Odin knew there was far more to him than met the eye.

"I was doing freelance work for Uncle Sam," Jinx finally replied. "By the time I actually *got* the invitation to War's wedding, it was too late. But then I heard about the mess that went down with that killer he was chasing, heard about how he'd started his own PI business, and I thought I might see if he needed an extra hand." He lifted his fingers. Wiggled them. "I've always been good with my hands."

Good with his hands, understatement. The things that man could do with a knife were chilling. But Jinx was also good at picking locks.

Cracking safes. Stealing highly classified and confidential information from enemy officers...

The guy had incredible luck. Most days. But when Jinx was lucky, others usually weren't.

"Anyway," Jinx shrugged. "I headed down this way. Found War's cabin all dark and empty, so I thought I'd go amuse myself for a bit. The next thing you know, fate is smiling on me—you know she likes to do that—"

Odin snorted.

"And you were walking right into the same bar I was in. Just like that, two best friends were reunited." Jinx's gaze darted to the right. To the hallway. His stare sharpened.

Odin whipped around to see Maisey padding down the hallway. Her cheeks were flushed, her hair tousled, and her eyes—*so beautiful*. Her gaze seemed to swim with emotion, but for the life of him, he could not figure out exactly how she felt. The emotions were a tangle he couldn't read. Not that he'd ever been particularly good at understanding how women felt. They were generally a mystery to him.

As he watched her, Maisey slowed to a stop. She'd put her jeans back on. Straightened her shirt. Her lips were swollen and red from his mouth, and for a moment, all he could think of was the way she'd tasted when he'd had his mouth between her legs and she'd come for him.

"Oh, are you missing something?" Jinx called out to her. "I think you are. I think you are missing—"

A growl broke from Odin.

"Your shoes," Jinx finished. He scooped them up and hurried toward Maisey. "Very Cinderella-like, I must say." He offered the heels to her. "I'm Jinx, by the way. But you probably figured that out earlier."

Slowly, she took the shoes. "Thank you?" The words seemed more of a question that anything else.

"I didn't catch your name," Jinx added. He waited, all expectant-like.

Maisey slid on the heels. Peered uncertainly at Odin. "He's a friend? You're sure of that?"

Jinx put a hand over his heart. "Only one of his most treasured friends on the planet. I know his secrets. He knows mine. We'd die to protect each other in a heartbeat." The words—and his tone—were mocking.

But Jinx was speaking the truth. He was one of Odin's best friends. And they would kill to protect each other in a heartbeat. Odin preferred killing to dying. "You can trust him," Odin told her. "I do."

"With his very life, he trusts me," Jinx assured her.

"Then I guess I will trust you, too." She offered him a tentative smile. A smile that hinted at her dimples. "I'm Maisey Bright." She extended her hand.

It was immediately engulfed by Jinx's. "A pleasure to meet you." His gaze slid over her, and he gave a low whistle. "I have to say, I am impressed. Odin usually scares off most women within five minutes of meeting them."

"Why?" Maisey appeared genuinely perplexed.

Jinx released her hand. "I don't know. Could be the one-word answers he likes to give. The weird shit he can sometimes say. His complete lack of a sense of humor—"

Maisey's shoulders stiffened. "I *thought* you were his friend."

"Uh, yeah, we just covered—"

She glared at him. Her dimples were completely gone. "He has a wonderful sense of humor, and he doesn't say the wrong things. Maybe you just don't listen the right way when he talks." A sniff. "There is nothing weird about him. Odin has been exactly what I need, and I will not just stand here and let some—some *bad luck* guy say rude things about him!"

"Bad luck?" Jinx took a step away from her. He sucked in a breath. "Take that back."

Jinx was superstitious as hell. "She didn't mean it," Odin hurried to reassure him. "Relax, man. No need to pull out salt and start sprinkling it everywhere." He'd already seen Jinx's hand dart toward his pocket.

Maisey kept glaring.

But Jinx slowly seemed to relax. "You passed the test, too." He inclined his head toward Maisey. "Good for you."

Maisey's glare wavered. "What test?"

But Jinx just shrugged. Then he turned back to Odin. "I like her."

Odin felt a warning was in order. "Don't go liking her too much."

Maisey darted to Odin's side.

Jinx took note of the movement. "Message received." His hand dipped into his pocket. Quickly, he tossed something over his shoulder.

"Was that salt?" Maisey asked at once. "You're only supposed to throw that over your left shoulder if you spill some of it." A considering pause. "Of course, there are many civilizations that believe salt itself can help to act as a talisman against evil spirits, so I suppose if you felt something evil was coming at you, then tossing a little salt might help you to—"

"Maisey." Odin tangled his fingers with hers. "Don't give the man more justification than he needs." Not that Jinx ever needed justification for the things he did.

Jinx rubbed his chin. "Are we gonna talk about salt all night or are you two gonna tell me what in the hell is going on? You know, what with the whole bar that was attacking you, Odin? I swear, O, if I've told you once, I've told you a thousand times...If you can't learn to play well with others, then you shouldn't play at all."

"The bar scene happened because of me." Maisey's voice was clear. Odin slanted her a fast glance and saw that her delicate jaw had tightened. "Odin had to fight tonight because I hired him. We're hunting a killer, and the hunt led us to that bar."

Jinx didn't show so much as a flicker of surprise. "A killer, hmm?" He did a little bounce. Seemed to bubble with energy. "Then count me in."

CHAPTER ELEVEN

"It's not a game, Jinx," Odin said as he walked Jinx to his motorcycle.

"Life's a game, man. I've told you that very thing numerous times. We're all playing, every single day. Whether we want to do it or not, we're in the game."

Odin glanced back at War's cabin. Maisey was inside. He'd wanted to speak privately with Jinx. *Don't want to alarm her.* "It's just us, so you can cut the act."

"What act?"

"The act where you pretend you don't care about anything." Everything. "This case is serious."

"Three victims sounds very serious."

"He almost took Maisey," Odin snapped. "The bastard nearly had her yesterday. He was trying to load her into a truck and drive away with her. *She's* his next target because Maisey was the one doing all the investigating—on her own until I took the case—and now he's locked on her."

Maisey and Odin had given Jinx a fast run-through of events. But what mattered most to Odin... "Look, if you really want to help on this one, then I could use you. Nothing can happen to her."

Jinx slapped a hand on his shoulder. "It won't. We got this." His hand tightened. "You want me checking out her neighbor? The guy Maisey seemed so certain was guilty? I can tail him while you stay close to her."

"That would be great. Thanks." He could sure use another set of eyes. "Guess it was lucky you were in that bar." His head tilted as he came back to a point that bugged him. "Exactly *why* were you in that bar? I get that you came down here after you got the invitation—hell of a wedding you missed, by the way, because War had an open bar—but why go to that dive?" Though Odin had a suspicion.

"What can I say? I was bored. Looking for something to amuse me."

The amusements in that place weren't exactly safe. And that was Jinx's secret. The man had always been pulled to the dark. Safe and easy—not in his vocabulary. "Something illegal?" Now he was even more suspicious. "You *are* done with the freelance work for the government, aren't you?" Jinx was good at undercover ops. Too good. Especially with those tricky hands of his.

"At the moment, I'm working with you. Your case is my priority."

That wasn't exactly a clear answer, but Odin decided not to push for more. "You got a place to crash?"

"Well, I *was* intending to stay at War's place. You know how he said his guest room was always open..."

War had said that, numerous times. Until recently, Odin had been crashing in that guest room, too. But then War had gotten married and War's new bride, Rose, had wanted to sell her condo. Since Odin had decided to stay in the area, he'd jumped in and purchased the place from her.

The condo wasn't exactly Odin's style, but he'd fix it. Eventually. At the moment, it was just filled with boxes he'd finally had moved in and furniture that had recently been delivered. He reached into his pocket. Pulled out—

"Those had better not be panties you are handing me."

"Shut the fuck up." He pulled War's spare key off the ring. "I'm taking Maisey with me tonight. You can have War's place."

"Yeah, so…first, I think I'll get started with a little digging." He did a quick maneuver with his fingers—one of those sleight-of-hand magic tricks that he was always showing off with—and made the key vanish in a blink. "I won't be back until later. You know, as in much, much later. Plenty of time for you and Maisey to finish up what…" He *ahemed*. "Whatever you started earlier."

He didn't want *plenty* of time. Odin wanted the whole freaking night. "Maisey will be at my place tonight." His place. In his brand new bed. "And don't worry, I absolutely intend to finish what we started."

"Oversharing." Jinx jumped on his motorcycle. He started the engine, but didn't leave. "Be careful with her."

Odin's eyes narrowed. "What's that supposed to mean?" He would never physically hurt her. He'd never hurt any woman.

"She likes you. I mean, really likes you. It's not one of those things when we get the women who just want to screw around because they think we have a dangerous edge, and they like that freaky thrill." His head turned toward Odin. "She was ready to tear into me because she thought I wasn't being a good friend to you."

About that... "You need to stop testing people."

Jinx revved the engine. "When people fail you often enough, you can't help but test them." His voice roughened as he added, "You never failed me. So know that I'll always have your back. If things go dark, call me. I'll be there in an instant." Another rev of the engine before Jinx drove away.

For a moment, Odin just watched him go. Then he turned back to the cabin. His steps were slow and certain as he headed back to Maisey. He found her waiting for him on the screened porch. The waves were thundering and he and Jinx had kept their voices low, so he didn't worry that she'd overheard them.

He *did* worry about what the hell he was supposed to say to her.

I want to fuck you and I'm barely keeping my hands off you. We need to get to my place, or I will take you right where you stand.

"So...Jinx, huh? Is that his real name?" A pause. Her arms had wrapped around her stomach. "Is *Odin* your real name? Because I just realized that maybe it's a code name. Maybe I almost had sex with a guy and I don't even know his real name, and you should know the real name of your lover. That's important information."

He closed the distance between them. "Odin is my real name. My parents are Scandinavian, and my dad was big into the Norse myths."

"Good to know," she murmured. "Because if your real name was something like Burt, then I'd need to make sure I called it out at the right ah, moment."

His lips were pulling up. She was doing it again. Making him want to smile. To laugh. His chest warmed as he gazed down at her.

See, Jinx, I do have a fucking sense of humor.

"Odin? You're looking at me oddly. Is something wrong?"

He shook his head. "Jinx isn't his real name. But we don't use his real name. Ever. The last two guys who tried? Jinx made sure they didn't repeat that mistake." He wouldn't go into specifics. "We should go."

"Go?" She looked back over her shoulder. "I thought we were..." Her words trailed away. "We should go." Her shoulders straightened. "Long day. Long night. Definitely time to go home and—"

"Fuck."

She sucked in a sharp breath. "Excuse me?"

Yeah, way too blunt. And it had been a one-word response. He could do better. "I want you to come home...with me." *Was* that any better? He sounded rough and demanding as hell. He cleared his throat. "If you want me...if you want to be with me—"

"Yes."

Had she spoken? Or had he just wanted so badly for her response to be yes that he'd just imagined it?

"Yes," Maisey said again. She stopped hugging herself. The bracelets on her wrist jingled as she pressed her hand to his chest. "I want you. More than I have ever wanted anyone else."

"Then give me tonight." Because he needed her too much. Couldn't hold back. He wanted to take and take... and have her break apart with pleasure beneath him.

"I'll give you anything you want."

His hands fisted. "Keep saying things like that, and I will take you right here."

"Promises, promises..."

"Maisey—"

She stepped back. "How far away is your place? And just how fast can you get us there?"

***

Maisey wasn't home. Clay cast a quick glance at her parked car. Her car was there, had been there all night, but the house was dark. Quiet.

He'd gone to the door. Knocked a few times. Not received any response.

He knew she must be gone with the guy who'd been skulking around her. Odin. The man with the gaze that was unnerving. Odin had seemed like trouble to Clay.

Maisey was good. Sweet. The innocent type. She wouldn't have anything in common with a guy like that.

Surely, she'd be home soon.

He'd just keep watch on her place. When she returned, they needed to talk. He was worried about her. And after the attack on campus, he figured that Maisey could use a friend...

She could use me.

He would be there for her.

***

"Ignore the boxes," Odin said as he locked the door behind them. "Just getting moved in. Was supposed to unpack last weekend, but then a new case came up." Maisey had come along and changed everything.

Maisey stood in the middle of the boxes. She had been quiet on the drive over. He hadn't said much. He'd been too busy keeping his hands on the wheel and off her. He'd found his gaze sliding to her legs. He'd imagined parting her thighs. Putting his hand on her and stroking her through the denim of her jeans.

"I didn't expect you to be the condo type." Maisey glanced around. "I mean this place—it's really fancy."

Was she trying to say he wasn't fancy? Odin considered the matter. Guilty. He wasn't. "I needed a place to stay. It became available so I took it. I liked the view." Money wasn't an issue for him. He didn't mention that. Maisey didn't care what he had or what he didn't, so he didn't see the point in telling her about the money he had piled away.

Maisey crept toward the glass balcony doors. It was dark out, so he knew that she couldn't see the stretch of beach and the waves that pounded below.

As if reading his thoughts, she said, "During the day," Maisey motioned toward the door, "I'm sure the view is beautiful."

"Beautiful," Odin echoed, but he wasn't talking about the view of the beach, and he'd pretty much reached his limit on small talk. He'd gotten them to his place. They were locked in. The alarm was on. No one would be bothering them. For the rest of the night, he had Maisey all to himself.

She glanced over her shoulder to look back at him. "I'm nervous."

He'd been stalking toward her. At those words, he froze.

"I shouldn't be. I mean, not after what we did at War's place, but, ah—" Her hand lifted. Waved vaguely toward him. "I am."

He wanted to rush to her, but her words had stopped him cold. "You're afraid of me?" Shit. He should have thought of this. After the way things had gone down in the bar, of course, she was afraid of him. She'd had time to think on the car ride over—that silent, tense ride—and now she wanted to back away. To put some distance between them, and what the hell was he supposed to do about that?

His stomach twisted. "I would never hurt you."

"What?" Her eyes widened. "I know that! Why would you say..." She rushed toward him.

Reached for him. Curled those soft hands of hers around his arms. "I'm nervous. *Nervous.* As in...having sex is a big deal and you obviously have way more experience than I do. Sex has *never* been that good for me—not like it was when you were, ah..." She sucked in a breath and said, "Going down on me. So if it was that good when you were using your mouth, I am pretty sure I will go absolutely crazy when, you know, another part of your body is in me. And I just want you to know that this is all..." She blew out a breath. "I don't want to disappoint you."

He squinted at her.

She squinted back. "What is it?" Her fingers let him go.

"Making sure you didn't hit your head." His hand lifted and curled under her delicate chin. He tipped her head back so the light slid over her face. "Don't see any new injuries. Still don't like that damn scratch." The sight of it on her cheek pissed him off. "Didn't think you were hurt at the bar." If someone *had* hurt her...

"I wasn't hurt. Why would you suspect that?"

He kept right on cupping her chin because he liked touching her. "Because you're saying crazy shit." He made sure he was staring straight into her eyes. "You could never, ever disappoint me. That doesn't need to be a worry that ever whispers through your mind."

She smiled at him.

Those dimples would be the end of him one day.

"I don't have a lot of experience," she told him in a voice that wobbled in an oddly sweet way. "I just—I want you to enjoy it as much as I did. I mean as I will. As I did and I *will*."

She was so damn cute. "I'll be with you. I'll enjoy the hell out of it." He had no doubt she would be the best lover he'd ever had. How did he know that? Because he couldn't remember wanting anyone as badly as he wanted Maisey. "But you have to be honest with me." He kissed her. A quick press of his lips against hers. "If I get too rough, tell me."

"Odin…"

"I'm big, Maisey. You're fucking breakable next to me. If I scare you, if I'm pushing too much, tell me."

She inched closer. "On one condition."

"What's that?"

"That if I'm too rough," she whispered, "you tell me. If I push too much, tell me."

Yeah, that was never gonna happen. She could push and be as damn rough as she wanted. She was teasing, but Maisey didn't get it. He wanted to pounce on her. His dick was still just as hard as it had been when he'd been back at War's place. When he'd been so close to having what he wanted most. When he'd tasted her. Gone crazy because she was so delicious.

Her hands slid to his waist. "I think I remember where we left off." She undid the button, reached for the zipper.

But he caught her hands and stopped her. "No." A growl.

Her eyebrows lifted. "Odin?"

"Baby, I am hanging on by a thread. You touch my dick, and I slam into you two seconds later."

Her tongue slid over her lower lip. "That's, ah..."

He kissed her. Took her mouth because her sexy tongue was driving him insane. Maisey had no idea how close to the limit he was. Hell, he wasn't even sure how much longer he could hold on. It had never been like this for him. He'd never wanted someone so intently. So completely.

He kissed her with a frantic lust and when she gave that sweet little moan in the back of her throat, the sound just urged him on all the more. He wanted to yank her jeans off. She wasn't wearing panties—he still had those—so all he had to do was get rid of the jeans. Then he could plunge into her. Drive them both straight to oblivion.

But she has to be ready.

Maisey was tiny compared to him. He didn't want to hurt her. Couldn't hurt her. He had to make it good for Maisey because he didn't just want one fast fuck with her.

Odin needed so much more.

He forced his mouth to tear away from hers. Forced himself to take a step back. "My bedroom..." A rumble. "Down the hallway, to the left." He wanted their first time to be in a bed. Not up against a wall. That could be the second time. Or the third. Whatever she wanted. The first time, he had to use care.

Have to make her ready.

"Go," he urged her when Maisey stared up at him with eyes that had gone even more golden than normal. He could see the desire shining in her stare. "Go in there." He swallowed. "Strip. I'll be right behind you."

"You want me to strip without you?" She didn't move.

"Baby, if I touch your clothes, I'll rip them off you." He was that far gone. The rest of her clothes would wind up as torn as her panties.

Maisey didn't look intimidated. She tipped back her head and murmured, "Promises, promises..."

Maisey!

"But if you want me to go, I'll go." She turned away. Paused just long enough to kick off her heels. Then she began walking toward his bedroom.

Only...she lifted up her shirt as she strolled down that hallway. Strolled as if she didn't have a fucking care in the world. Then she let the shirt fall.

She'd told him that she was nervous just moments before. Now she was walking away with a sexy sway of her hips and dropping her shirt. *Teasing* him. He'd been trying to hold back, and she was doing this to him?

She unhooked her bra. Let it fall.

He stalked behind her. He saw the beautiful, bare curves of her back. "I thought you were nervous."

She paused at his bedroom door. Her thick hair tumbled over her shoulders as she angled her head and looked back at him. "I was. Then I realized that when you touch me, nothing else matters."

Yes, no doubt about it, Maisey was trying to destroy him.

She turned back to the front. But she didn't enter his bedroom. He was five steps behind her. Watching. Transfixed. Obsessed.

With a soft rustle, her jeans slid to the floor. She kicked them away. Not that he was looking at her feet. His gaze was on her ass. Her perfect, round ass. An ass that he wanted to feel against his hands, just as he wanted to feel every single inch of her body.

Maisey walked into his bedroom. Slow and easy. Still moving as if she didn't have a care in the world.

His breath was ragged. His body felt too big. Too rough. He jerked off his own shirt and threw it. Kicked off his boots. Yanked away his socks. When he got to the bedroom door, his hands were reaching for his zipper.

Maisey was in his bed. A big bed, the biggest he could special order. She waited in the middle of the bed, lying on the crisp sheets with her body completely uncovered. Her breasts were full, her nipples tight, dusky peaks. She'd turned on the lamp, and the light drifted over her body.

He'd wanted to be careful with her.

Not gonna happen.

I will take and take and—

He didn't move. *Make sure she's ready. Make sure she's fucking ready.*

"Odin?" Her head tilted as she pushed up on her elbows. "What are you waiting for?"

He ditched his jeans.

Her gaze dropped. She sucked in a quick breath. The gold of her eyes gleamed even more.

"Spread your legs," he ordered as he stalked forward.

Slowly, she did.

So pretty and perfect. And...was she wet? He slid onto the bed. Caught her legs. Spread them more and put his fingers to her core.

Wet.

"You're...really big." A hint of worry.

"And you're absolutely perfect."

"Like, not saying this to flatter you or anything, but you are seriously bigger than the other guys I have been with—"

His growl cut through her words. The last thing he wanted to hear about was any other guy she'd ever been with. His head bent and he took her sex with his mouth. His tongue slid over her clit.

She heaved against him. "Odin!"

His hands clamped around her thighs. He tasted. Licked her clit over and over, then drove his tongue into her sex. She twisted against him, not to back away, but to get closer.

He lifted his head. Replaced his mouth with his fingers and stroked her. First one finger, then a second. He stretched her. Made sure she was open and ready to take him.

"If you don't fuck me, right now, I will go *crazy!*"

He couldn't have that. He also couldn't hold back, not another moment. Not with her sensual taste on his tongue and not with the hot, tight way her sex squeezed his fingers. She was going to feel like heaven around his dick.

He withdrew his fingers. Grabbed his cock and—

Condom.

"Do not move," he ordered her.

"Odin!" A cry of frustration.

He shot from the bed. Grabbed a condom from the nightstand. Had it on and was back to press against her. His cock lodged at the entrance to her body. She'd grabbed the sheets and fisted them. He locked his hands around her hips and began to push into her.

But Maisey tensed. "It's...ah..." She bit her lower lip. "Been a little while for me."

He'd gone in an inch. Maybe two. Every cell in his body screamed for him to *drive* deep.

His left hand slid down. His fingers strummed her clit, just the way he'd learned she liked.

"Oh, that's good, Odin, that's—" Her hips did a little shimmy. "That feels—" And then she was the one to surge up against him. Her hips arched.

He drove into her. Thrust past the initial resistance of her inner muscles and sank all the way inside of her.

That was the moment when he lost his mind. Because Maisey didn't just feel good. Good didn't begin to describe it. *Insane. Fucking fantastic.*

He loomed over her. His mouth bent to capture hers in a long, drugging kiss as his cock retreated, then plunged deep. The rhythm was fast, faster, and her legs lifted to curl around him.

Maisey's hands freed the sheets as she grabbed for him.

"Okay?" Odin rasped. It was all he could manage, but he needed to be sure he wasn't hurting her.

"Do not *dare* stop."

He didn't. He let go of his control, completely. Both of his hands went back to her hips so that he could haul her up against him as he thrust. Over and over. Hard. Deep. She was moaning. His heart was pounding. And he could feel the avalanche of pleasure coming.

He wanted to fuck her forever, but that wasn't going to happen. *Too intense. Too powerful.* Too strong to hold back.

Maisey gave a sharp cry, and he felt the contractions of her inner muscles around him as she came. *Hell, yes.*

He thrust again and again. Lost, blind, to everything but the way she felt. And when his climax hit, the eruption slammed through him with so much force that his breath choked out. The whole damn world seemed to shatter around him and the only thing that remained—

Maisey.

CHAPTER TWELVE

She'd been doing it wrong.

Maisey understood this truth with one hundred percent certainty. Sex had never been like this for her. It had never felt this good.

She'd been doing it way, way wrong before. Or maybe her partners had. Whatever. This—*this* was a whole other level of pleasure. So good that her body still quivered. So good that aftershocks were exploding through her. So good that she wanted to have sex with Odin a million more times, please.

"Thanks for straightening that out for me," Maisey murmured.

Odin's head slowly lifted. His expression was both savage, and sated. He was heart-stoppingly gorgeous, and he was also still *in* her.

"I won't make the mistake again," she added. Nope, she would not be repeating that error. Never, ever again. He'd gone and ruined her for the amateurs.

His lips brushed over hers. "What the hell are you talking about?" But the words were oddly tender. Almost like an endearment.

"Now I know what it's supposed to feel like. Won't be able to settle for anything less ever again." A glow seemed to spread through her, and she just had to ask, "Was it...was it really good for you, too?"

Odin shook his head.

Her heart squeezed. "I'm sorry. I, uh, if you show me what you like, then I can do better."

"The hell you can."

Her eyes widened.

"It wasn't *really good,* Maisey. You were the best ever. Got it? *Ever.* So good, so make-me-crazy-perfect, that I need you again."

He was still in her. Still *big* in her. "Again, as in...right now?"

But he withdrew. Pulled out of her and she winced because she might be the tiniest bit sore. Not that she'd noticed the soreness before, but—

He strode away. Didn't say anything. She rolled over and watched his ass and almost whistled because, damn, every single inch of him was muscle. Steel. Strength. And—he was back. Already heading toward her and now she had a view of his front.

Maisey swallowed.

He bent. Reached into the nightstand drawer. Pulled out another condom. Staring at her, he slowly rolled it over his thick length.

Then he waited.

Her gaze rose to catch his.

"Right now," he said flatly.

That was some admirable recovery time. She made a mental note of it even as she scrambled upright. "Are you always like this?"

He eased onto the bed. Stretched out. "Right now, I can't think beyond you, so I have no clue." He motioned toward her. "You're up."

"Excuse me?"

"On top. You control it this time. Otherwise, I'll be too hard."

She rather thought he was already too hard. But she wasn't exactly sure that was a problem.

"I don't want to be too rough with you."

Oh, he'd meant hard *that* way.

"You show me what you need," Odin added.

"That's simple." But she crawled on top of him. Straddled him and pressed her hands to his chest. "I need you."

His eyes widened. "Maisey, what am I supposed to do with you?"

Everything. His cock pressed to the entrance of her body. But she didn't move to take him inside. Not yet. Instead, she leaned down and her tongue licked over one tight nipple.

Odin hissed out a breath.

She took that as a sign that he liked what she was doing, so she licked him again. Opened her mouth. Sucked.

"Baby, you are pushing..."

Yes, she was. And she liked doing it. Her hips arched down against him, taking the head of his cock inside of her just the smallest bit. She tensed a little, worried about pain, but...

Only pleasure.

She was wet and sensitive and every small push of his cock into her was sending off little waves of pleasure. She kept rocking against him, taking him in deeper. Ever so slowly. She worked him inside of her even as she licked and played with him. Her hands slid down his chest. Felt the raw power beneath her touch.

"*All the way, Maisey.* Take all of me." His hands clamped around her hips.

She looked at him. His expression was so fierce and hungry.

Did she look the same way?

Her hands pushed down against his chest. She lifted her upper body and pressed down with her hips.

All the way. He lodged fully inside of her. Maisey's head tipped forward and her hair fell around her face as she took a moment to savor having him all the way inside of her. He filled her completely. So tight. So full. Curious, experimenting, she deliberately clamped her inner muscles around him a little more with a squeeze.

"*Maisey!*" His hold hardened on her.

She did it again.

And saw Odin break.

He heaved up against her. His hips pounded with fast and frantic thrusts and she held on as she enjoyed the hell out of the ride. He drove deep. She felt him in every inch of her core. He was driving into her, she was shoving down against him, and they were racing toward release. Maisey could feel the climax coming. It was bearing down on her even as he thrust into her again and again.

She cried out Odin's name when she came. One moment, she was flying desperately toward release, and in the next instant, her whole body seemed to be going supernova as the pleasure lashed at her.

Odin tumbled her back onto the bed. He grabbed her legs. Lifted them higher. Slammed into her and just had the pleasure increasing. Soaring higher. She didn't even know if this was another orgasm or if he was just intensifying her feelings. All Maisey knew was that the pleasure was so good it seemed to be consuming her.

Then he was there. Erupting into her. Shoving hard with his hips right before his body stiffened against her. She was staring straight into his eyes when he came. She saw the pleasure wash over his face, and she knew she would never, ever forget the possessive look in his gaze as he whispered, "Mine."

***

A phone was ringing somewhere. Blearily, Maisey cracked open her eyes. Something big and warm was on top of her. She pushed against it. Realized it was...an arm?

Odin's arm. He'd curled it around her stomach.

A phone rang again.

"Yours," Odin rumbled.

Hers?

"Your new phone." He slid from the bed. The room was in darkness, but he seemed to know exactly where he was going. She strained to see him as her eyes adjusted. He was bending down, picking up a phone from her bag. When had he brought her bag in the room? She didn't remember. She'd kind of passed out after the second round.

Or had it been the third?

"No caller ID." He put the phone to his ear. "Who the hell is this?"

The glow from her phone's screen let her see the hard angles of his face.

Maisey sat up, pulling the sheet with her. They'd just gotten that phone, but it had been programmed with her old number. So anyone who knew that number could call her—or it could just be some random, spam call.

"Hung up." Odin lowered the phone. He took a step back toward the bed.

The phone rang again.

"Sonofabitch," Odin began. His finger swiped over the screen.

"Put it on speaker," Maisey urged him as tension snaked through her.

He came closer to her. Tapped the screen to turn on the speaker.

"Who is this?" Maisey demanded. The clock on her phone told her it was almost one a.m.

"I need you..." A woman's voice. A voice that was somewhat distorted, but still familiar.

Goosebumps rose on Maisey's arms. "*Who is this?*"

"You have to help..." Again, the same voice. But it sounded funny. As if the voice was coming from very far away.

Maisey shook her head because this couldn't be right. She had to be confused. The caller could not be...

"*Maisey?*"

Her heart squeezed in her chest. "I'm here. Tell me what I can do." Her eyes filled with tears. "Tell me where you are. I will help you. I will do *anything*."

She could feel Odin's eyes on her, but he wasn't saying a word.

"Have to help…" The woman's voice was even softer.

"How?" Maisey demanded. "Tell me how, and I will. Tell me where you are—I will come to you right now! Please, tell me. Where are you—*where*—"

The call ended.

A tear leaked down Maisey's cheek. "No." She grabbed the phone from Odin's hand. "We have to call her back."

"Who was on the phone, Maisey?" Careful. Quiet.

The light from the screen glared up at her. "How do I call her back?" Because there wasn't a number listed. It had been blocked. "How?"

"Who was on the phone?" Odin repeated.

Her breath came too fast. Her chest burned. And hope had her feeling dizzy. "That was Whitney's voice." She hadn't thought it was possible. She'd been so horribly certain but… "My God, Odin. She's alive. *Whitney is still alive!*"

And she wanted Maisey to help her.

***

"I don't like it," Jinx announced the next morning as he stood on Odin's balcony and peered down at the beach. "The woman is missing and suddenly, right after *your* lady is nearly taken, she calls Maisey?"

Odin glanced back toward the closed balcony doors. Maisey was showering. She hadn't been able to sleep after the call. She'd had him pull every string he had in order to try and get a trace on the caller.

So far, his strings weren't doing any good.

But he did have a monitor on her phone now. If she got another call...

"Is Maisey sure the caller was Whitney?"

He focused back on Jinx. "She says it was her friend's voice. Swears she is one hundred percent certain." She'd been crying by the time the call ended. Silent tears that had leaked down her cheeks and made his chest ache.

"Sonofabitch." Jinx shoved his hands into his pockets. "And how long has this woman been missing?"

"Two months."

Jinx closed his eyes. "If she's been held for that long..."

"Maisey's coming," he said quickly because he'd glanced back once more and seen her approaching the door. "Don't paint any damn pictures. The last thing I need is for her to get those images in her head about what might have happened to her friend."

The door opened. Maisey stood there, her feet bare, her hair still wet, no makeup on her face. She'd put back on the clothes that she'd worn the previous night. She looked lovely and delicate and so damn breakable.

No one will break her. Odin wouldn't let that happen.

"What's the plan?' Maisey's shoulders squared. "How do we find her?"

Jinx and Odin shared a long look.

"No," Maisey said instantly with a shake of her head. "Not happening. You two aren't running off and leaving me to sit and twiddle my thumbs. This is *my* friend." Her voice thickened. "I'm the one who gave up hope and thought she was dead. I should have kept going, kept hoping, and I will. I swear, I will do it now." Tears filled her eyes. "You won't shut me out. I will help on this. I *will*."

He couldn't watch her cry. Odin reached for Maisey and pulled her into his arms. His hand patted her shoulder.

Over her head, Jinx winced. "That is like watching a bear swipe at someone. Try a gentle stroke. It will work way better."

He *was* gently stroking her. Couldn't the man see that?

"And, Maisey, I'll be the one to say this because Odin doesn't want to crush your dreams and tender feelings but..."

Oh, hell. Frantic, Odin tried to glare the guy into silence—

Jinx ignored his glare. "But it's too convenient."

Maisey's head whipped up. She spun to face Jinx. "Excuse me?"

"Too convenient," he repeated and enunciated it extra slowly. "Sorry, but I'm a suspicious bastard even on my best days. All of a sudden, right after you're nearly abducted, your missing friend reaches out and calls you? Nope. Not legit."

"It was *her* voice. I know Whitney's voice."

"And voices can be faked. They can be altered. They can be digitally changed in a thousand different ways. Give me five minutes and your phone, and I'll download an app that lets me sound exactly like my great-grandmother."

Her body trembled. Odin could *feel* her pain.

"Jinx," he warned.

"What? I'm telling her so that you don't have to do it. So that you don't have to be the one to watch the hope shatter in her eyes."

Maisey whirled to face him. "Odin?"

But Jinx wasn't done. "Look, you contacted the cops last night. Did the whole due diligence bit after you got the mystery call, but, O, you and I both know this is shady. The odds of it actually being the missing woman calling—those odds are so low that no one would take that bet."

Maisey's eyes were on Odin. Hope was still clinging to her expression. He didn't want to destroy the light in her eyes.

"Do you think it was her?" Maisey asked. Then she held her breath.

I don't want to hurt you. He also didn't want to lie to her. "I don't know."

"Fuck me," Jinx called out. "Odin, get your balls back. You are as doubtful as I am and allowing Maisey to hope now does nothing but make her vulnerable."

He couldn't look away from Maisey. "Sometimes, people need hope." Maisey needed it. "Until I see a body—"

Maisey flinched and retreated from him.

Yeah, he was back to his usual level of tact.

"Until then," Odin added, "I can't know for certain. None of us can."

Some of the tension slid from her shoulders. "Thank you," she whispered.

"But..." He just had to say this. "It is suspicious. It could damn well be the perp, Maisey. You should prepare for that."

"Why?" She tried to blink away the tears in her eyes. "Why would he do this?"

Jinx moved to her side. "To jerk you around? To torture you? Because he's a sadistic prick who gets off on playing with people's pain? Lots of reasons come to mind for me."

She frowned at him.

"Could be another reason." Jinx shrugged.

Jinx had even less tact that Odin did. Odin cleared his throat. "It could be a trick. Could be that he thinks he might have a way of luring you to him. If he offers you Whitney, then you'd come running."

She nodded. "Yes, I absolutely would."

No, baby, you absolutely will not.

"If my friend is out there, if she is still alive and this guy is willing to let her go..." Now Maisey grabbed Odin's hand. "I will help her. I have to help her!"

Jinx sighed. He peered woefully at her. "That's why it's called a trap. The perp dangles some bait at you. You run ahead, not even looking at the danger, and the next thing we know, bam, you're the one who has been missing for months and no one knows what the hell happened to you."

A dark rage burned within Odin. "Not happening." There was no way anyone would take Maisey. If he had to chain her to him, he would do it. Maisey was not going to run into danger. She sure as hell wasn't going to vanish on him.

"What do you want me to do? Ignore the possibility that Whitney might be alive?" She let go of Odin and gestured between him and Jinx. "What if it was the two of you?"

Odin met Jinx's stare.

"What if someone had Odin?" she asked Jinx.

Jinx gave a rough laugh. "Then the guy is a damn fool. He made the worst mistake of his—"

"Would you risk everything to save Odin? If you thought there was a chance he might be alive, would you risk yourself for him?"

Jinx's lips pressed into a thin line. After a beat of silence, with his eyes still on Odin, he said, "If she has the chance, your girlfriend will rush off into who-the-hell-knows what kind of situation. She's going to do anything she can to save her friend." A pause. "Because it's the same shit you and I would do for each other."

It wasn't the same. Not even close. "We've had training. We know how to protect ourselves."

"Train me!" Maisey piped up.

"We know how to kill." Flat.

Maisey sucked in a breath.

His gaze locked on her. "That's the thing, sweetheart. When you're in one of these situations, when you're going up against some sadistic asshole who doesn't care how badly he hurts you or the people you care about, you have to be willing to cross that final line. You have to be willing to take a life." He stared at her. "You can't do that." Maisey had an innate goodness about her. That goodness burned like a light whenever he looked at her. Maisey wasn't the kind of person who could take a life. She wasn't a killer.

But I am.

Her body had trembled, but her stare hadn't wavered. "Yes, I can do it. You don't know me well enough to make that call."

"After last night, I'd say I knew you damn well." He took a step closer.

"Oh, jeez," from Jinx. "This just took a very awkward personal turn. I think I should step inside—"

"Don't move a muscle," Odin ordered him. Because he wanted Jinx to back him up. His gaze remained on Maisey. "You kill someone, and that will stay with you. The blood will be on your hands for the rest of your life."

"I am prepared for that." Her chin jerked up. "If this guy has hurt Whitney, if he's hurt those other women—I will stop him. I won't think twice about what I have to do!"

Easy to say. But killing was hard. "And he won't think twice about hurting you. Once he gets you, what do you think he'll do?" He didn't want to scare her, but there wasn't a choice. This was her life.

And she matters too much.

"He won't let your friend go. He isn't going to magically trade her for you. He'll get you. He'll hurt you." Just the thought had Odin's hands fisting. "That's not happening. Not on my watch. There is going to be *no* running off when you get mystery calls, do you understand? No trying to be the hero. No thinking you can do this on your own." *Because you can't, baby.*

Her eyes shot sparks at him.

"Every step, we take it together." There was no debate on this. *Your life matters too much, Maisey.* "You keep Jinx and I in the loop."

From the corner of his eye, Odin saw Jinx make a little circle with his hand. "This is the loop."

Odin ignored him. "You try to hide something from us, you try to lie to us...you put yourself at risk..." His nostrils flared. "And you and I will have a very big problem."

"She is my friend!"

"And you are—" He caught himself just in time. Stopped right before he growled *Mine.* And he sure wouldn't have meant that Maisey was his *friend.* She was one hell of a lot more than that.

"Ahem." Jinx cleared his throat. "How about we all take a big breath? We want the same thing here, people We're on the same side. In the same big, old loop of trust." Once more, he made a loop with his fingers. "How about we come up with a game plan that works for everyone?"

"We need to find Whitney," Maisey said empathically. "That's the game plan. Look, I get that isn't why I originally hired you, Odin. I went to you because I thought Clay was guilty. I wanted proof one way or the other."

Proof they still didn't have.

"If you need more money, I'll give it to you," she added quickly. "I will give you anything. *Please.* Just help me find her."

Oh, hell, no. "Don't." Bit off. "You don't have to plead with me for anything. I'm on *your* side. Always. Remember that." He shifted through possibilities. They had to start somewhere. They had to get moving. And the place that seemed to keep connecting dots for him? "The college."

Maisey's brow furrowed. "I don't have a class today—"

"You work there. Clay is there. Whitney *was* there. And you were almost taken from that location. It's a central point. I want to go back and start rattling cages in that place." Cages that belonged to other staff members, students. Whoever the hell came into his line of suspicion. His head turned toward Jinx. "And I want you to keep shadowing Clay. Stay on him."

"Done." He strode for the door. But stopped just before he left the balcony. Jinx threw a glance over his shoulder. "And what about the new friend you made at the club last night? Do I need to worry about him?"

Ramsey? Hell, they all needed to worry about him.

"We need to tell him," Maisey said. "If Ramsey thinks Whitney might still be alive..."

He'd be even more desperate. Ramsey would be frantic in his efforts to locate her. Did Maisey understand just how dangerous and unrelenting Ramsey could be?

"He has a right to know about the call," Maisey added stubbornly.

"Provided he's not the one who *made* the call." Jinx's voice was carefully expressionless. "Granted, I don't know everything that went down in that closed-door meeting last night, but Odin did give me a few of the highlights this morning." He sniffed. "Just because a man says he's innocent, doesn't mean he is. Just because a man pretends to be in love...doesn't mean he is." He inclined his head toward Odin. "Your girl is too trusting. It's a good thing you're not."

No, Odin wasn't the trusting sort. His thoughts had already dipped along the same path about Ramsey. "Maisey, it's awfully convenient that call—basically a proof of life call—came right after we had our meeting with Ramsey."

Her lower lip trembled. "You think she's dead."

"I think it's convenient," he repeated. "I also think things are about to get a whole lot more intense. From where I stand, Clay and Ramsey are our lead suspects. They know we're hunting, and it's time to step it up even more." He wanted her to be ready for what would come. "If I had the option, I'd send you someplace safe with Jinx. I'd get you out of the way while I learned the—"

"*Get me out of the way?*" Her voice had risen. A lot.

Jinx whistled. "Wrong thing to say. Typical you." He glanced at Maisey. "Let me translate. Odin is worried about you. If something happens to your sexy self, he will lose his shit. When that happens, when Odin goes off book, bad things happen." A shrug. "So, judging by your expression, going to a safe house is off the table?"

"Off," Maisey affirmed. "Way, way off."

"Then you need to make sure that you follow orders to the letter. When things get intense, you do what Odin says. Hell, it's what I do." A roll of one shoulder. "And Odin has saved my hide more times than I can count."

Her gaze darted back to Odin. "I won't be put aside. I am in this with you." An exhale. "But I can follow orders. It's not like I *want* to get hurt. You're the professional. I get it. I'll follow your lead, but I won't be cut out of the investigation."

Jinx clapped his hands together. "Fabulous. We're in agreement. So, I'll go and snoop on Clay, and the two of you will tackle the college and we'll catch the bad guy and everything will turn up roses."

Yeah, Odin didn't think things were gonna be that easy.

But Jinx walked out.

Maisey stayed there, staring up at Odin. "You saved his hide?" she finally asked.

"We saved each other. It's what you do." When you're in war zones and the world is exploding around you.

"He was...Delta, with you?"

Jinx had been many things. "Classified." That was the truth when it came to him. "I can't tell you. I'm sorry."

She peered toward the closed balcony door. "He doesn't seem serious enough for classified work."

"Jinx is hell on wheels in the field. Don't let appearances fool you."

Her attention shifted back to him. "I'm not too trusting."

Uh, yes, she was.

"I trust you," Maisey said after she did a little nibble on her lower lip. "And I'll trust Jinx, if you vouch for him. But I know the world is dangerous. I know dangerous people are *out* there." A long exhale. "I won't take unnecessary risks, okay? But I need to be in this. I need to help. I get that you're in charge, and I'll follow orders."

Would she? He wasn't so sure. But before they left his place... "I think some instruction is in order."

"Instruction?"

"Yes, you keep asking for some tricks, so I'll show you a few." He turned away. Headed inside. Heard her hurry to follow him. He waited just inside the door, and when Maisey came in—

Odin pounced. He grabbed her in an instant and shoved her back against the nearest wall. He held her easily. One of his legs was between hers so she couldn't knee him in the groin, and with one hand, he'd chained both of her wrists over her head.

"What are you doing?" Maisey's voice was breathless.

"Far too trusting," he muttered. "Baby, you never know who will attack..."

"Odin?"

"I want you to hurt me."

"Excuse me?" She jerked beneath his hold. He didn't let her go.

"Or *try* to hurt me," he amended. "We don't have a lot of time, but we need to go over some quick and dirty techniques."

"Quick and dirty? Now?"

"Right now." His right hand moved to her throat. His fingers curled over her. "I've got you. Pretend I'm the bad guy. What would you do? How would you get away?"

"Odin, look, I don't like this—"

"You want to waltz right into danger." Anger hummed through him. A fear that he didn't want to acknowledge. "You want to put yourself out there when we know the perp is focused on you. Then you damn well better show me what you've got. If he comes at you, if something happens and I'm not there...what the hell will you do?"

CHAPTER THIRTEEN

"I'm not helpless." Is that what he thought?

"No?" Odin's eyes glittered at her. "Compared to me, you sure seem that way. I had you against the wall in seconds."

"That's because I didn't expect you to grab me!" She'd thought they were about to leave the condo.

"Not like the perp will announce his intentions, sweetheart."

Her heartbeat doubled. "Do you mean that?"

"Hell, yes, I mean it. He won't tell you he's going to attack. You have to be ready. And, dammit, yes, I do think you're too trusting. You don't know the shit I've done. You don't know the blood on my hands." His gaze dropped to the hand around her throat. "If you did, you wouldn't let me touch you."

"I like it when you touch me," she snapped back.

His gaze *burned*. "And I fucking like having my hands on you."

He had to feel the frantic racing of her pulse beneath his fingers.

"But right now, I want to see what you've got. I want to know that if we get separated, you at least know one or two moves that will help you get that sweet ass of yours to safety."

"First, thanks for calling it sweet. I appreciate that."

He blinked.

"Second, you want to know what I'd do? Fine." Maisey considered her options. "To try and get out of this hold, I'd slam my head into your nose. You're leaning down toward me, you're in my range, so I would hit you as hard as I could."

He raised one brow.

"That's how I'd attack. If it was someone else holding me this way. Not you. I-I don't want to break your nose." She rather liked his nose. His whole face. Him.

"You wouldn't break it."

He shouldn't be so sure. "I'd hit you in the nose with my head. You'd stumble back, and I'd get away." She'd seen that move in plenty of movies. There. Done. She wiggled her fingers. It was time for him to let her go.

Odin leaned even closer toward her. "Try it," he murmured.

Hadn't she just covered that she didn't want to hurt him? "Odin—"

"Try it. Prove it. You show me that you can take care of yourself, and we'll get the hell out of here."

"I happen to like your nose! I don't want to break it! I don't want—"

"You're scared." Flat. "If you're scared in a real attack, you know what will happen? You'll get shoved into a truck and taken away, and I won't ever see you again. Do you know what that will do to me?"

She couldn't quite name the emotion that had entered his voice. "Odin..."

"*Attack*."

She slammed her head forward, but he just jerked away.

"Not very effective, baby."

First sweetheart, now baby? Her breath huffed out as she tried to ignore the endearments. "It's not like I will broadcast my plans to the bad guy. You knew what I was going to do. You freaking *told* me to attack so you were prepared for my move."

"Get loose. Do whatever the hell you need to do. Break free of my hold."

Fine. With a burst of energy, she twisted and heaved against him. She tried to bring up her legs. She tried more head-butting. She tried yanking her hands free. But, no matter what she did, Odin didn't let go. He didn't even seem to be putting any effort into restraining her.

His gaze stayed on hers. Never wavered. His expression never altered. He just stared at her with eyes that seemed to burn with a banked fire.

Her breath came faster. Harder. "This isn't funny."

"Not supposed to be," he tossed right back.

"You're huge, Odin. Way bigger than any guy I'm probably going to face."

"Size doesn't matter." A slight pause. "In this particular instance."

Her eyes narrowed. "Odin..." A lock of hair had slid over her left eye.

"From this position, you can't go for my groin or my eyes, two of the most vulnerable areas on a man's body."

Yes, she knew that.

"Head-butts don't work so well if your attacker can put enough space between you. Obviously, I can do that."

Because Odin was huge.

"You have to think about maneuverability. What parts of your body are free right now?" His voice was all calm and cool.

Like he held women pinned against walls all the time.

"What?" His head tilted. "Why are you staring at me that way?"

"No reason." Her breath still came too quickly. "Parts of my body that are free?" She evaluated. "My legs. I mean, you're between them." That had her tensing because it reminded her of last night and how he'd been between her legs plenty during those hot hours. "But, ah, I can still move them."

"You can't kick me with them. Not from this angle."

"No." She'd tried. Failed.

"Your attacker isn't gonna just stand still while he holds you. He won't be a statue. You have to watch his body. Pay attention to every single movement, no matter how small. *Feel* where he touches you. When my weight shifts, when my hold shifts, notice it. Look for those telling signs because that's when you attack."

She pulled in a breath. Tried to focus.

"Feel me," Odin told her.

Then she waited.

His left leg slid back, as if he were trying to get better balance.

"From this position, you can work your foot closer to mine. Go for my ankle. You can pound your heel into it as hard as you can. Ankles and knees are always good for kick attacks—provided you can reach them."

She gave a little nod.

Waited more.

Felt the faint ease of his grip on her wrists. She prepared herself. Got ready and—

His hold dropped to her shoulders in a flash. Now he had her shoulders pinned to the wall.

"Sometimes, it's not about fighting back. It's just about getting the hell away. Remember that. The priority is saving your ass. When you're this close to someone, you won't have a lot of mobility. So if you're going to break for freedom, break, baby. Break and don't look back."

She was still waiting. Still focusing. She could do this. She would get out of his hold.

"Make him think you're scared. Make him think you're weak. Do whatever you need in order to get him to lower his guard, and when he does…"

There. She felt it. He'd just eased the hold on her right shoulder.

Her hand flew up, but Odin caught it.

"You don't have to use a fist." He opened her fingers. "Palm strike. Go for the chin, shove his head up. Or slam the heel of your palm up into his nose. The goal is to make him back away. To give you time to haul ass."

He stepped back.

Maisey started to spring past him.

His arm immediately curled around her stomach, and he jerked her back against him. "If he has you this way…" His breath blew against the shell of her ear. "Hit hard with your elbow."

Maisey shivered.

"I'm going to show you how to get out of different holds. Don't get scared. Remember to focus, and you are going to break free."

Then he showed her. Over and over. From the back, he had her use her elbow to drive into him. Then he flipped her around. He grabbed her from the front, with his hand curling around her neck. He had her swing her arm—first her right, then her left—across to break his hold when he was in front of her. She wasn't hitting hard enough at first, but he kept going until she was.

He flipped her around again. Grabbed her in what felt like a tight bear hug. "Drop your weight," he gritted. "Someone has his hands and arms around you like this, you want to be a dead weight. Drop. You can also stomp the hell out of your attacker's feet. And don't forget, fingers are weak. You want to inflict some fast pain, you grab your attacker's pinkie fingers and snap them like twigs."

That seemed oddly brutal. Maisey's stomach twisted.

"There are a thousand ways to attack." He let her go.

Maisey turned to face him. The knots in her stomach were worse.

"But the major thing when defending yourself…" His expression hardened even more.

"Fight with everything in you. Know that you will hurt him. Embrace it."

How long had they been at this? "It's not like I can learn everything right now."

"No, you can't. You and I are gonna start daily lessons. Even after this case is done, we're gonna stay at it."

"Why?" She was certainly all for learning as much as she could, but Odin seemed particularly obsessed.

"Because you matter." He didn't blink. "Because I need to know that you are safe, *always*."

"I like to know the same thing about you," Maisey admitted. Did he understand that?

"I can defend myself."

Obviously. "It's one thing if it's hand-to-hand, but what if it's a gun or a knife? You're not bulletproof." She thought of the scars on him, and a lump rose into her throat. Odin had been hurt badly in the past.

What if...what if she'd never met him? What if he'd died on some battlefield and their paths had never crossed?

"I'm always armed."

He was? "Since when?"

His lips curled. "Always, baby. I have a knife in my boot right now. I've got a concealed carry license, so I keep my gun at the ready."

"I didn't notice..."

"Because I didn't want you to. Because I don't want you to be afraid of me."

A light sweat covered her body. Not so for Odin. The man hadn't even broken a sweat as they tangled together. "I'm not afraid of you."

"Good." He rolled his shoulders. Exhaled.

"I should have a weapon." Something more than her mace.

"If the perp takes the weapon away from you, you just went from bad to worse."

Yes, she got that, and she also got that she was getting his down and dirty self-defense guide because he was afraid. It was almost sweet. No, correction, it *was* sweet. He was insisting that she learn these techniques before they left because he wanted her safe. If she didn't know better, she'd think that big, fierce Odin was starting to care for her...

I don't know better...because I hope that he does care. I hope this isn't just some sort of standard Trouble for Hire package thing that they teach everyone. She bit her lip, then blurted, "Does Trouble for Hire provide these lessons to all clients?"

He'd turned away. Headed toward the counter in the kitchen. "I know War taught Rose. He wanted to make sure she could be as safe as possible."

Yes, but Rose and War had married so...

He flattened his hands on the counter. "Are we going to talk about it?"

It? "Could you be more specific?" She peered at his broad back.

"Last night."

Right. That was what she'd thought. He was referring to the sex that had left her in a melted puddle of bliss. "What, exactly, do you want to discuss—about it, I mean?"

He turned and looked at her. "Was it too much?"

She shook her head.

"Do you have regrets?"

Again, Maisey shook her head. Then, "Do you?"

"Only that I didn't make love to you the first day we met."

Oh. "I kinda regret that, too." She offered him a smile. "But better late than never, am I right?"

His gaze fell to her mouth. His expression shifted. Became even more inscrutable.

"Odin?"

He gave a little jerk. "You stay with me. You follow my orders. You don't go rogue for even a second, got me?"

A light laugh slipped from her. "As if I'm the going-rogue type."

Now he quirked a brow.

"Fine. I'll stay with you. Happy?"

"Not yet. But I think I know how I fucking will be."

***

"All of Whitney's files and belongings were boxed up and moved down here." Maisey shoved her key into the lock on the storage room door. The storage room was in the basement of the Humanities building, and being down there again gave her goosebumps. She kept looking nervously over her shoulder, but each time she did, she just saw Odin's reassuring form behind her. "I've actually been through her files at least four times," Maisey confessed. "It's not like we're going to find anything new." She shoved open the door and hurried unerringly through the towering shelves. "Her sister packed up her house, but I was the one to take care of things here. Her sister didn't want the items from Whitney's office on campus, so I secured them." She rounded the corner.

Came to a quick stop.

Behind her, Odin swore. "Guessing things aren't supposed to look this way?"

Papers were strown across the floor. Boxes had been overturned. Ripped apart. There was a smashed photo of Whitney in the middle of the wreckage. A photo that had been taken right after she received her Ph.D. Whitney was smiling broadly in the photo even as heavy cracks streaked across the image.

"No. *Not* supposed to be this way." Maisey dropped to her knees. She started to reach for the papers.

"*What are you doing?*" A woman's voice. Sharp. Angry.

Maisey looked up and saw Heather Blass rushing toward her. Heather was an intern in the psychology department. She'd worked closely with Whitney. Been lost when Whitney vanished. The overhead light glinted off the glasses she wore. Heather's short, blond hair was cut in a pixie style to frame her delicate face.

"*Why* did you do this?" Heather staggered to a stop and gaped at the sight before her. "This is Whitney's!"

Maisey realized the scene appeared bad. How could it not? She was kneeling in the middle of the chaos. "I didn't—look, I'm not the one who did this!"

"We just arrived," Odin said from behind Maisey. "Found it this way."

Behind the lenses of her glasses, Heather's eyes bulged when she got a good look at him. "Who are you?" she whispered.

Maisey rose. She was gripping the framed photo. "He's—"

"The boyfriend." Odin's arm curled around her shoulders. "I'm Maisey's boyfriend. After what happened the other day, I'm sticking close to her."

Heather's body quivered. "I heard!" Now she scampered toward Maisey, darting through the files and boxes on the floor. Her hands fluttered in the air, as if she'd reach for Maisey, but she stopped herself. "Everyone is talking." Her voice was an overly loud whisper. "You were almost kidnapped! And the truck was just abandoned and the bad guy got away and no one knows where he is..." A shudder. "*My* boyfriend is insisting on walking me home at night. And I know the other interns are making sure no one is alone, either. Using the buddy system."

"Good idea," Odin said. "Better safe than dead."

A quick, bobbing nod from Heather. "That's exactly what I said! Um, actually, no, I think I said better safe than sorry, but I see your point. It's a good point. Very strong." She looked back down at the floor. "What is going on?"

Maisey thought it was pretty obvious what was going on. Someone had been looking for something. Searching inside the boxes that belonged to Whitney. With the way everything was thrown and scattered, would they even be able to tell if files were missing? And that was where it seemed the culprit had focused. On Whitney's case files...

Heather bent down. "I should clean these up—"

"I think we need to call security," Maisey said.

Heather's fingers were on top of two files. "Yes. Right. I should get Sandy down here." She shook her head. "I was here last night. Everything was fine. Nothing was out of place." She continued to crouch near the scattered papers. "Oh, God, what if...what if he was here, when I was?" She bolted upright. "What if he was hiding in the shadows..." Heather looked over her shoulder. "While I was inside? My boyfriend wasn't with me. He was outside, and...would he have heard me if I screamed?"

Maisey reached for her hand. Gave it a quick squeeze. Heather had always been the nervous type. Very shy, too. But she was a great intern, at least, according to Whitney, she had been. Thorough. Knowledgeable. "Nothing happened. You're safe."

Heather looked as if she might pass out.

"Why were you down here last night?" Odin wanted to know.

"Because Dr. Prescott asked me to pull some old books for him."

Clay.

"He didn't have time, so I came down and grabbed the books for him. Didn't think it was a big deal." She swept her stare over the floor. Squeaked. "Seems like a way bigger deal now." A bracing breath. "I'm going to find Sandy. I'll tell him what happened and get him down here to help."

"Excellent idea," Odin muttered. "You go do that."

She bolted.

Maisey waited a moment, then sidled closer to Odin. "What are you thinking?"

"That there was something in these files that the perp didn't want us to see."

"That's what I was thinking, too," Maisey admitted. Damn it. She'd *been* through those files. What had she missed?

A door slammed. Heather must have left.

Odin assessed the scene. "He scattered the stuff to throw us off. With it so disorganized, we'll have a hard time figuring out what was taken."

Yes, they would. Her gaze darted to the left, then to the right. To the towering shelves that surrounded them. Those shelves had been there forever. Or, rather, for as long as the college had been in existence. Some of the thick boxes and storage items were covered with a heavy layer of dust and some of them—

Were weaving?

Yes, yes, the boxes on the top of the closest shelf were weaving because—"Odin!" She shoved him, as hard as she could.

And it was like shoving a brick wall. He didn't move. The boxes were tumbling down. The whole shelf was tumbling down, and it was too late. The whole thing was falling down *on them.*

She tried to scream even as Odin's arms closed around her.

CHAPTER FOURTEEN

Maisey's breath choked out. Another box hit the floor. Another shelf. She heard a terrible groan, like metal screeching, and then the pounding of more boxes. The shattering of glass. The sounds seemed to echo around her. Over and over. And then—

Thuds.

Not her heart. Not boxes falling. But...like feet. Running away?

"Baby..." Odin's voice. His breath blew lightly over her cheek. "Are you okay?"

No, she was not okay. The shelves had come falling down, and he'd thrown himself on top of her. He'd covered her with his body, and not a single thing had hit her because everything had fallen on him. "Forget me—"

"Fucking never."

"How are you?"

With a heave, he rose up, and she realized that he'd just dislodged a ton of random crap that had fallen onto him. Books, equipment, half a heavy shelf. "Fine," Odin snapped.

Fine? He didn't sound fine. He sounded pissed.

She scrambled to her feet.

"When I catch that bastard, he will pay." Odin curled his fingers with hers. "Come on." Then he was kicking his way down the aisle. Shoving whatever the heck was there out of his path as he gave chase.

He'd obviously heard the fleeing footsteps, too. He knew that their prey had been in that storage room with them. The jerk had waited and then shoved those shelves onto them.

Now their attacker was running, but he was still close. *We can get him.*

Odin threw open the storage room door. Then almost ran straight into Clay. A Clay who had just spun toward them.

"Maisey?" Surprise sharpened Clay's voice. "What's going on? What's—*ah!*"

Odin grabbed him. Slammed Clay back against the nearby wall. "No more," Odin snarled.

Maisey glanced down the hallway. Didn't see anyone else. Wasn't Jinx supposed to be keeping an eye on Clay? Hadn't that been his one big assignment?

"Were you in that storage room?" Odin demanded of Clay.

"What? No, no, I was *going* in there. Had to return some books. But I haven't been in there yet." His voice was strained. "Maisey? What is wrong with your friend?"

Maisey saw books scattered on the floor. She realized Clay had dropped them when Odin grabbed him. Old psychology texts.

"*Maisey!*" Clay was insistent. "Call off the guard dog! Tell him to get his hands off me!"

She eased closer. "Someone just attacked us in the storage room. Shoved shelves down on top of us." She could see scratches on Odin's powerful arms.

"It wasn't me!" An instant denial. "Look, I don't know what you think is happening here, but I just arrived! I was bringing back some books!"

"I will fucking *end* you." Odin's voice was low and lethal. "Do you think I will put up with this shit? Do you think I am going to let you hurt her? Do you think I will let you *touch* her?"

The stairwell door burst open. Sandy stumbled out, with Heather hot on his heels.

"Get him off me!" Clay shouted. "He's crazy!"

"I will show you crazy," Odin promised grimly. "You hurt Maisey. You hurt *my* Maisey, and I will show you how crazy I can be. I will rip you apart. There won't be anything left of you when I'm done. You think you're so good at making people disappear? I will make *you* vanish."

Clay stilled. Then...went wild. He heaved and twisted and punched at Odin. "*You don't scare me! You don't scare—*"

"Just wait, I will." Odin held Clay with ease. The same ease he'd held Maisey with back at the condo.

But Sandy was fumbling and grabbing for his taser. "You two—break it up!"

Odin leaned in even closer to Clay. "Different when you're not going up against them, isn't it? When you don't have a woman who is smaller and weaker than you are, it's harder."

Clay's face went absolutely white.

Sandy's fingers were shaking as he lifted the taser. He cast a desperate glance at Maisey.

"Why are they fighting?" A loud shriek from Heather.

Because we think Clay is a killer. And I'm pretty sure Odin is trying to scare a confession from him.

But, again, dammit, where was Jinx?

The shaking in Sandy's fingers was getting worse. She was afraid he was going to accidentally tase Odin. Carefully, she edged her body between Sandy's taser and Odin.

"I haven't hurt *anyone!*" Clay yelled. The veins in his neck bulged. "If you're talking about that bullshit story that used to circulate about me and my old girlfriend, you've got it all wrong. She left *me.* I didn't hurt her! I would never hurt anyone!"

"Then you didn't just shove those shelves onto me and Maisey?" Odin charged.

"No! But I wish I had shoved something on you—you are *insane!*"

"Push me more," Odin dared. "Like I said, you're not the only one who can make people disappear. You got away with it before, but it ends. *You're* ending."

Clay looked as if he might faint. "He's threatening to kill me! Get the cops. Help. *Help me!*"

Maisey grabbed Odin's arm when he drew back his fist to punch Clay. "Stop."

His head turned toward her. She'd thought that he'd been deliberately pushing Clay, toying with him, but...

His eyes told her that she'd been wrong.

Odin's eyes burned with a fury she hadn't seen before. One that had her breath catching. One that almost made her think she was staring into the eyes of a stranger. "Odin?"

He blinked. Slowly lowered his hand. Let Clay go.

"He's insane, Maisey," Clay snapped. "Your boyfriend is out of his head. You need to be smart and get the hell away from him before he hurts you or someone else!"

"Shut up, Clay," she ordered. Her fingers still pressed to Odin's arm. His muscles were rock hard beneath her touch. This situation was going from bad to worse, and she wondered what could possibly happen next...

An alarm began to sound. A high, shrieking alarm.

Sandy backed up a step. "That's the fire alarm." His eyes widened as he glanced around feverishly. "Everyone, out, *now!*"

***

Chaos.

Odin was dead certain the chaos was deliberate. Students and faculty flooded out of the Humanities building in a thick crowd. There was no way to keep track of anyone. *Anybody* could have been in that throng that burst outside.

It was the perfect cover for a killer. The perfect way for him to escape.

"I had eyes on Clay until he went downstairs." Jinx stood near Odin. "I knew you were down there, so I figured I should just hang back. That you had things covered."

Odin turned his head to stare at him.

Jinx winced. "You're looking a little crazy-eyed, my friend."

"Maisey tried to shove me out of the way."

"Okay."

"She noticed that the shelves were falling before I did." He was speaking between clenched teeth. "Then she tried to shove me."

"The nerve," Jinx muttered. "How dare she?"

Did it look as if he was laughing? "It's not a damn joke." Odin knew he had bruises all over his back from the stuff that had come raining down on him. He didn't want to think about what that heavy crash would have done to her delicate body. "The shelves were massive, nearly touching the ceiling. They were stuffed with boxes, equipment, you name it. That stuff could have knocked her out." Or, if something had slammed into her head...*No, do not. Do not go there.* But he was seeing red. Blood red. As in...*I want Clay's blood. I want to make that bastard pay.* "She shouldn't be trying to protect me. That's not happening."

"Maybe you should tell her that."

He intended to. Loudly. Clearly.

"By the way, if we were trying to keep a low profile with Clay, I think that ship has sailed. He's currently glaring at you, and I heard that blonde over there..." He motioned to the woman that Odin now knew was Heather Blass. "She was saying that you'd accused him of making people disappear. Is that true? You just threw that charge at him?"

"I was baiting him."

"Is that what you were doing?" Jinx didn't sound convinced. "And did he take the bait? Did he break down and confess his crimes?"

"No." But there had been something in Clay's eyes. A flicker, a break that showed emotion. Fear.

"You probably don't want to hear this, but I think we have another problem."

No, he didn't want to hear about another problem. He had enough going on at the moment.

"If you look due south, you'll find a friendly face."

Odin took his time and casually glanced due south. *Dammit.* "How long has he been there?" Ramsey was casually leaning against one of the massive trees near the Humanities building. Like everyone else, he acted as if he was just watching the scene. A curious bystander.

Firefighters had rushed inside.

Odin hadn't caught even a whiff of smoke.

"Noticed him right after everyone else came scrambling out. Interesting, isn't it? That he's here at exactly the same time someone attacked you?"

Not interesting. Infuriating. Suspicious.

Ramsey lifted his hand.

"Did that guy just *wave* to you?" Jinx demanded.

"No, I think he flipped me off. Better get your vision checked." Ramsey had turned away and was casually walking from the scene. "Maisey is talking to the security guard and the cops. Make *sure* your vision is clear enough that you see her every second until I get back, got me? Do not let her out of your sight."

"On it."

Odin grunted and gave chase. There was no way he was letting Ramsey leave that scene without having a talk with the bastard. In moments, he and Ramsey had left the crowd behind. Ramsey was heading for a dark SUV.

He opened the door. Started to slide inside—

"Don't make me drag you back out," Odin warned.

Ramsey's shoulders stiffened. He turned. Slowly. "You truly think you could?"

"With minimal effort." Fury infused his veins. "You don't want to test me right now."

"Why? Because your Maisey almost got hurt today? Feeling a little bit tense, are you?" Ramsey closed in on him. "Then imagine how I feel. My Whitney wasn't just hurt. She was taken. Killed. That means I feel a million times angrier than you do. So I will tell you...you *don't* want to come at me."

As if Odin would ever back down. "Maisey thinks you should know about a phone call she received last night. I think you might have *made* the phone call, so I wasn't exactly rushing to contact you but then I looked, and surprise coincidence, here you are."

Ramsey frowned. "I didn't call Maisey."

"No?"

"*No.*"

Odin measured him.

"I don't have time for this." Tension blasted in Ramsey's words. "What the hell was the phone call about? Did you get a lead?"

"Whitney."

Ramsey's jaw tightened. "Do you know how annoying it is when someone gives you a one-word answer? Nothing pisses me off more."

"The caller was Whitney." He dropped this bombshell and waited.

All of the color drained from Ramsey's face. He staggered. Caught himself. "*Don't lie.*"

That reaction was real. Hell, Ramsey *hadn't* been the caller. "The voice on the line was Whitney's. Maisey confirmed it."

The pain that flashed in Ramsey's eyes was so intense. There was no denying the obvious. *He really does care about her.*

"What did she say?" Ramsey rasped.

"The caller asked Maisey for help."

Ramsey grabbed him. Fisted his fingers in Odin's t-shirt. "Then we help her! We do anything necessary to get Whitney back!"

"The call was probably fake. You take a breath for a second, and you'll remember how easy it is to fake someone's voice with those cheap apps that float around."

Ramsey's grip tightened. "You don't know it was fake."

"And you don't know it was real." He looked down. "You're wrinkling one of my favorite shirts."

Swearing, Ramsey let him go. "If you think it was fake, what was the point in even telling me?"

"To see your reaction."

Ramsey stalked back to his vehicle. Jumped in. Before he could swing the driver's side door shut, Odin caught it. "Why were you here today?"

Ramsey turned his head. "You're wasting your time with me. Cross my name off your list. I didn't hurt Whitney, and I haven't done anything to Maisey."

Odin just waited. Ramsey hadn't answered his question.

"You should be afraid of me," Ramsey suddenly said. "Smart people are afraid. Dumbasses, too. You don't want me for an enemy."

"Well, I don't want you for a buddy, either, so..."

"You're fucking insane."

Odin considered the situation. "You are the second person to tell me that today. Funny thing is, I feel completely sane. It's the rest of the world that's crazy." He paused. "Why were you here?"

"She said she thought someone was following her," Ramsey muttered. "I didn't mention it last night, but Whitney—she said that she thought someone was following her one night when she left campus." A muscle flexed along his jaw. "I wanted to put a guard on her right then and there, but she laughed. Told me that I was being too protective. That she probably had just imagined it, but that she'd be sure and exercise more care in the future." His jaw hardened. "Said she'd get the security guard to walk her out if she stayed late again." His fingers curled around the steering wheel. "I let it go. Some creep was following her, and *I let it go*. If I'd just put one of my men on her, she'd be safe right now."

"She told you that she'd go to the security guard?" As far as he knew, Sandy hadn't mentioned anything about Whitney needing protection.

"Yeah. That's why I was here today. Wanted to have an up close and personal chat with the guy. Turns out he's pushing ninety and couldn't protect a damn fly. Whitney never told me that." His knuckles whitened.

"You mean you came to threaten his ass then realized that if you used your usual tactics, you'd probably kill Sandy in minutes."

Ramsey didn't respond.

"Who's next on your hit list?" Odin asked.

Ramsey angled his head so that he was looking at Odin. His smile was ice-cold. "Thanks to you—and a helpful blonde who talks very loudly—I now know the identity of your other chief suspect. I think I'll see how long he can hold out against my, ah, 'usual tactics,' I believe you called them."

Shit. The situation had just gone from bad to clusterfuck.

"Let go of the door," Ramsey directed.

He didn't. "Leave him alone. I'll deal with Clay."

"After I'm done with him, have a freaking field day." He started the car. "Let go, or you'll get dragged along. Your choice."

The sonofabitch—

"*Odin!*" Maisey's voice.

He let go. Ramsey shot away with a squeal of his tires even as Odin spun to find Maisey running toward him.

Jinx was trailing a few feet behind her. "Got eyes on her!" he called in his cheerful voice. "Perfect vision."

She hurried to Odin. Her breath rushed in and out. "You were interrogating him without me!"

Guilty. He tossed a glare back at Jinx. "Couldn't you keep her away for a little longer?"

"Didn't realize that was part of my job. Thought I was just supposed to have my eyes on her. You need to make sure you're clear when you give orders."

Maisey's hands flew to her hips. "Keep me away? Odin, why do you have such trouble understanding this is a partnership?"

He surged toward her. Loomed over her. "Ramsey is dangerous. Whether he's tied to what's happening or not, I don't want you anywhere near him."

"I can handle some danger. Haven't I proven that?"

Why didn't she understand this? "I don't want you around danger." *You're too important*. And too vulnerable.

"Yes, well, I don't want you running off and leaving me in the dark."

"I'm the damn PI! I'm supposed to investigate."

"And I'm the one who just realized *why* Whitney's files were ransacked in the storage room." Her lips tugged down. "It wasn't her."

He slanted a hard glance at Jinx.

But Jinx shrugged. "I have no idea what she's talking about. Maisey just came running up and said she had to talk to you, ASAP. I pointed in the general direction you'd taken, and the game was afoot."

Seriously?

One of Maisey's hands flew up and pressed to Odin's chest. "The caller last night wasn't Whitney." Sadness whispered in her voice. "You were right about that."

"How do you know?"

"Because there were a few old tapes in those boxes of hers. Interviews that she'd conducted a long time ago. I remembered them when we were running out and the fire alarm was shrieking." Her hand was right over his heart. "I told Sandy about them. He went back in as soon as he had the all clear. He searched, but said the tapes are gone."

Jinx positioned himself beside Odin. "It would be easy enough to take a recording of Whitney talking and splice pieces together in order to make that call to Maisey."

Yes, it would be. Too easy.

"It wasn't her," Maisey said once more. "He's jerking me around. Trying to manipulate me."

"More than that, sweetheart." Her touch seemed to burn through his shirt. "He's trying to kill you." He hadn't just wanted to injure her with the "accident" in the storage room. Or with the attempted abduction. The bastard's goal was clearly to take out Maisey.

And that shit was never gonna happen.

CHAPTER FIFTEEN

"Now that you mention in it…" Sandy rubbed his chin. "I do remember Whitney coming to me and saying something about feeling a little nervous when she was heading to her car."

They were in Sandy's cramped office. The fire trucks had left. The crowd had finally vanished—and so had Clay. When Odin had returned to the Humanities building with Maisey, he'd discovered that Clay had cut and run from the scene.

Except Clay hadn't been able to go too far. Jinx had tagged his car. They knew the man had just driven back to his house. *And I'll be seeing you soon to finish our talk.*

But first…

Sandy.

"Whitney didn't mention this to me," Maisey fumed.

Sandy shrugged. "It was a one-time deal. I walked her to her car that night. After that, she came and said it had all been a misunderstanding. That she'd found out who'd tailed her, and it was just someone who'd needed a little help."

"Help?" Maisey pounced on that. "Did she tell you what kind of help?"

He scratched his chin again. "No, and I didn't ask." His gaze fell. "Sure wish I had now, though."

Odin let his gaze drift over the small security office. Stacks of paperwork. Campus flyers. A cold cup of coffee on the ancient desk. "What about the security cameras in the Humanities building? Did they catch anything useful today?"

"They were shut off."

His gaze jumped back to Sandy. "Say that again."

"Shut off, son," Sandy raised his voice. "Shut. Off."

Odin narrowed his eyes. "Who shut them off?"

"Heck if I know. Was trying to pull up the stuff for the cops—you know, they need to investigate all that vandalism—but just got static. Looks like the whole campus system went down around eight. Thought we might see something, but...nope."

Great. Fabulous. He glanced at his watch. They were wasting time. He needed to confront Clay, before Ramsey got to him. "Come on, Maisey."

She took his hand immediately. His fingers curled around hers. Touching her seemed to steady some of the pulsing tension that coursed through his body. He didn't speak, and neither did she, not until they were out of the building and the warm sunlight was hitting down on them.

"Convenient, isn't it?" she finally murmured.

"It's a lot more than that." Odin turned toward her. "He's on campus. An employee. A student."

"Has to be," she agreed with a quick glance around them. "It has to be someone who is familiar with the layout of the college. Someone who knew about those tapes in Whitney's storage boxes."

"That takes us back to Clay." Round and round they went. "He knows we suspect him now."

"Because you wanted to rattle his cage," she noted with a crook of one eyebrow.

Oh, he hadn't just been interested in rattling. "I want to shove the fucker *into* a cage." Just so they were clear.

Her lips tightened. "But when you were doing all that rattling, he didn't give up anything to you."

For a moment, Clay almost had. "There was something in his eyes. When I talked about making people vanish—I could have sworn that for just a moment there, I saw fear."

She inched closer. "Fear doesn't equal guilt."

"But you're only afraid if you have something to hide."

"Excellent point." She shivered. "Okay. So maybe we need to rattle him a little more."

"Yeah, but the problem is that Ramsey is ready to go after him, too. We need to get to Clay first." His Jeep waited. They turned as one and started rushing toward it.

"*We're done.*" A woman's voice. Angry. Sharp. "I don't care anymore. I don't want to hear your excuses. You are never there when I need you. I have put everything on the line for you, but now I don't think you're worth it."

Odin glanced to the left. Saw the blonde from earlier—Heather—arguing with a thin, lanky guy in the parking lot. As he watched, Heather spun away from the man and started to storm off. But the man—with thick, brown hair and a swirling tattoo sliding up his neck—grabbed her. He whirled her to face him.

"Hey!" Maisey immediately called out. "Is everything all right?"

Odin was already closing in. When the man had grabbed Heather, he'd grabbed her a little too hard. "Let her go."

The guy didn't. "Mind your business!"

"This is my business. You're being an asshole in public, so that makes it a public concern." He looked at the hard grip on Heather. "Let her go."

"Let me go, Steve," Heather snapped. "Right now. God, this is so embarrassing."

Steve let her go. But he was glaring for all he was worth. "Don't come crawling back to me!"

Heather straightened her shoulders. "I don't crawl to anyone. You must have mistaken me for someone else."

Steve's hands were fisting. Odin stared at them, then looked up to lock eyes with Steve. "What you're gonna want to do is take some breaths, calm the fuck down, then get the hell out of here."

Steve's face flushed a deep red. It was easy to see the other man's intent. It was also apparent that Odin had about eight inches and nearly seventy pounds on the guy. "Try it, though," Odin invited.

Steve apparently thought better of trying anything. He bolted. Jumped in a sports car and flew out of there like his life depended on it.

"He is such a dick." Heather sniffed. "Sorry you had to see that, but he needed to know we were done."

Odin swept his stare over her. "He get physical like that a lot?"

"Steve? No. First time." She straightened her glasses. They'd already been straight. "You think you know someone, and then they have to go and show you their true colors. Disappointing."

Maisey touched her shoulder. "Do you need a ride home?"

"No, I got it, but thanks. I appreciate you trying to look out for me." A quick smile. "You remind me of Dr. Augustine. She was always looking out for people, too, you know. Her interns weren't just her students. We were family." She swiped at her cheek. "I need to go. I-I'll see you around soon." She scampered toward a parked four-door car.

Odin could tell Maisey was worried as she watched the younger woman. "What do you know about that guy?"

"Not a lot. Steve Barrington is a computer science grad student. I don't see him much. Just when he comes around and I happen to pass him and Heather in the halls. He always seemed quiet. Pretty devoted to her." Maisey met Odin's stare. "But sometimes, we can all trust the wrong people."

Odin thought about the scene that had gone down between him and Clay. Maisey had seen every brutal second of it. "I'm not like—" Odin stopped. "I would never hurt you."

Her brow furrowed. "You don't need to tell me that." She walked around. Jumped into the Jeep.

He found himself lingering by the passenger side of the vehicle. "But I want to tell you. I don't want you thinking that I could turn on you. That's not me. I would never do that."

Her hand slid against his cheek. "Big, tough Odin. I know who you are." She leaned forward. Pressed a kiss to his lips. "And I know what you would and wouldn't do. I know you wouldn't hurt me. But I also know that you *would* hurt anyone who tried to come for me."

Yes. He would. In a heartbeat. "Do I scare you?"

"Do I look scared?" Her hand lingered against his cheek.

"I think you look absolutely beautiful." But then, he always thought that about her.

Her smile bloomed. Her dimples flashed for him. "Careful, or I'll start to think there's a whole lot more between us than just the case."

She didn't get that yet? "What do you think last night was about?"

Her lips parted. She didn't speak. He realized he needed to get his ass in the vehicle and move. He hurried around the ride. Leapt inside. Had the engine growling moments later.

But Maisey touched his hand. "Last night...why don't you tell me what it was about?" She seemed to hold her breath.

His head turned toward her. "It was about me wanting you more than anything else in the world."

"I felt the same way." A whisper.

"I *still* feel that way." It was all he could do not to pull her into his arms. "It's not about the damn case. I want you, and I intend to have you, over and over again. When the case ends, you're not getting away." Shit. That had come off way too possessive and hard, but he *felt* that way. "Ah, Maisey..."

"Neither are you, Odin. You're not getting away from me just because the case gets closed."

Warmth spread through his chest. Did it look as if he wanted to get away? Hell, no. What he wanted...

Odin wanted to figure out a way to keep Maisey. For as long as he possibly could.

I had one night. I want one hell of a lot more.

***

"So the plan is to just confront him?" Maisey paced in her den. "We have zero evidence. He'll laugh in our faces."

"He wasn't laughing earlier. And either we confront him, or Ramsey does."

She rocked back on her heels. "That sounds bad. Is it as bad as I think it is?"

He peered through the window to stare over at Clay's place. "Sweetheart, I suspect it's a thousand times worse."

"Great. Wonderful." She began pacing again as she tried to work off some of the nervous tension making her stomach quiver. "Okay. So am I the good cop? Or the bad one?"

He looked back at her. "I'll be bad enough for us both."

Maisey swallowed. "I don't see him confessing."

"We just need to trip him up. Get him to say one or two things that can help us to nail his ass to the wall. When we do that, we're golden."

If only. Maisey wasn't exactly feeling golden at the moment. She turned and walked toward him. Stopped when she was right in front of Odin's towering form. "I didn't thank you."

"You don't have anything to thank me for."

Uh, yes. She did. "What about being a human shield? Can I thank you for that?"

His jaw hardened. "I'm bigger. It only made sense for me to get on top when the shelves came down. You want to know what *didn't* make sense?" He reached for her hand. "When you tried to shove me out of the way. If that move had worked, *you* would have been the one getting the brunt of that weight as the shelves rained down on you."

"I-I know that."

"You know?" He pulled her ever closer. "Then why the hell would you do something so dangerous?"

She thought it was obvious. "To keep you safe."

Shock flashed on his face. But in the next instant, he'd schooled his expression. "You don't need to do that."

"I think I do." On this point, she wouldn't back down. "I think you need someone watching your back, and I'm not just talking about Jinx." She wanted the job. If possible, she'd like to put in an application, please.

"Jinx." The faint lines near his mouth deepened. "You know he's outside right now, keeping an eye on Clay's place? He's gonna make sure Clay doesn't leave—or have any unexpected visitors—before we're done with him."

She actually hadn't known that. Jinx had kind of disappeared when she and Odin had gone to talk with Sandy. Maisey figured Jinx must be well hidden because she hadn't seen him when they'd driven home. A faint sigh escaped her. "It's a miracle you weren't hurt when that stuff fell on us."

His gaze cut away from her. "Yep. A miracle."

Red flags started flying. "Odin? Odin, are you hurt?"

"Nothing I can't handle."

Hell. That meant he *was* hurt. "Show me. Right now."

He let go of her hand. Marched for the door. "Let's get this interrogation scene moving. The sooner we can toss Clay's ass in jail, the better."

"Odin! If you're hurt, I want to help you!"

He glanced back at her. "Just some bruises. Nothing I can't handle."

She rushed to him. Shoved up the back of his t-shirt. Saw the already darkening bruises that mottled his skin. "Oh, Odin..."

"Not a deal. Don't even feel it."

He was such a liar. Maisey leaned forward. Her lips feathered over the skin. "I'm so sorry."

"Don't."

She pressed another kiss to him. "I'll do what I want. You're hurt. You got hurt protecting me."

"And what are you doing?" His whole body was taut. "Kissing it better?"

"Yes," she said simply. Another press of her mouth against his back.

Odin shuddered. Then he spun around. "You make every damn thing better." He caught her hands. Pulled her against him. Crashed his mouth down on hers.

You make every damn thing better. That might just be the nicest thing anyone had ever said to her.

But she didn't get to linger too long on that because his tongue was driving into her mouth and, as always when Odin kissed her, need and lust seemed to burst to life within her. Her mouth met his eagerly, greedily, and she pressed as close to him as she could possibly get.

"Fuck." Odin ripped his mouth from hers. "See—this is what happens if you put your mouth on me. *Anywhere* on me."

She gazed up at him.

"You're dangerous," he accused.

She was? He was the first person to ever say that.

"We have a job. A suspect we need to push, before a crime boss comes along and tortures his ass." His eyes blazed. "We have that shit happening, but I want to fuck you up against the wall."

That was an option?

"But we have to go. Dammit." His gaze cut to the wall. She could tell he was considering his options.

And she thought he was about to go for the wall when his phone rang. He whipped it out of his pocket and pushed it to his ear. "Jinx, tell me the bastard isn't on the move…"

Her shoulders tensed.

"What? You're shitting me." A pause. "Huh. Yeah, that is interesting. We're on the way. You hold your position." He ended the call and glanced back at her. "Your neighbor just got a surprise visitor."

She would not look at the wall. She licked her lips and still tasted him. "Do not leave me in suspense." Her voice was way too husky.

"Heather Blass." His voice was like gravel.

Heather was at Clay's house? Right then?

"She and her boyfriend broke up," Odin mused still in that gravel-rough voice that sounded like rough sex. "And now she's at her professor's house. Not hard to connect those dots."

He was saying—Heather and Clay?

"You ready for this?" Odin asked.

She was more than ready. And the wall was apparently not an option now. Right. Of course. They had a job to do. The sex could wait. *But I will so come back to it.* Her head moved in a jerky nod.

"He could be dangerous," Odin warned. "If he does or says anything that seems like a threat, get back. I'll deal with him."

They'd deal with him.

They raced over to the house next door. As they approached, Maisey could hear the raised voices from inside. Heather and Clay were having an argument.

"I did it for you!" Heather cried out. "Can't you see that?"

Odin slanted a fast glance back at Maisey. Then he reached for the door.

It yanked open before he could knock. "You need to leave!" Clay bellowed. His head was turned away from the door so he didn't see Odin and Maisey. "Go now, before it gets worse—"

Now his head turned and he could see them. His mouth gaped open.

"Before what gets worse?" Odin asked, tone ever so cold. "Because from where I'm standing, things are definitely bad enough."

A gasp came from Heather.

Clay's stare jumped from Odin to Maisey. "This isn't what it looks like."

Odin advanced, and Clay seemed to automatically step back—or retreat—for him. Maisey slipped right inside after Odin.

"It's not?" Odin's voice was mild. "What do you think it looks like? That a professor is having a personal relationship with his intern?"

"I'm not—" Clay said.

Just as Heather cried out, "I love him!"

Maisey schooled her expression. Sure seemed like those two were not on the same page.

Clay spun toward Heather. "For the last time, there is nothing between us! I was helping you on a project. I don't know how you got the idea that we were romantically involved, but we are not."

Forget being on the same page. From the sound of things, they weren't even in the same book.

Heather's lower lip trembled. "But I broke up with Steve. I'm free now. I did that so we could be together."

"It's *not* happening, Heather."

Her eyes flashed with fury. "Is it because they're here? Are you just saying this in front of them?" She rushed to Clay. Grabbed his hand. "Because you were different with me last night. You felt the same way, I know you did."

"You need to go." He pulled his hand away from her. "Before this gets worse. You are an intelligent, beautiful young woman, but I cannot give you what you need."

She sucked in a pained breath and jerked back, as if he'd hit her. Then she bolted for the door. Maisey hurriedly stepped out of the way so that Heather wouldn't careen into her. As Heather ran out, Maisey caught the gleam of tears behind her glasses.

Heather slammed the door. The slam was so hard it seemed to shake the frame.

Clay cleared his throat. "That's—it's not what you think."

Maisey wasn't sure what to think.

Odin, apparently, was. He said, "You mean you aren't screwing your intern?"

Maisey wrinkled her nose. Obviously, Odin was not going to be coy with this interrogation. But then again, he hadn't been *coy* even once during their association.

Clay flushed. "I am not screwing her. Heather developed a-a crush on me recently. It happens sometimes with students. I just needed to set her straight." He rolled back his shoulders. "I certainly didn't expect her to show up here."

"Sometimes, people just don't live up to our expectations." Odin crossed his arms over his chest.

Alarm flashed on Clay's face. "Look, I am not in the mood to deal with more of your madness." His attention shifted to Maisey. "How about you take your crazy boyfriend out of here?"

"How about you don't call him crazy?" Maisey fired back. She took a quick step toward Clay.

Clay's jaw dropped. "Maisey, the man attacked me and basically accused me of murder earlier! It doesn't get crazier than that!"

"Oh, it could get a lot crazier," Odin assured him. "Especially if you're the killer we're after."

Clay blanched. "Killer? Are you for real?"

Maisey made sure she stood at Odin's side. "We are. We have questions for you."

"Oh, for shit's sake." Clay threw his hands into the air. "Maisey, you're cute, so I've let you get away with some crap, but it ends, okay? I'm over it. I get that you do your little podcast and you talk about killers, but this is going too far." His hands dropped. "You're in my house now? Accusing me of—of—"

"What happened to Hannah Martinez?" Maisey asked. She was going right to the point.

Anger flashed on Clay's face. "I knew you were talking about her." But his words weren't directed at Maisey. They were thrown at Odin. "Back on campus today, when you were talking about making people disappear, I knew you were talking about Hannah." His breath heaved out. "What? Did the two of you dig into my life? Is it because of those break-ins that Maisey had? You thought her only neighbor must be the culprit, so you tore into my past?"

Odin just stared back at him.

"She left me." Clay swallowed. "We were freaking kids. It wasn't some big, epic romance. Hannah broke up with me. Said she wanted more out of life than to stay in some tiny, Tennessee town forever. The next thing I knew, she was gone. I thought she'd run away. I told her parents that. I told the sheriff. Hannah wanted more than she could get in that town." He raked a hand over his face. "But then she never came back. She never contacted anyone. Everybody started looking at me suspiciously, like I'd done something to her."

"Did you?" Odin asked.

"No!" A yell. Then, softer, "No." Adamant. "I've been accused of hurting her so many times now, you'd think I'd be over it." A shake of his head. "Let me be clear. *I did nothing to Hannah Martinez.*" A muscle jerked along his jaw. "I liked her, okay? I didn't love her. We weren't soul mates. I didn't go into some jealous frenzy because she broke up with me. That's the most popular story, by the way. The old jealous rage." He puffed out his cheeks and exhaled. "After a few years, her family decided she was dead. Not missing. Dead. And maybe she is—I don't know. *I have never known what happened to her.*"

Emotions vibrated in his voice. Rage. Pain.

"If that's all," Clay snapped, "how about you get out of my house?" He jerked his chin toward the door.

"Jenny Lynch." Odin didn't move. His arms were still crossed over his chest.

Clay's face hardened even more. "You are not seriously suggesting—"

"You took her job when she vanished," Maisey noted as she continued to carefully watch him.

His gaze cut to her. "What the fuck am I?" he breathed. "A podcast for you?"

Maisey didn't flinch. "Three women tied to you have vanished. There is no overlooking your connection to them."

He stalked toward her.

Odin moved into his path. "Jenny Lynch," Odin said again.

"Get the fuck out," Clay ordered.

"Were you involved with her?" Maisey asked as she shifted to the left in order to get a view of him around Odin's massive form.

"Yes. So the hell what? Jenny and I hooked up a few times at conferences. No big deal." He had a sneer on his face. "Oh, wait, was that the wrong answer? Should I have said...we hooked up and then she broke up with me. In a rage—because, you know, apparently, I suffer from jealous rages—I killed her. I took her body out on my boat and I weighed her down and I dumped her."

Odin's hands dropped to his sides. "What kind of boat do you have?"

"*Get out of my house!*" Clay snarled as his face mottled. "I am two seconds away from calling the cops." His hand lifted and he pointed at Maisey.

"The only reason I haven't is because of you. I thought we were friends, Maisey. But all along...what? You just figured I was killing women? First Hannah, then Jenny, and—"

"Whitney," Maisey supplied as she held her ground. "You took Jenny's job, then Whitney's. Both women disappeared. Just like Hannah disappeared. I couldn't ignore what happened to them. Whitney was my friend."

Disgusted, he shook his head. "And here I thought there might be a chance for more between us." A rough exhale. "Guess we were both wrong." He drew himself up to his full height. "Let me be clear. I did not kill Whitney Augustine. I have no idea what happened to her." His lips pulled down. "Just like I didn't kill Hannah or Jenny. Now, that's all I'm going to say. You two aren't cops, and I don't have to answer more of your BS questions."

Maisey glanced at Odin. His intent stare was still on Clay. They hadn't learned anything new, and Clay's anger seemed more than real enough. "Let's go." Because she knew that if they didn't leave, Clay *would* be calling the cops on them.

Odin turned with her. She reached for the door.

"I know you were in my house."

Her hand froze in mid-air.

"When I left town? I know you were here. At first, I thought maybe I'd had a break-in, just like at your place, Maisey. But then I realized nothing was taken. Just some things knocked over in my closet. Like someone was searching the place."

She looked back at Clay.

His stare was locked on her. "Didn't find anything, did you?" Almost a taunt. "Because there is nothing to find."

"We have no clue what you're talking about," Odin said, sounding bored. "But if you had a break-in, I think you need to be calling those cops you keep mentioning. Maybe they can come out here, check every inch of your property, do a thorough search, and see—"

"I'm not calling the cops. For Maisey's sake. But my good will only goes so far." He glared at Odin. "I blame you for this mess. Some wannabe PI. Yeah, I can dig, too. And I did. All you are is a burned-out soldier who thinks he can get a second shot at your buddy's PI business. You have no clue what you're doing. Maisey made the worst mistake of her life when she hired you. And that's what happened, isn't it? She hired you to find Whitney. Then you seduced her. Now you're just stringing her along. You can't find her friend. Can't solve the case. All you can do is screw Maisey over—"

She grabbed Odin before he could take a step back toward Clay. "Rule one, remember?"

His eyes glittered down at her. But he wasn't lunging at Clay, so she took that as a win. And they were gonna make their exit. Definitely. After she got a few things straight. "He's not a burned-out anything, just for clarification." Maisey gave Clay a brittle smile. "He didn't seduce me. I pretty much jumped him." She'd definitely been the one stripping in the hallway.

Clay's face twisted in a mix of shock and anger.

"As for Whitney, we will not stop. Odin isn't the kind of man who gives up, and I am certainly not that type of woman. My friend is out there, and we will find her. We will make certain that the person who took her is caught and spends the rest of his life in jail."

Done. Her fingers wrapped with Odin's. Or, rather were swallowed by his giant grip. She kept her spine straight and her head up as they left. She was conscious of Clay moving to the doorway. Of his gaze following every single step that they took.

She didn't look back. Her steps were slow and steady. As if she didn't have a care in the world, when she really had about a million of them. Maisey waited, pretty much biting her lower lip in two as she held back the words that wanted to tumble from her. As soon as they were safely inside her house, as soon as the door was closed and locked behind them, she whirled to face Odin. "He didn't give us anything—"

"He has a boat, Maisey."

Her eyebrows shot down.

"I searched—had one of my contacts dig, too, but there was no boat registered to him. But the guy just told us he has one. That means he's got it registered under another name. He was hiding it from us." Odin pulled his hand from hers and yanked out his phone. "I'm finding it."

"Wait...when he was saying that about Jenny, about dumping her body..." Her gut twisted. "You don't think he was serious?"

His expression told her how he felt even before Odin said, "I think I'm finding his damn boat."

CHAPTER SIXTEEN

The prick had been taunting him. Odin knew when he was being baited, and Clay must have been feeling freaking bulletproof to say that shit to him about Maisey. For the moment, though, Odin shoved aside his simmering fury at the jerk. He had a job to do. *Wannabe PI, my ass.* Odin kept talking to his contact, knowing the woman would be able to dig through databases in record time.

"He's got a boat," Odin said into the phone. "It's gonna be close by. Start with the marinas in the area. You already have his description. The boat isn't registered under his name because I checked before. So try looking under different last names, but with the same first name." In his experience, that was often the easiest way to fake a new identity. You kept your first name because when people called out to you, you responded. Your head turned automatically. If you just wanted a quick and dirty fake ID, you altered your last name.

"You're gonna owe me," his contact said. "You and War because I've been doing a ton of favors for him lately. I prefer payment in the form of super expensive chocolates and luxury vacations."

He shook his head. "Ali, consider the chocolate done, but you gotta talk to War about the vacation trip." He hung up the phone. One item down. Had Clay tripped up when he said that bit about the boat? Odin sure thought he had.

This could be the break they needed. *A boat.*

They were on the coast. Hell, yes, he'd considered the option—dark as it was—that maybe Whitney's body had been dumped in the Gulf of Mexico. And in order to do that, Clay would need a private vessel. His own transport so no one would see what he was doing.

"His anger seemed real."

He turned his head. Odin found Maisey with her hands twisted in front of her.

"It was." Odin didn't doubt that. "When you're the bad guy and people are closing in, you get mad." He advanced relentlessly toward her. "You get scared." And, what worried him... "You get desperate." He tucked a lock of her hair behind her ear. "That's why we don't lower our guard." Why he would not be leaving Maisey. He'd be sleeping at her place that night. He'd keep watch over her and keep tabs on Clay.

And it's not about fucking seducing her. Having sex with her was bonus. Keeping her safe? *That* was the priority. "I'm not screwing you over."

Her long lashes lifted. "I never thought you were. In fact..." A faint smile teased her lips. "You tried to reject me as a client, remember? Told me that you couldn't take advantage of me."

He'd said that and then had her in bed with him at the first opportunity. "I couldn't keep my hands off you." They weren't off her now, either. His palm slid over her cheek.

"I don't want them off." Soft. Husky.

Did she know that he was hard for her? Simply being near Maisey made him hard. Her scent. Her touch. Everything about her sent him into overdrive. She had, from the very first.

"I like it when you touch me," she told him. "I actually like everything about you, even your overprotective ways."

Good to know. Because his overprotectiveness? Not going anywhere, not when it came to her. In a short period of time, Maisey's life had come to mean more to him than anything else.

"What is it?" She rocked toward him. "You aren't thinking about what Clay said, are you? Because you're not a burned-out anything, and I know you aren't stringing me along. He was trying to mess with us, just like we were there to rile him."

Like Odin gave a flying fuck what the other guy believed. "He can think I'm burned out. He can think I'm an amateur who has no clue what he's doing. I don't care." He was staring at the person who mattered. "Not gonna change anything for me. I will do the job. I won't ever back down or give up." Not when Maisey needed him.

I think I will always need her.

He wanted her. Wanted to strip her and take her. Feel her against him and know she was safe.

But he stepped back. "It could be a while before my contact gets back to me. She's good, but there are still plenty of records to search." He inclined his head toward Maisey. "Jinx is gonna keep watch on Clay's place. Clay won't move without us knowing. So if you want to rest, now's the time."

"I'd like to shower." Her face scrunched. "I think I'm covered in dust from the storage room, and I probably smell terrible."

"You smell delicious." An automatic reply. "Like strawberries and cream, and it makes me want to eat you up." *Like the friggin' big, bad wolf that I am.*

Maisey licked her lower lip. "Ah..."

He took another step back. "Go for your shower. I'll have a turn when you're done."

"I have two showers. You can use the one in the guest bath." She held his stare. "Or you could just join me."

His fingers fisted. Released. Fisted again.

"If you wanted," she added uncertainly.

There was nothing he wanted more than her naked with him. "I'm in the shower with you..." His voice deepened even more than normal. "Then I'm *in* you." No way could he hold back if she was naked and wet in front of him.

"Yes. That's kind of the idea, isn't it?" Maisey seemed to hold her breath. "I'll just go get the shower started. If you want to join, follow me."

He'd follow her anywhere, any damn day.

Maisey turned away, and he took a step after her.

His phone rang. It buzzed and vibrated and he yanked it up to see Jinx's grinning image on his screen. Odin shoved the phone to his ear. "What?" he barked.

Maisey stopped. Glanced back.

"Well, hello to you, too, sunshine," Jinx drawled in his ear. "Did I interrupt something?"

"Is there a problem?" Odin demanded. "Is Clay on the move?"

"No. Take a breath. I'm just checking in."

He lowered the phone. "It's okay," he told Maisey. "Go ahead."

She hesitated, but finally nodded. She headed for the bathroom. Where she'd be getting naked and wet while he talked to Jinx.

Freaking Jinx. Odin put the phone back against his ear. "Make your check-in fast."

"Grumpy." A sigh. "And here I am, out doing the grunt work. Hiding and staring at a house all night while you're snug and cozy in there with Maisey."

"PI work *is* grunt work. It's doing the dirty deeds so you get the case closed." He couldn't see Maisey any longer. "Maybe it's not the line of work you want to get into."

"I don't know. Perhaps if I were the one close to the hot client, it would be different…"

"*Jinx*. Do not go there. Ever."

"Check. She's off-limits. I meant another hot client. I'm sure there are others, you know. Not like you magically got the only one in the whole world." A pause. "But I'm off topic."

"You are."

"Learn anything useful on the visit next door?"

"I learned that Clay Prescott has a boat somewhere. A boat I didn't discover on my first hunt. I've got Ali looking for it."

Silence. Huh. He'd finally managed to shut up Jinx?

"Didn't know you were still working with her." Mumbled.

"Ali is freelance, and you know hacking is pretty much second nature to her. War had me pull her in for a few jobs, and the relationship has been good. So far."

"Has she mentioned me?"

"Why in the hell would she mention you?" He did not have time for this shit. "Look, I have to go. I have—" A hot, naked Maisey. "Something waiting. You see activity on the house next door, you call me. I'm afraid Ramsey is gonna be closing in, and the last thing I want is for the guy to kill our suspect before I can get to the truth."

"Fine. I'll make sure Ramsey doesn't kill him. But if Ali mentions me, I want to know it."

What-the-hell-ever. He hung up. Tried not to run down the hallway. He flew through Maisey's bedroom, then drew to a quick stop. The bathroom door was shut, but when he approached, he could hear the heavy stream of the water. Maisey was in there. Naked and wet. And she wanted him with her.

He put the phone on the table near the door. Lifted his fingers to knock. Holy hell. Were his fingers actually shaking?

Yeah, they are. Because you want her so badly you can barely hold back. He knocked lightly.

"It's not locked," Maisey's voice called out.

He grabbed the knob. Twisted it and threw open the door. Steam drifted in the air. And Maisey, completely naked, with the water rushing around her, stood in the shower. She'd left the glass door open, and he had a perfect view of her.

She smiled at him. Her dimples dipped in her cheeks. "Now, we're even."

He barely heard her words. His heart jackhammered too hard in his chest and echoed in his ears. He grabbed for his shirt. Yanked it over his head. Kicked off his boots and socks and tossed away his jeans.

Her gaze slid down his body. Widened. There was a gleam of feminine appreciation in her eyes that had him surging toward her. He stepped into the shower with her. Hauled the door shut behind him and pulled *her* up against him. The water poured on him. Slid over his skin. Maisey's hands curled around his shoulders as she tipped back her head.

He took her mouth. Thrust his tongue inside even as his leg moved between hers. He lifted her up, had her riding his thigh as he kissed her with fierce demand.

Maisey.

He loved the way she tasted. Loved the way she smelled. Loved the way she felt against him.

Love the way she feels when I am balls deep in her.

He wanted to drive into her until she was screaming and he was coming as the pleasure lashed them both.

But Maisey pushed against him. "We…need to get clean."

Did they? He was in the mood to be dirty as hell.

She stared up at him with her molten eyes. "I was hoping to clean you off."

Okay, he wasn't sure exactly what that meant, but he was down for it. Slowly, using all of his control, Odin released her.

Maisey started cleaning him off. Sliding the soap over his body. Smoothing her fingers over his skin. Working him ever so carefully. He didn't move. His body had turned to stone beneath her. She carefully caressed his back, murmuring over the bruises there. Fluttering that soft mouth of hers over his skin. Every gentle touch was driving him crazy, but he wanted to see where this was going. Sure, it was his own version of torture, having beautiful Maisey caress his body—

She eased in front of him. Her fingers slid down to his eager, bobbing cock.

Torture. But it was also heaven.

His breath hissed out as she began to stroke him.

Absolute heaven.

"You are so big."

And you are tight and hot and perfect. Speaking was beyond him. Growls were pretty much all he could manage.

Her fingers slid over the broad head of his cock. "I want to taste you."

Maisey's mouth around his dick? He'd be a goner.

She pumped him again. Her fingers and his cock were slick from the water and the soap and her squeezing hands felt so incredibly good.

She was lowering toward him. Her lips were parted. He knew what she was gonna do—

"Need you." Did he actually say the words? Just sounded like more growls to him. He grabbed Maisey. Lifted her up. Held her against the tiled wall.

He kissed her. Drove his tongue into her even as he put his cock at her hot core and shoved into her.

Her nails bit into his shoulders. For a minute, he stiffened, afraid he'd hurt her. He hadn't given her enough care. He should have—

Her legs locked around his hips. "Do not stop."

He withdrew. Thrust deep. Over and over. His hand slid between them. Rubbed her clit. Squeezed. Strummed her.

"Odin!" She was holding on tight. Her mouth went to his neck. She kissed him and sucked his skin. Gave him a savage bite that had him pounding even harder into her.

She felt so good. Better than anything in the world. She was wet and hot and tight and her bare skin was against him as—

Bare.

His left hand slammed into the wall beside her. "No...condom..."

Maisey's head lifted. Drops of water streaked down her face. Her neck. She stared at him in confusion. Her eyes shone with need and passion.

"I don't..." He broke off because she'd just squeezed him with her delicate, inner muscles. His eyes wanted to roll back into his head because that squeeze felt so freaking good. "Don't have protection. Have to...protect..."

"I'm on birth control." Whispered. "I don't—I've never been with anyone without a condom." A pause. "Until you."

He could not look away from her eyes. "I haven't, either. I'm clear."

"Then don't stop," she said. "Because I like the way you feel."

Done. Gone. He lost it with her words. His fingers went back to stroking her clit. He made sure to work her into a frenzy and soon her nails were scratching over him as she thrashed against him. As soon as he felt her climax hit her—

"Odin!"

He pounded into her even deeper. Even harder. He couldn't let go. Couldn't pull back. Nothing in the world would have stopped him. He was surging toward paradise, and there was nothing better. Nothing but—

"Maisey." The orgasm tore threw him and obliterated everything else. But then, wasn't that exactly what she'd done to him from the beginning?

Tore into his life...

And obliterated everything else.

CHAPTER SEVENTEEN

Maisey's eyes opened. The water kept pounding down on her, and it felt good. Not as good as Odin, of course, but...

Did anything else feel this good?

His head lifted. Very slowly, with his eyes on hers, he eased out of her. He lowered her until her feet touched the bottom of the shower, and then *he* was carefully washing her. A gasp sprang from her lips as his big fingers slid over the folds of her sex.

Was she supposed to get turned on again, so soon?

Before she could push against those wicked fingers, he'd pulled back.

His bright eyes pinned her. "What am I going to do with you?"

Love me forever. The words just rolled through her mind, and she almost said them. *Almost.* They almost burst out of her the way so many rambles did, but Maisey caught herself at the last second. Her lips clamped together, and she stared at him in horror.

OhmyGod. When had it happened? When had she done this? When had she fallen for her PI?

"What is it?" His knuckles slid over her cheek.

I love you. This was too soon. If she said those three words, she'd probably freak him out. She didn't want to freak out Odin. She just wanted him.

Maisey shivered. Even though the water was warm, the shiver rocked her body because she was suddenly aware that she was in way, way deep with Odin.

"You're cold. Come on, baby. I'll take care of you."

And he did. He got her out of the shower. Dried her off. Carried her to bed and eased her under the covers like she was something precious and fragile. He handled her so carefully. As if she mattered.

Maybe she did. Maybe this was more than sex for him. It was certainly a hell of a lot more for her. But she didn't know what to say. So she stayed quiet.

Odin turned off the lights. Climbed into bed with her. Pulled her into his arms. "Did I hurt you?"

"No."

His hold tightened. "You're scared."

Absolutely terrified. She'd never been in love before. Never come close. But she *knew* this was it. Odin was it. "Wh-what do you mean?"

"You talk when you're nervous. You go dead quiet when you're scared." A pause. "Did I do something that made you scared?"

No, I did. I went and fell in love with you.

"Maisey?" He pressed a kiss to her temple. "I can't fix it if I don't know what it is."

"I feel like I fit with you." A whisper.

A soft laugh. "I think we happen to fit pretty damn well."

No, she, um, didn't mean sexually. Though—*yes*. Maisey turned in his arms. "I've been alone a long time."

He brushed back her hair.

"I told you that I was left at a hospital when I was a kid. I never knew my mom. Never knew if she was the one who put me there or if it was someone else. I was left, and whoever left me never looked back." It was too dark for her to see his face. Too dark for him to see hers, so he wouldn't notice if a tear or two slid down her cheeks. "It was a small town. You would have thought that someone would notice a pregnant woman who was suddenly minus her baby, but that didn't happen. Maybe—Pop thought perhaps she'd been someone who drove through town. Someone who was looking for a safe, good spot for her baby girl to grow up."

"Pop?"

"My adoptive dad." His image slid through her mind. His grizzled cheeks. The humor that had always sparkled in his dark eyes. "He was the sheriff. He and his wife adopted me. Pop told me..." He'd told her this a hundred times. "That he looked at me and knew I was his. He told me that some people just fit you, and you know it."

Another press of Odin's lips against her temple.

"It's because of him that I first started watching crime shows. We'd stay up late watching them together. Get lost in them. He would always want me to try and solve the cases with him." She could see him so clearly in her mind as he sat on the edge of that old, sagging couch. "My mom was the town's librarian. When I wasn't trying to solve crimes with him, I was reading with her. My life was good. It was quiet. It was safe." A slow exhale. "Until that safety ended."

"Baby…"

"The town was supposed to be perfect. A place where you know everybody and everybody knows you." She swallowed. "But how well can you really know anyone? I told you before, I get that evil can hide. And Pop figured out that one of the guys in town—this fellow who went to every PTA meeting and city council meeting—he'd been pulling robberies left and right two cities over. Pop went to confront him, and instead of surrendering, the guy ran." *And that was when things ended.* "But he didn't run far. He blamed my dad for destroying his world. For making his perfect illusion shatter."

"It was the bastard's own fault. Your dad was doing his job."

She nodded. Yes, that was what she thought, too. But… "He went to the library. The only library in town. He knew my mom worked there, you see. The sheriff's wife. He went there, and he shot her."

"Fuck. Maisey."

"His name was Jeremiah Harrison. He'd bought candy from me when I did school fundraisers. And he shot my mother."

"I'm so sorry."

"There was a standoff at the library. Biggest thing the town had ever seen. Jeremiah just wouldn't give up. He would not surrender. He came out shooting. Pop stopped him, but Pop...he didn't live long after that." A ragged breath as the pain squeezed her heart. "He wasn't wearing his vest. He should have been wearing his bulletproof vest, but I think he didn't care about himself. Not after he knew what had happened to Mom."

She could feel the tears on her cheeks. She hadn't told anyone else about her parents. She'd moved away. Started fresh. Tried to leave the pain behind. But Odin wasn't other people. She needed to tell him this. "I buried them both on the same day, and I never went back to that town."

His fingers slid over her cheeks. Tenderly wiped away the tears that she knew he couldn't see. "I want to take your pain away."

"You do. You have." That was why she had to finish. So he'd understand. "Pop said certain people fit you, and you know it." *Just say it.* "You fit me, Odin. Fit me in a way no one else ever has. I'm scared because I haven't felt this way before, but the truth is...I think I'm falling in love with you." Then she held her breath because...

It's too soon. He won't feel the same way. I should have just held back. But once she'd started talking...

"Can you forget what I said?" Maisey blurted into the silence. "Sometimes, I overshare. That was obviously a major overshare. You don't need to feel that you have to say anything back to me. I mean, you can just be like, 'That's nice' and sort of leave it at that. There is no pressure. I don't expect anything."

His hand slid under her chin. "You should."

"I should—what?"

"You should expect the whole damn world. And that's what I want to give you."

What was he saying?

"I don't know what I feel, Maisey. I just know that I feel *more* for you than I ever have with anyone else. I like it when you smile. Sometimes, I think I'd do just about anything to see your dimples wink at me."

He would?

His lips brushed over hers. He'd found her mouth—unerringly—in the dark.

"I like it when you're excited about something that you're telling me and your eyes get extra golden as they light up. You've got the most gorgeous eyes I've ever seen."

That was so sweet.

He gets grumbly when I tell him that he's sweet.

"I like the way your body responds to mine. Like you were made for me. I was made for you."

"I'm rather fond of your body, too," she confessed.

"I don't feel too big or rough when I'm around you. Everything feels just right." Another kiss. "Like we fit."

She blinked quickly so that more tears wouldn't fall.

"I don't know much about love. Didn't have those teen romances in school. Most girls steered clear of me. Then it was battle after battle. No time for anything lasting." His words were careful. "I would like to try something lasting, with you."

Could he feel the frantic pounding of her heart?

"I want to try everything with you." Odin's voice seemed to fill the darkness around her.

"I would like that very much." She was the one to arch up toward him. To find his lips in the dark this time. Happiness was blooming inside of her. When she'd walked into Trouble for Hire, she'd never expected her life to change this much. Now, she couldn't imagine her life without Odin.

She was in his arms. Safe. Warm. And he wasn't saying he loved her. She truly hadn't expected the words back. But *what* he was saying sure sounded good to her. It sounded like a beautiful start.

***

A phone was ringing. The quick peal of sound yanked Maisey from sleep. She jerked upright, pulling from Odin's arms.

"Yours," Odin rumbled.

Hers. Her phone. Ringing on the nightstand. She squinted at the glowing screen of her clock. Two a.m. A late-night call again. She knew it had to be the jerk they were after.

"Keep him talking," Odin ordered as he sat up beside her. "We'll get the trace." He jumped from the bed. Grabbed his own phone and sent out a quick text to someone.

Maisey reached for her phone. Swiped her fingers over the screen as she took the call *and* turned on the speaker. She wanted Odin to hear every word. "Hello?"

"*Help me...*" Whitney's voice.

A pang shot through Maisey. All sleepiness had vanished. Her mind was ice-cold and awake.

"*Come...help—*"

"Stop it," Maisey ordered bluntly as she shoved back hair that had tumbled over her eye. "I know this isn't Whitney. You're using a recording, and you're jerking me around. Either talk to me for real or I end this call."

Silence.

She stared fearfully at Odin's shadowy form. Had she just screwed up? Would the caller hang up on her?

"You think you're clever." Not Whitney any longer. But still, not the caller's real voice. Distorted. Robotic. "Solving the big mystery. Hunting the killer."

She sucked in a breath that just seemed to chill her lungs. "What do you want from me?" Her hand fisted the sheets and pulled them against her chest.

"I *wanted* you to stop playing Nancy Drew. But you didn't. I tried to warn you off, but you just couldn't take a freaking hint."

Her heart hammered frantically in her chest. "What did you do to Whitney?"

"She's gone. She won't be coming back."

Dead. Whitney is dead. That was what Maisey had feared all along.

"Soon, you'll be gone, too, and you *won't* be coming back."

"I'm not scared of you," she said.

"Yes, you are."

Her fingers were shaking as she clutched the covers.

"You think you can hide behind the boyfriend, don't you?" A taunt from that robotic voice. "But you can't hide behind a dead man."

Her fingers stopped shaking. Her whole body stiffened. "Don't you dare touch him."

Laughter.

"Don't!" Maisey snapped.

But he hung up on her.

"Got him," Odin said with satisfaction.

Her head whipped up. Maisey realized she'd been glaring at the phone. *He threatened Odin.*

Odin had turned on the lamp. His phone was pressed to his ear, and he was listening to someone. One of his contacts? The cops? She didn't know.

"You're kidding me," he snarled. His eyes turned to slits. "Hell, yes, I know the location. I'll be right there." He dropped the phone.

"Where?" Maisey leapt from the bed. Hauled the sheet with her.

"Armageddon."

She had no clue what he meant. Frantic, she shook her head.

"That's the name of War's bar. The bar that is located right beneath the Trouble for Hire office. The caller is either at the bar or at our PI office."

She dropped the sheet and ran for her closet. "If he's there, then so are we," she called out as she hauled on clothing as fast as she could. "We should call the cops. Get them to close in."

A phone was ringing again. Maisey shoved her head out of the closet just in time to see Odin take the call.

"What is it, Jinx?" His words were snapped out. "Shit. Now? Are you serious? Yes, we're coming. Hell, yes, you need to keep Clay alive. Keep Ramsey *off* him." He shoved down the phone and hauled on his own clothes. In seconds, he was racing for the door.

Maisey ran with him. She grabbed his arm. "Stop! Tell me what's happening." Though she had a scary feeling she knew.

"Ramsey just arrived. He's storming for Clay's door. If we don't stop him—well, we both know what he'll do."

"But it's not Clay." Not if Clay was next door. Not if the call had come from the bar or the PI office. "It's not him." He couldn't be in two places at once.

"We need to make sure Ramsey realizes that. Before he does something he can't take back."

Something like...killing Clay Prescott.

CHAPTER EIGHTEEN

"Get the fuck out of my way!" Ramsey bellowed.

Jinx didn't move. Odin knew he'd always been good at standing his ground. "Can't let you go in," Jinx said, his raised voice drifting to Odin as he barreled toward the house. "Because if you go in, you'll do something stupid like try to kill the guy."

"I won't try." Ramsey grabbed Jinx's shirtfront. "I'll succeed."

The door behind Jinx flew open. Clay gaped at the sight before him as the porch light glared down on the scene. "What in the hell is going on?"

Odin rushed up the porch steps. "Get back inside, Clay. Lock the door. Stay there."

"I don't take orders from you!" Clay snarled as he shoved Jinx to the side and strode onto his porch. "I don't—"

That was as far as he got. Because Ramsey was on him. He drove his fist into Clay's jaw and sent the man stumbling back. One hit. A second. Then Clay was down and Ramsey was crouched over him, holding a knife to Clay's throat.

"What did you do to her?" Ramsey asked, voice hollow. "What did you do to my Whitney?"

"Stop!" Maisey's frantic shout as she flew up the porch steps. "He didn't do anything! I was wrong. We're all wrong! *It wasn't him!"*

A drop of blood trailed down Clay's throat.

"Let him go," Odin ordered. "I don't want to have to hurt you, Ramsey. Let him go!"

"Nothing else can hurt me. She's gone." Ramsey stared down at Clay. "I don't think you're innocent. I looked at your past. Saw the skeletons. I see the lies beneath your skin."

"The man who took Whitney just called me!" Maisey yelled.

The knife jerked. Clay whimpered.

"He just called," Maisey added, voice softer but still strained. "We have his location. Odin and I are going there now. We don't have time to waste because he could be gone if we screw around. We need backup. You can come with us."

Odin's head whipped toward her. "Uh, Maisey..." *That's a terrible idea.*

"It gets his knife away from Clay's throat!" she threw at him, as if reading Odin's mind. "We can't do this. We can't just waste time. He *called* me. We have him, we just have to go. *Now.*"

Ramsey angled his head so he was looking back at Maisey. His grip on the knife didn't waver. "Are you telling me the truth?"

"Yes. He just called. Odin traced the call. We have him."

Jinx glanced back and forth between Ramsey and Maisey. "I don't think she's lying, man. And do you really want to slit the throat of the wrong guy? That shit will be hard to live with."

"I've lived with worse." Ramsey's flat response.

Odin got ready to attack him.

But Ramsey pulled the knife back. "Give me the location."

"No." Odin reached for Maisey's hand. "You follow us. And when we get there, you stand back until we know what we're dealing with."

Ramsey's mocking laughter told him that wasn't gonna be the case.

"Jinx," Odin said with a quick incline of his head. "Stay with him. Keep him in check."

"Are you kidding me?" Jinx demanded. "*I* have to ride with the obvious psychopath? How is that fair?"

"*What in the hell is happening?*" Clay shouted.

Odin stopped. Lasered his stare on Clay. "Maisey just saved you from dying. Now we're going to destroy the man who took Whitney Augustine. Lock your door. Stay inside."

"I'm calling the cops!"

"Good idea." Odin started moving. "Send them to Armageddon, would you?"

***

No cops were at Armageddon. Actually, no one seemed to be there. When Odin pulled his Jeep to a stop near the bar, the street was empty and the bar appeared shut down. Closing time had been at one a.m., and it looked as if everyone had already cleared out.

"We're too late," Maisey said as she leaned forward to stare at the building.

No, they weren't. The bar was dark, but the second level in the building wasn't.

"There's a light on upstairs." In the Trouble for Hire office. A light that shouldn't have been on. No alarms had gone off. No alerts had been sent to him. *Someone disabled our system.* "I'm checking it out."

She grabbed his arm. "You mean *we* are checking it out."

Not like he was going to leave her behind with Ramsey due to arrive any moment.

"Don't worry," Maisey rushed to assure him. "I will stay close to you. There is no other place I plan to be."

He checked his gun.

"Please, be careful," Maisey urged worriedly. "If you get shot right in front of me, I am going to lose my mind."

"Not planning to get shot." But he would be shooting at anyone who threatened them. "Come on." They moved quickly across the street. There were exterior stairs that led up to the Trouble for Hire office, but if someone was up there—and it sure as hell seemed someone was—then Odin wanted to catch the perp off guard.

He slipped inside Armageddon, using the keys War had given him. Then Odin and Maisey accessed the private stairs inside and crept up to the second level. But as they climbed, he heard shouting. Distorted at first. Damn. Whoever was up there didn't seem concerned about staying quiet—

"Help!" A sudden, sharp shriek that was clearly discernable. A woman's voice. Terrified. *"God, please, help—"* The words were choked off.

Odin glanced back at Maisey. "Stay here," he ordered. "I'll see what's happening. Jinx will be running in any moment."

Another high-pitched cry. Pain-filled this time. Gripping his weapon, Odin stopped creeping up the stairs and flew up them. He kicked open the door to Trouble for Hire. Rushed through the small hallway and turned to find a woman standing in his office. Her back was to him, and her shoulders were shuddering with sobs. He recognized the short, blond hair, and his gaze swept around the room as he looked for threats. "Heather?"

She jerked. Turned her head to look at him. He could see the tear tracks on her face.

"What's happening?" Odin barked. "Are you hurt?" He took two fast steps toward her. Her arms were wrapped around her stomach.

"I'm hurt so badly," she whimpered.

He didn't see her attacker. Was she holding her wound, was that why she was hugging herself so tightly? He began to lower his weapon.

"I'm hurt..." She slowly angled her body toward him. "But, not as badly as *you'll* be hurt."

He stiffened and aimed his gun at her. "What the hell are you talking about?"

With tears on her cheeks, she smiled at him. "Just where is Maisey? Did you leave her all alone?"

Fuck. He spun and ran for her. *"Maisey!"*

But when he got to the stairs, when he peered down them as fear twisted inside of him, Odin realized he was too late. The lights were on in the stairwell, shining brightly when it had been dark moments before. Maisey was still on the stairs. She'd followed his instructions. Stayed where he'd thought she'd be safe.

But Maisey wasn't alone.

Steve was with her. *The asshole boyfriend?* He had a gun pointed at Maisey's head.

Steve lifted his brows. "I'll need you to ditch the weapon or I'll have to shoot her."

***

"So, this will be hard, but I'm going to need you to *not* be a psychopath, okay? For just like, ten minutes or so." Jinx turned to Ramsey. "Do you think you can handle—"

Ramsey jumped out of the car—Ramsey's SUV, though Jinx had been driving—and ran toward Armageddon and the PI office.

"Wonderful," Jinx sighed. "Obviously, ten minutes was too much to ask for. I should have just gone with five." He leapt out of the vehicle and gave chase. It was apparent that Ramsey wasn't stopping, so Jinx launched at him. Tackled the guy to the ground. "We have to play this scene right," Jinx snarled at him, trying to keep his voice low. "You go in there all crazy, and who knows what the hell could happen."

Ramsey heaved Jinx aside. Mostly just because Jinx let him go.

Lightning flashed overhead in the dark sky, and in the distance, thunder rumbled.

"I know what will happen." Ramsey's hands fisted. "Someone is going to die."

"Yes, well, I don't want that *someone* to be a friend of mine. Calm your ass down. We're handling this the right way."

"There is no right way!"

"Debatable." Why had he gotten stuck with the hothead in this scene? He tried to figure out how to calm the crime boss down.

A gunshot rang out. One followed by a shattered, desperate scream.

Jinx lunged for the building, leaving Ramsey in his dust.

***

"What in the hell are you doing?" Heather fumed. "We have a plan for this scene, and that plan doesn't involve you shooting random shit!"

Maisey's breath shuddered out. They were in Odin's office—the same office where she'd met him just a few short days ago. Steve had forced Odin inside first, *after* Odin had dropped his gun in that stairwell. Then Steve had dragged her inside.

He'd made Odin take up a position near the wall, then the guy had raised his weapon and *fired*. Maisey had grabbed Steve's arm and shoved as hard as she could because he'd appeared to have been *aiming* at Odin. The shot had blasted and a broken scream had torn from her.

But the bullet had missed Odin.

Steve laughed as he swung the gun back toward Maisey. "Just a warning shot. Wanted to see how scared he would be."

The shot had missed Odin's head by about a foot. The bullet had thudded into the wall.

Odin didn't look scared. His blue eyes gleamed with an icy rage that promised retribution.

Steve shoved the gun's muzzle into Maisey's side. He had one arm around her neck, and the other hand held the weapon.

"Wasn't a warning," Odin said. His voice was gravelly. Cold. "You just can't shoot for shit."

Steve's hold tightened around her neck. "I'll show you what I can do, you bastard!"

Odin...laughed.

Was that a normal thing for him? Did he laugh in the face of danger or something? She should know, for future reference.

"Why is he doing that?" Heather demanded. She stalked close to Maisey. "Doesn't your boyfriend get that you're both about to die?"

Maisey wet parched lips. "I don't think he believes that will be the outcome."

"He *should* believe it. We've been steps ahead of you all along." A smirk. "We got you here, didn't we? Steve suspected your phone was being monitored. Told me that was like, PI 101 or something. So we just made sure that you traced us back here. We wanted you here. We got you here. And—"

"And what?" Maisey cut in to demand. "You obviously don't want me to just die here or I'd already be dead. You lured us here because this part of town is deserted at this time. Fine. Got it. But before you go patting yourself on the back too much, you should know that the cops are coming."

Heather shook her head. "No, they're not."

"Uh, yes, they are," Maisey fired right back. Had Odin just taken a step forward? She thought he had. She needed to keep talking and distract Heather and Steve. If she could keep their attention, then Odin could figure out a way to attack. A way that did *not* involve him getting shot. "We left Clay and told him to call the cops! They are on the way here now."

"Clay isn't calling the cops. He can't."

"Why not?"

"Because Clay doesn't have a landline. Steve knocked out his internet earlier, and when I was there, I managed to swipe his phone."

Maisey switched gears. "He can just get in his car and go for help." From the corner of her eye, she saw Odin take another step. "Did you not consider that obvious move in your master plan?"

Heather's face hardened. "Why would he want to help you? You think he's a killer. Your boyfriend attacked him. I took his phone as a precaution, but in the end, we both know Clay won't do a damn thing for you."

"Granted..." Maisey lifted her hands and tugged on Steve's arm. His hold on her neck was starting to hurt. "I *did* think he was a killer, but he'll do the right thing."

"No, he won't. People don't *do* the right thing. I learned that working with Whitney. Seeing the cases she studied. Give them a chance, and anyone will screw you over." Her chin notched up. "She was gonna screw *me* over. Me and Steve."

Odin's hands had clenched into fists. "You killed her?"

Heather's head swung toward him.

Dammit! Why was Odin drawing their attention? Maisey had planned to be the distraction.

"I didn't *kill* her," Heather clarified with a slight shift of her shoulders. "We just left her to die. There's a difference, you know."

"No. I don't think there is." His eyes glittered.

Steve's hold on Maisey's neck tightened even more. "She saw me making a deal. She shouldn't have even been in that bar, but she was. She saw me, and she was going to tell the dean at Dunson. I would have been kicked out of school. I would have lost everything I'd worked for!"

"I couldn't let that happen." Now Heather's stare flew toward Steve. "She wasn't going to do that to him."

Right, okay, so...these two had faked the fight scene at the college. It had been a trick. They were a deadly duo, and they had to be *stopped*. Or else Maisey had the feeling that they would be *leaving* her to die soon, too...Her and Odin.

"We waited until she was vulnerable." Apparently, Heather was in the mood to confess all. A bad sign. "We hit her in the head, knocked her out. Then we made sure she vanished."

"How." From Odin. Not a question. A demand.

"Steve's dad has a boat. We took her out, drove as far as we could, then dumped her over the side. She was just waking up," Heather hurried to say. "So she was alive when we put her in the water. We didn't *kill* her—"

"You just left her to die," Odin finished coldly. "Right. Heard you the first time."

Maisey's stomach was in knots. "Is that supposed to make it better? That you didn't kill her with your own hands? Because drowning isn't better! It's not like she just slips under the water and that's all there is!" Rage poured through her. "*How could you do that to her? How could you make her suffer like that?*"

"We didn't." From Steve. He seemed much more controlled than Heather. Cold. "Clay did. At least, that's what you thought, isn't it? And that's what the cops will think, too."

Heather gave a jerky nod. "When I took his phone, I made sure to leave Whitney's earrings at his place. Those will be part of the evidence we use to nail him for Whitney's death. Later, we'll plant evidence that ties him to you, too, Maisey."

Because they are going to leave me to die.

"He's the perfect fall guy," Steve said. His body trembled the faintest bit against Maisey.

He's not as confident as he appears.

"Heather found out about his past. Heard Whitney talking one day about how tragic it was. When we needed to take her out, I came up with the idea of just making sure she vanished, instead of having her body turn up." Steve sounded quite proud of himself. "Knew that if anyone asked too many questions, we could point back to him."

And she'd asked questions.

"When Clay got promoted to her job, it was even more perfect. Suddenly looked like he had a motive."

Yes, it had.

"Didn't think you'd get a freaking PI, though," Heather muttered as she cut a glance toward Odin. "That screwed things up."

"So sorry," Maisey choked out around Steve's squeezing arm. "Didn't mean to mess up your murder plan. My bad."

"*Do you think this is some kind of joke?*" Heather lunged toward her.

Steve tightened his arm even more. Maisey couldn't suck in a breath.

"*You're hurting Maisey.*" Odin's voice was guttural. "Ease up on your grip. Now."

Steve's hold jerked in automatic response. Jerked, then eased, just for a moment...

The moment Maisey had been hoping would happen. She knew that Odin had given that order deliberately, and Maisey wasn't going to waste a second. Odin had taught her how to get out of this exact hold. Granted, a gun had not been involved at the time, but she didn't have an option.

Can't let them kill Odin. Can't let them do this!

Heather and Steve thought they could use her to control Odin. They were about to see how wrong they were. No one could control Odin.

And no one controls me.

She shoved back with her elbow. Dug it into Steve's ribs as hard as she could even as she shoved her heel toward his ankle and kicked down *hard.*

He screamed and let her go. A reflex. She surged away from him.

"You bitch!" Steve yelled.

Maisey saw the horror on Heather's features and knew Steve was aiming his gun at her. "Don't shoot her!" Heather yelled. "We're supposed to dump them like we did—"

Bam. The bullet exploded from the gun. Maisey froze, but she wasn't hit. She whipped around and saw that Odin had slammed into Steve. The gun had been tossed toward the desk, and Odin was pounding his massive fist into Steve's face. It only took two blows before Steve crumbled and didn't get up.

Maisey jumped for the gun.

"*No!*" Heather's cry.

Maisey scooped up the weapon and whirled to aim it at Heather. But Heather had run for the door...only to be blocked by Ramsey and Jinx.

"What the fuck?" Ramsey glared at Steve's prone form. "I know that little asshole. He got kicked out of my bar because he thought he could sell his shit drugs in my place."

Heather whimpered.

Ramsey turned his stare back to her. "Who the hell are you?"

"She's the woman who killed Whitney," Odin said as he strode toward Heather.

Ramsey's eyes blazed. He grabbed for Heather.

"*Don't.*" Maisey's yell. "I'm the one with the gun, and I'm telling you all—stop. I want the cops here. I want Heather and Steve going to jail. I want this to end." But she could see the killing rage in Ramsey's eyes. "Whitney wouldn't want you doing this," she added desperately. "Ramsey, just...stop."

Ramsey didn't see it, but Jinx had moved behind him. She could tell that Jinx was about to launch at the guy.

"What did you do to her?" Ramsey snarled to Heather.

"She was alive when I left her!" Heather cried out. "I swear, she was!"

Alive, but sinking beneath the waves of the Gulf of Mexico.

Ramsey wasn't going to stop. Maisey could see it. And she—she couldn't shoot him. Odin was too close. So was Jinx. What if she hit one of them?

A wild cry broke from Ramsey as he surged at Heather.

Jinx grabbed him from behind. Shoved into the nearest wall, and when Ramsey came up with his fists flying, Jinx pointed a gun at him. "Don't." Low. "I am not your enemy."

"You are now," he vowed.

In the distance, a siren shrieked. Either Clay had finally gotten somewhere so he could use a phone or someone had heard the gunshots and reported them to the police. Hell, maybe Jinx had called them.

What she *did* know...it was almost over. Odin had just pulled cuffs out of a drawer, and he was slapping them around Heather's wrists. Heather was crying, saying that it was all Steve's fault. Steve was unconscious, and from the look of things, he'd probably be that way for a while.

Odin glanced up at her. "I can take the gun."

"That would be great, thank you." Her fingers were quivering so badly that she was afraid she might accidentally shoot someone.

He took the gun from her trembling grip. "Baby? You okay?"

He'd almost been shot in front of her. "I don't want to lose you."

"You won't. Not ever."

The siren's call was growing louder. "I love you."

His eyes flashed. "*I fucking love you, too.*"

CHAPTER NINETEEN

"Why do you get to be happy?" Ramsey was in the shadows. Away from the cops and the flashing lights and growing throng of reporters.

It was gonna be another big story. Trouble for Hire had captured two killers. Jinx was currently handling the explanations. Smiling his easy grin. Twisting details just the slightest bit so that Ramsey was left out of the story.

Maisey inclined her head as she listened to a cop. He knew she was telling him about Heather's confession. Hell, Heather was confessing left and right to everyone. She liked to keep telling everyone that they hadn't actually killed Whitney.

As if that made it better.

"You get to go off into the sunset with your lady. Have the whole picket-fence ending. The kids. Probably a freaking dog. You get all of that..." Ramsey turned toward him. "And I don't even get Whitney's body. I can't even bury her."

There was fury in Ramsey's voice. On his face. But there was also pain. It was the pain that got to Odin. "I'd be lost without Maisey."

Ramsey stiffened.

"I'd be lost and I'd be furious, and I would want to destroy anyone who had ever hurt her."

He motioned toward Ramsey. "We aren't so different, you and I."

"Yes, we are." Ramsey turned away. "You get to sleep with your woman tonight. I'll never see mine again." He took two steps forward. Stopped. "Make sure Jinx stays the hell away from me."

"He was saving you from jail. If you'd killed Heather and Steve, you would have spent the rest of your life behind bars."

"Maybe. But I would have also felt one hell of a lot better."

"I'm not so sure about that."

Ramsey looked back at him. "Why do you get to be happy?" he muttered again. Then he shuffled away.

Odin exhaled. He didn't know why he was lucky that night. He *did* know that he hadn't been lying to Ramsey. He would be lost without Maisey. When he'd gone down those stairs and seen Steve with the gun to her head, his whole world had stopped. In that instant, he'd forgotten his training. His plans. He'd been helpless and terrified and willing to do anything in order to get that gun away from her.

Maisey darted away from the cop. Her gaze swept the scene. Odin knew she was searching for him, and he hurriedly stepped from the shadows. Thunder rumbled in the distance. A storm was coming.

When she glimpsed him, relief flooded across her delicate features. She ran toward him. He caught her. Pulled her close. Felt her warmth and softness.

You get to sleep with your woman tonight. I'll never see mine again.

Ramsey's words rang through his head. Odin held her tighter. Maisey was alive. Safe. He had her in his arms. He *would* be sleeping with her that night. That night and every other night that followed.

He had no idea what he'd done to deserve her. He didn't know why he got a happy ending. But he would never let anyone take that ending from him. He would never let anyone take Maisey.

"I love you," he said, and the words were natural. Easy. He didn't stumble. Didn't screw up and say something stupid. He just told her how he felt.

Maisey was his world. He loved her.

He *loved* her.

***

There were explanations to give. Statements that had to be taken by the cops. Maisey spent more hours than she could count at the police station. Odin was by her side. Jinx was there, too, in an oddly helpful mood with the cops. Giving smooth replies to everything.

She didn't mention Ramsey. Neither did Odin or Jinx. Steve hadn't seen him, as for Heather...

Well, she'd been talking plenty so far. She'd confessed to attacking Whitney and leaving her to drown in the Gulf. She'd admitted that Steve was the one who'd tried to abduct Maisey at the college. That Steve had been the one to shove the storage shelves onto Maisey and Odin.

According to Heather, everything had been Steve's idea.

Maisey wasn't so certain of that. Heather was playing the traumatized, terrified victim now, but Maisey remembered how well the other woman had acted in the parking lot of Dunson College. How she'd pretended so effectively to be in a breakup. How she'd acted as a desperate lover at Clay's house.

Maisey thought that Heather had been *fully* involved in everything that had gone down. But the cops would be the ones to press the charges. The cops and the DA. The Coast Guard was doing sweeps in the Gulf, over the area where Heather had told them that she'd left Whitney.

Not that those sweeps would do much good. Not at this point...

Not after so long.

We'll probably never find her body. Maisey knew that, and it broke her heart.

"You should go home. Get some rest." Jinx stood in front of her. "I can get a cop to drop you off." He jerked his thumb over his shoulder. "Odin and I have to tie up more loose ends, but the detective said you were clear to go."

Falling into bed seemed like a wonderful idea to Maisey, but she hated to leave Odin. Her gaze automatically searched for him.

"Thank you," Jinx said.

Her attention jumped to him. "For what?"

"Odin."

She shook her head, lost.

"You don't know what he was like after those last few missions. How he pulled away. Shut down. He was hurt badly, and the darkness was pulling him under."

Maisey rose from the sagging chair. "I saw the scars on him."

"Those are the ones on the surface. The wounds I'm talking about are on the inside. He saw too much blood. Too much war. And he came far too close to dying."

He'd come too close to dying just hours ago. When Steve had been taunting him and fired that bullet, her heart had nearly shattered.

"He put up a wall between himself and the world. You shattered that wall. When he looks at you, his eyes change. I see it. I mean, not like the man goes around grinning from ear to ear now or anything, but his eyes are different. I swear, they fucking light up when he looks at you."

She put a hand to her chest. "I love him."

"And that's why I'm saying thank you. Odin is one of the good ones. He's always had my back, and it's nice to see he found a woman who will always have his."

She would always have his back. In a heartbeat.

Odin came around the corner. She turned her head and watched him, and as he approached, she realized Jinx was right. His eyes did seem to light up when he saw her.

She smiled at him.

Odin walked right up to her. His hand slid under the fall of her hair, and he bent and pressed a kiss to her lips.

"Oh, yes. He's different." Jinx's voice held its usual teasing edge as he added, "That's like, a super suave move. Odin is never suave. I could be staring at a stranger."

"Fuck off," Odin muttered.

"Fucking off. And, hey, I'll get that ride ready for Maisey. She needs to crash, man."

Odin's head lifted. He stared straight into Maisey's eyes. "I know what she needs."

I need you. I want you. Forever.

Her arms rose to curl around his waist. "It scared me to death when he almost shot you."

"You knocked his aim off me, baby."

Her breath caught. "H-he said he was deliberately missing."

Odin shook his head. "Thanks for saving my ass."

"Anytime," she whispered.

He kissed her again. Deep. Slow. So good that she was pressing against him before he pulled away. "A cop is staring at us," he murmured.

They were in a police station. There were probably lots of cops staring at them.

"I think Jinx asked her to take you home. I'll be there to meet you as soon as I do some more paperwork. Probably need to call War and update him, too, before he sees the stories on the news."

If he hadn't already.

Another tender kiss from Odin. Then he let her go.

The cop cleared her throat.

Right. Time to go. Maisey squared her shoulders and advanced toward the waiting cop.

"You found out what happened to her, Maisey."

Odin's voice stopped her.

"You're gonna get justice for Whitney, too."

Yes, yes, they were. Her steps seemed lighter as she joined the cop.

***

Maisey watched the patrol car drive away. Wind blasted against her, and she felt the light touch of raindrops on her skin. The promised storm was finally about to hit.

Even though the sky was dark—nearly pitch black—she figured it had to be close to noon. There had been so many questions. So much drama.

But it was all over.

She heard the slam of a door. Her head turned toward Clay's house. *Almost over.* Her hands pressed against the front of her jeans. This wasn't going to be easy, but she needed to do it. She'd been colossally wrong, and he deserved an apology. Her stride was determined as she headed for Clay's house. She ignored the light drops of rain that fell against her skin.

His trunk was open. The big duffel bag was tossed back there again. He must have a basketball game that evening that he needed to coach. She peered down at the bag.

"Maisey."

Her gaze lifted and her head turned. Clay was jogging toward her.

"Where's the boyfriend?" A curt question.

"At the police station. He's still answering questions."

He crept closer to her. Darted his stare toward the trunk.

"You heard, I guess?" She tucked a lock of hair behind her ear. "About Heather and Steve?"

"Cops were here earlier." He stopped less than a foot away from her. "Heather had left earrings here. *She'd set me up.* And the cops were here to collect them as evidence." He cast a glance over his shoulder. "I think they are going to come back and do a whole crime scene sweep, just in case more evidence was left behind."

She realized he had another duffel bag slung over his shoulder. "Got a game today, huh?"

"Yes." Again, he was curt. "Now if you don't mind...?"

"I'm sorry." There. She'd said it. "I was wrong about you. I thought you were behind Whitney's disappearance."

"Yes, I know. You broke into my house, Maisey. Your boyfriend attacked me. You thought I was a *killer.*"

"Heather was setting you up. She found out about what happened in the past, and she and Steve were trying to put the blame on you." *Don't half-ass the apology. Go all the way.* "I found out about your past, too. Instead of seeing you as the victim, I put you in the role of the killer. I'm sorry."

"Sorry doesn't really change much, does it?" He moved around her. Dumped the bag in the trunk. Something banged.

Automatically, Maisey glanced toward the trunk. Something had fallen out of the second duffel bag.

Something...

Wait, is that my laptop? She moved closer and dipped her head toward the open trunk.

"Besides," Clay added, "you weren't entirely wrong."

The top of the trunk slammed down on her. Maisey fell forward and her upper body careened toward the bags.

He hit her again with the trunk, driving it into her shoulders and back, and Maisey screamed. She tried to kick back at him, but he grabbed her legs and shoved her fully into the trunk. Before she could jump out, he was plunging a syringe toward her. He drove it into the side of her neck.

"Got this from a med student. Nothing too strong, don't worry. Just a little something to knock you out for a bit."

She scraped her nails over his face. She'd been aiming for his eyes. She'd missed.

"Fucking hell!" He surged back. "You are such a pain in the ass, Maisey. I'm going to make you pay for that."

He slammed the trunk.

And Maisey's eyes sagged closed.

***

Odin's phone was ringing. He had a detective waiting to talk to him, but he automatically glanced down at the screen. When he saw the caller, he realized that he'd almost forgotten...

"Excuse me, would you?" He turned away from the detective. Took the call. "Ali, hey, look, I don't need the intel any longer. We got the perps."

"Are you kidding me?" Ali demanded. "I was up all night long looking for your info. All night. I need beauty sleep, and I didn't get any."

He winced. "Yes, well, I'll make it up to you. But right now, I have a cop waiting so—"

"He didn't have his own boat, but he did have a membership. That's why you didn't find it the first time around. You didn't look at boating club memberships. *I* looked because I am awesome like that. FYI, the membership is under his dad's name, which made it trickier."

"Clay isn't the killer."

"It's a membership in one of those boating groups," she continued, as if he hadn't spoken. "You know, you pay a flat fee to get *in* the club, then a monthly bit for dues, and bam, you get access to all the boats in the fleet."

"Okay. Good to know, but I've got to go—"

"I pulled up all the dates he took out boats. Thought you might be interested to know that the day Jenny Lynch disappeared, he took a boat out that night. Coincidence, sure, but thought that was something to note."

The detective called Odin's name. "I have to go," he told Ali. "Thanks for your help." He shoved the phone into his pocket.

The detective motioned toward him. "We need you to sign your statement."

He didn't move. "You figure out how Steve and Heather got past the security system at War's place?" Because War had a top-of-the-line system installed both at the bar and at the PI office.

"Heather told us her boyfriend is some kind of tech whiz. He disengaged the setup, the same way he disengaged all the security cameras at the college."

Odin advanced. Picked up the statement. Scanned it. Then he slashed his name across the paper. A sudden, hard intensity was riding him.

Maisey.

"What about the break-ins at Maisey's house?" Odin asked, keeping his voice casual. "Did Heather cop to those, too?"

"No, actually." The detective tilted her head as she considered the matter. Her dark eyes were thoughtful. "She denied that. Weird, because she seemed more than happy to talk about everything else. She's angling for a deal, but we're not exactly in the mood to bargain with a murderer."

Why wouldn't Heather admit to the break-ins?

The detective took the signed statement. "Thanks. We'll be in touch if we need more."

Jinx came up and clapped a hand on Odin's shoulder. "And that, my friend, is a done deal. Case closed."

"It doesn't feel closed." Something was off.

"Uh, sure it does. The bad guys are in jail. One is confessing to pretty much everything under the sun. That means—done."

Not to everything. "Heather didn't confess to the break-ins at Maisey's place."

"Well, give her time." Jinx didn't seem concerned. "I'm sure she'll get around to it."

Odin broke from him and hurried for the door.

Jinx scrambled to follow him. "Where is the fire, O?" Jinx wanted to know as soon as they stepped outside.

Odin yanked out his phone again. Rain pelted down on him. The fact that Clay Prescott had a membership in a boating club didn't change the situation—Heather and Steve had been the perps who attacked Whitney. And maybe it *was* just coincidence that Clay had taken a boat out on the same night Jenny Lynch disappeared.

He dialed Maisey. Her phone rang and rang. "She's not answering."

"Maisey?" Jinx side-eyed him even as he flipped up his collar. "Uh, probably because she's asleep. She went home to crash, remember? Dude. You need to take a breath. I get that we had some big drama, but all is well. Your lady is fine, so calm down."

He didn't feel calm. Not at all. His instincts were screaming at him. "Clay didn't call the cops."

"What are you talking about?"

The rain was coming down harder.

"When we left last night, we told him to call the cops. He didn't. Somebody reported gunshots. That's how the cops knew to come to Trouble for Hire." Maisey wasn't answering. Fuck it. He made a different call. This time, it was to Ali.

She answered on the second ring. "I think I just stopped talking to you. There is no way you are missing me already."

"I want to know where the hell Maisey is. Ping her phone or do whatever the hell you need to do." They were still monitoring her phone. He hadn't ordered that to halt.

"I *can* ping it, as long as it's on. I can hit the different towers and give you a location, but...why?" In the background, he heard the sound of her fingers tapping a keyboard. "I thought you told me that you had the bad guys."

"I need to know where she is," he said from between clenched teeth. "She should be at her house, resting. Make sure that's where she is."

"Stalker," Jinx muttered. "Just when I thought you were getting better—"

"Uh, she's not at home." A faint note of alarm entered Ali's voice. "You sure that's where she's supposed to be?"

He nearly shattered the phone. "Where is she?"

More tapping on the keyboard. "So, this is gonna sound crazy, but remember when I told you that Clay had membership in the boating club? I just pinged her phone, and it's coming up about one mile away from that place."

Odin took off for his Jeep at a run.

"Odin!" Jinx shouted after him.

CHAPTER TWENTY

The car had stopped. Maisey was aware of throbbing pain in her back and shoulders, and she felt sluggish as hell. She'd opened her eyes just moments before. Been aware that she was moving. *They* were moving. She didn't know where Clay was taking her, but Maisey knew she was in trouble.

She'd shoved her hand into the big bags around her. Found the laptop. Now she gripped it as tightly as she could. Maisey figured she'd have one good shot at this. One chance to catch him off guard.

She heard the slam of a car door. Footsteps. He was coming around the car. She lowered her head. Closed her eyes. Turned so that she was partially hiding the laptop with her body, but she didn't let it go.

There was a screech as the trunk popped open. "No one is around," he told her roughly. "So don't waste time screaming."

She didn't make a sound.

Thunder rumbled.

"Maisey?" His voice was louder. Closer. As if he'd leaned into the trunk. Then she felt his hand curl around her hip as he gave her a hard shake. "Hey, wake up!"

I'm awake, you bastard. Her eyes flew open just as she lunged up with her laptop. She slammed it into his head as hard as she could. He swore and stumbled back. Maisey leapt out of that trunk. Hurtled forward and ran as fast as she could.

It wasn't fast. She didn't get far. Her legs seemed to immediately collapse under her. Whatever drug he'd given her was still in Maisey's system. She shoved upright. Staggered. Rain was pummeling down on her. "Help!" she cried. "Help!"

But he was right. No one was around. They were in an empty parking lot. She could hear the splash of water. She spun, frantic, and realized—

Marina. We're in a marina's parking lot.

There *had* to be someone out there!

Lightning flashed overhead. A huge bolt that lit the scene.

Wait, was that a store up ahead? Some kind of office? Maisey stumbled toward it.

"Maisey, you disappoint me." Clay lunged into her path. Blocked the office or whatever the hell it had been. Rain pounded against him.

The rain. That was why no one else was out. The weather was too bad. Everyone was inside, and she was alone out there with him. Wind whipped against her.

"I didn't expect you to attack me. That's something that jerk boyfriend of yours would do."

Was he serious? She backed up a step. Almost fell again. Her whole body felt so uncoordinated.

The rain wasn't making that coordination any better. "You kidnapped me!"

A shrug. "You got in the way." He advanced.

She scurried back. Almost slipped on a puddle.

"I don't really know how you even found out what I did. That murder board of yours was quite something."

There was a dock about ten feet away. Maybe someone was over there. In one of the boats tied close by. Desperate, Maisey darted for the dock.

He followed her. Shadowing her movements as the torrents of rain pelted down even harder.

"I didn't kill Whitney, though. You should know that. Never touched her." He was on the dock with her.

And, no, dammit, she didn't see anyone who could help her. The boats all appeared empty as they shoved up and down against the rough waves.

"But I did kill that lying slut Hannah. She cheated on me with my best friend. Can you believe that? So I took her out into the mountains—there are miles and miles of mountains near my old home in Tennessee—and I made sure she didn't come back." He laughed. "Didn't even have to hide her body. I let the animals take care of her."

She needed a weapon.

"I got the hell on with my life after that. Went to college. Got my Ph.D. Met Jenny Lynch. I liked Jenny, at first. We hooked up a few times, but can you believe *she* was seeing someone else on the side, too? I mean, what the fuck? Does anyone understand commitment these days?"

"You killed her." She was backing up as he advanced, and she was starting to run out of room on the dock. The water pounded on either side of them, and the bobbing boats sent waves splashing into the air.

"I did. Killed her, then took out a boat and dumped her. Figure the fish ate her. We've got some damn big sharks out here in the Gulf. I cut her before I put her in the water. You know, chumming her up some."

She was going to be sick.

"I'll have to cut you, too, so that they will come for you. But don't worry. You won't feel a thing. I'll make sure you're dead before you go in the water." He paused. "I heard on the news that Heather was saying Whitney was alive when she went in the water. Amateur mistake. You want to kill someone, then you kill them. You don't leave shit to chance."

She was at the end of the dock. There was nowhere to go but into the water. And, normally, she was a great swimmer, but Maisey was having a hard enough time standing upright. Her body swayed as the heavy blasts of rain fell down on her.

Clay held out his hand to her. "End of the line." He wiggled his fingers. "It won't be painful, I promise."

She was supposed to believe him?

"I had actually even thought about letting you live. But you interrupted me at the wrong time. Saw something you shouldn't have."

My laptop.

"I knew I had to get rid of the last bit of evidence from my break-in at your place. Especially since the cops were planning to come over with their crime scene teams and see if Heather left anything else at my house. So I just shoved the remaining murder board crap in my bags. I put basketballs on top of the evidence. That's what I did the other night, too, when Odin caught me leaving."

She swiped at the rain on her face. "What are you talking about?" But she knew. *I just need more time.*

"When your boyfriend was poking around in my trunk the other night, he just didn't look hard enough. If he'd jerked out a few of those basketballs from my bag, he would have found some of that murder board shit you'd had at your place. I stuffed the evidence in the bottom of the bag. I hauled it away and burned that shit." He laughed. "Oh, and by the way, nice try making me think you had a backup of the evidence on your computer at the college, but I looked, and you didn't have jack."

She saw movement behind his shoulders. Relief flooded through her. "Odin."

"Yes, Odin." His hand was still extended toward her. "He's a fool. He thought he was protecting you, but he failed. Now you're alone with me, and your big, bad, hulk of a boyfriend is nowhere to be found."

She shook her head.

"How long do you think he'll look for you?" Clay asked. Water streamed from his hair.

Dripped from his clothes. "I say he'll give you a month, then he'll give up. He'll move on. That's what people do, you see. They move the hell on. If you'd only done that, instead of digging and digging because of Whitney, then we wouldn't be in this—"

"I love you," Maisey said.

"What?" Clay's hand fisted. "You think—you think you can tell me that and I'll spare you? You think you can manipulate me? You think—"

"I think she wasn't talking to you, bastard," Odin snarled from his position right behind Clay. The pounding rain and the rough waves had hidden the sound of his approach.

Clay spun toward him. "What? How—"

"Because I'm a fucking PI. That's how."

Maisey fell to her knees. Nausea blasted through her. She was so damn weak.

"No." Clay shook his head. "*No!*" He launched at Odin. Flew at him in a fury of wild rage. His fists slammed into Odin. And Odin didn't so much as flinch.

"Odin," Maisey whispered.

He locked one hand around Clay's throat. Drove the other into his face. Broke Clay's nose with a sickening crunch. "Told you before, it's harder when you're not the one who is bigger and stronger."

Clay kicked him. Odin didn't let go. He punched Clay again. Again. Clay's head snapped back from the blows.

The rain hammered them.

Clay's hands fumbled. He seemed to be reaching for something.

Another syringe? If he stabbed Odin with whatever he'd given to Maisey, Odin would be helpless. "Odin, don't let him inject you!" Maisey cried. She surged to her feet.

Odin grabbed Clay's wrist. Yanked something from him. Threw it into the churning water.

"Stay back, Maisey," Odin yelled.

Maisey froze.

Clay and Odin were facing off. Their fists were clenched. Their bodies tight with fury.

"I warned you," Odin said, his voice echoing like the thunder. "I told you that I would make *you* vanish. You never should have touched her." He bent low. Pulled something from his boot.

"Odin?" she whispered.

"*You* shouldn't have touched her!" Clay screamed back. "You should never have been in the picture! I had plans for Maisey. She was going to be mine! She wasn't like the others. She would have been true—"

"No." Maisey's voice. Cutting through the storm.

Clay wrenched his head to look back at her.

"I would have never been with you." Was that why he'd moved next door? Because she'd been his next target?

"You would have," he shouted back. "Or you would be *dead*." Then he focused back on Odin. "Your fault. You are in the way. *Your damn fault!*" He ran at Odin. Uncontrolled. Frantic. He didn't even stop to look. He just launched forward—

And ran straight into the knife that Odin held.

Maisey shuddered.

"Guess this will help to—what did you call it?—chum you up, bastard," Odin twisted the knife. Yanked it up. When he pulled it out, Clay took one step back. His hands flew up to touch his chest as he half-turned toward Maisey.

Blood covered his hands. He looked at her. "Maisey?" He stretched out a hand toward her. Then he stumbled. Slipped on the wet dock. And fell. Before he hit the water, his head cracked into the bow of a bobbing boat.

Lightning streaked across the sky.

Odin rushed toward her. Scooped her into his arms. "Baby, baby, are you hurt?"

She looped an arm around his neck. "I have never, ever..." Her teeth were chattering. She was soaking wet. Her body kept shuddering. "*Ever* been so glad to see someone."

He squeezed her in a grip so tight that she couldn't breathe. "And I have never, ever been so scared in my entire life." He buried his face in her wet hair. "*Maisey.*"

"Cops are right behind me!" A loud shout pierced the rain. Jinx's voice. "Where the hell is Clay? Point me at that bastard and I will—*holy fuck.*"

Maisey pushed against Odin's chest. She lifted her head so she could see Jinx—he was gaping at something in the water. She didn't want to look, but she knew what he was probably seeing.

Clay's body.

"He shouldn't have taken Maisey," Odin said simply.

Jinx shook his head. "No, and that's a mistake he'll never make again."

***

"I don't need an ambulance." Maisey glared at Odin. "I need *you*."

"You're going to the hospital. You're getting checked out." And he was going to have a talk with the cops.

I killed him. If he had to do it all over again, Odin would change nothing.

She grabbed his hand before he could jump from the ambulance. "How did you know?"

Know that Maisey was in danger? Know that he was close to losing her?

"Pieces didn't add up. Heather wouldn't cop to the break-ins at your place. And Clay never called the cops after that mess that went down at his place last night." Too many jagged pieces that hadn't lined up.

"You saved my life."

He pressed a hard kiss to her lips. "You *are* my life." Then he pulled back. "You're safe now. He won't ever hurt you again."

She sucked in a breath. Her gaze darted to the ambulance's open rear doors. To the detective and the uniformed cops who waited. "Odin was defending himself. Saving me. Clay didn't give him a choice. Clay attacked. Odin did *nothing wrong*."

He'd killed a man. He'd known—as soon as he stepped foot on that dock—that he wouldn't be letting Clay escape. Clay had been a dead man walking.

"I can back that up," Jinx declared, voice ringing out. "I saw the whole thing."

No, he hadn't, but that wouldn't stop Jinx.

"I need to give someone my statement," Jinx added. "Tell you the whole sordid tale. Who wants to talk to me first?"

Odin glanced down at Maisey. She was safe. He brought her hand to his mouth. Kissed her knuckles. *I didn't lose her.*

Because for a moment there, when he'd been on that freaking, rocking dock, and Clay had been between him and Maisey, all Odin had been able to hear in his head had been Ramsey's damn voice.

Why do you get to be happy?

If anything had happened to Maisey, Odin knew he never would have been happy again. "I wouldn't have stopped after a month," he rasped.

Maisey stared up at him.

"Not one month. Not two. Not six. If I lost you, I would never stop looking." *Never.*

She smiled at him. Her dimples winked. "I would never stop looking for you, either."

He swallowed down the lump in his throat. "You're gonna need to marry me." *So I can stay sane.*

"I thought you'd never ask..."

"Never?" Jinx's shocked voice. "I'm pretty sure he told me that you guys met just a few days ago. Days, people."

Odin looked into Maisey's eyes. "When you fit someone..." He deliberately used her words from before. "You just do." Maisey fit him. She made him feel like he finally belonged somewhere. Not too big. Not hulking. Not awkward or out of place.

He belonged, with her.

Her smile stretched a little more.

He hoped that their kids would have her smile.

EPILOGUE

"So..." War sauntered into the office at Trouble for Hire. He had one hand shoved into his pocket. "What did I miss?"

Odin glanced up at him. "I'm engaged."

War laughed. "Bullshit."

Odin didn't laugh.

War's grin faded. "Are you for real?"

Jinx appeared behind him. "I know. I'm still in shock, too. Our little boy has grown up."

They were both assholes, but also damn good friends.

"It's the client, isn't it?" War cocked his head. "The one you told me about on the phone? I get that you tracked down the killers—good job, bro—but you seriously managed to get her to want to *marry* you?"

"I can be charming." Odin frowned at him. "You're the one who told me that."

"Yeah, but I was just lying to help your self-esteem!" War appeared dumbfounded. "I have to know everything. Let's go downstairs and get a drink because this is a story that I have *got* to hear."

War was such a gossip. The man always loved the nitty-gritty details. Odin began to rise, but his phone rang. It was the happy ring tone that he'd assigned to Maisey. He swiped his finger over the screen and put the phone to his ear. "Hey, baby," he said by way of greeting.

"*Baby?*" War repeated, voice strangled.

"War's back in town," Odin continued after he flipped off his friend. "Want to come meet him? Because I swear, he is dying to meet you—" He broke off because Maisey was suddenly speaking quickly. No, frantically. "Maisey. Slow down."

The two men who'd been ribbing him suddenly advanced toward his desk.

"Say it again, Maisey," Odin urged her. "Slowly. Baby, I know you're upset, take a breath."

She did. And she explained again. *Holy hell.* "I'm on my way. I will meet you at the hospital."

Maisey hung up before he could say more.

"What is it?" Jinx appeared to be nearly jumping over the desk. "Is Maisey hurt?"

Odin shook his head. "It's not her." He fired off a quick text. A text that he never thought he'd send.

A text to Ramsey. *Meet me at Angel of Grace Hospital.*

"What is happening?" War demanded.

Odin looked up. "Whitney Augustine has been found."

"Maisey's friend?" Jinx pounced on that. "The one Heather and Steve killed? They found her body?"

"Not exactly." He finished his text to Ramsey. *Whitney is alive.*

***

Ramsey shoved two security guards out of his way. "I want to see her! *Now!*" Ramsey bellowed.

Maisey ran into the hallway. She still couldn't believe what was happening. It was a miracle. Whitney was back. *Alive.*

A third security guard was running at Ramsey, and Ramsey was pulling back his fist to punch the guy.

"Stop!" Maisey yelled.

Ramsey froze. The guard scrambled to retreat as he called for more backup.

Maisey rushed toward Ramsey before the scene could deteriorate even more.

He grabbed her shoulders. "Is it her? Is it really Whitney?"

"Yes." There was so much to say. So much she still didn't understand. "She was pulled from the water by some fishermen. They were based out of Louisiana, not here, and that's where they took her."

A deep furrow tunneled between his eyes. "Why didn't they take her to the cops?"

"They did, in Louisiana. But she didn't know who she was. Her prints weren't in any system."

"Didn't know who she was—what the hell?"

"When Heather was describing the attack on Whitney, she told me they hit her on the head. The docs are examining her now, and Whitney said she was examined before. There are signs of severe trauma. The swelling has gone down substantially, and she started to remember who she was..."

He broke away from her. She knew he'd just caught sight of Whitney in the exam room behind her.

"No! Wait!" Maisey called.

He wasn't waiting.

Footsteps rushed toward her. When she saw Odin, relief filled her. He pulled her into his arms, and she drew in a steadying breath. She always felt safe when Odin was close. "Ramsey beat you here." She'd asked Odin to contact him, but Maisey wished Ramsey had just held on so she could tell him exactly what was happening. "I didn't get to explain everything." She pulled away, but made sure to hold Odin's hand as she tugged him toward the hospital room. "Most of her memory is back, and the doctors say that is a great sign, but she doesn't remember everything." Actually, what Whitney didn't remember...

Was the last six months of her life before the attack.

Maisey and Odin hurried into the hospital room.

"You can't be here," the nurse was telling Ramsey. "The patient needs rest, and unless you are family—"

"I am her fucking family," he snapped as he leaned over the bed. His fingers were shaking as he reached for Whitney. "Sweetheart?"

Her head turned toward him. Her green eyes were full of confusion.

"I missed you," he breathed.

She blinked. "I'm sorry." Her head tilted. "Do I know you?"

He jerked back as if he'd been stabbed.

"She doesn't remember," Maisey rushed to say. "That's what I was trying to explain. Whitney has no memory of the six months before her attack."

His head turned. He stared at Maisey. "Those were my months."

She knew that. She could feel his pain.

Whitney fisted the sheets. "I don't...am I supposed to know you?"

He looked at her again. The torment on his face was clear to see. After a long moment, he pushed away from the bed. "No. No, I'm no one that you should know." Then he turned and walked out of the hospital room.

***

Odin followed Ramsey to the parking garage. "What the hell are you doing?"

"For the first time in my life, the right thing."

Odin grabbed his arm. Spun him around. "The woman you love is in a hospital bed. You're leaving her. Maybe I'm just slow today, but I don't quite get how that is the *right* thing."

"She was too good for me." His voice was savage. "She should never have crossed my path. Now, she doesn't know that she did. She can be safe. My world won't touch her."

"You have a chance here. You can be happy."

Ramsey stared back at him.

"You asked me once why I got to be happy. You want the answer?"

"I want you to take your hand off me—"

"Because I'm willing to fight for my happiness. I will fight, I will steal, I will kill. I will do anything to make sure that I get to have Maisey at the end of the day. You want to be happy? Then stop being a coward. Do whatever the hell you need to do in order to protect the woman in that hospital bed." He shoved Ramsey away. "You just got a miracle. Those don't happen often." With that, he marched away.

Jinx waited until Odin was in the elevator, then he let out a long, low whistle as he stepped away from the stone column in the parking garage. "Someone just put you in your place."

Ramsey's hands fisted. "I am not in the mood for your shit right now."

Jinx took his time sidling from the shadows. War had already gone upstairs—he was no doubt in a rush to meet Maisey and find out what in the hell was going on. Jinx, though, he had a pretty good idea what was happening... "Your lady love is back from the dead."

"I told you to stay away from me. Warned you not to come close—"

Jinx threw an arm around Ramsey's shoulder. "But you're my brother, Ram." No humor filled his voice. Not this time. Because he wasn't kidding. He was dead serious. "And you need me right now."

The reason he'd been in Ramsey's the night Odin had found him? He'd been paying a visit to his older brother. The brother no one knew about.

"I'm doing the right thing," Ramsey rumbled.

Jinx shook his head. "After the life you've led, why the hell would you want to start doing what's *right* at this point? Makes no sense to me."

Ramsey's brows flew up.

"Don't worry. I've got your back." This time, he did. "I'll hang around town. I'll help you out."

"I don't want your help," Ramsey snarled.

"Of course, you do. Everyone wants my help. Haven't you heard? I'm freaking amazing."

"Jinx..."

"One day, you'll thank me for what's going to happen next."

"I doubt that."

Jinx smiled. "How about you just wait and see...?"

***

"She's alive." Maisey stared out at the blue waves of water. "I've got Whitney back." It was a miracle that still had her head spinning.

Odin's hands wrapped around her waist. He pulled her up against the strong warmth of his body.

"She's scared and she's lost," Maisey continued, "but she's back."

"And you're going to help her." His breath blew lightly over her ear.

Maisey could feel a tear sliding over her cheek. But—it was a happy tear. She still couldn't believe it. "I am going to help her." Maisey turned in his arms. Stared into Odin's beautiful eyes. "We're going to help her." Because she wasn't alone any longer. She had Odin. They were a team.

She searched his eyes. "Thank you for taking my case."

He smiled at her. She *loved* his smiles. So rare and so beautiful. "Maisey…" He said her name as if it were a caress. "Thank you for changing my whole damn life."

He bent his head and kissed her.

THE END

NOTE FROM THE AUTHOR

Thank you for reading DON'T PLAY WITH ODIN!

I love the strong, tough heroes...especially those who fall so very hard. Ever since he made his first appearance in NO ESCAPE FROM WAR, I was itching to give Odin a happy ending. Now, of course, there are a few other guys that are teasing me with stories, too (guys who just appeared in Odin's tale...).

If you'd like to stay updated on my releases and sales, please join my newsletter list.

https://cynthiaeden.com/newsletter/

Again, thank you for reading DON'T PLAY WITH ODIN.

Best,
Cynthia Eden
cynthiaeden.com

ABOUT THE AUTHOR

Cynthia Eden is a *New York Times*, *USA Today*, *Digital Book World*, and *IndieReader* best-seller.

Cynthia writes sexy tales of contemporary romance, romantic suspense, and paranormal romance. Since she began writing full-time in 2005, Cynthia has written over one hundred novels and novellas.

Cynthia lives along the Alabama Gulf Coast. She loves romance novels, horror movies, and chocolate.

For More Information

- *cynthiaeden.com*
- *facebook.com/cynthiaedenfanpage*

HER OTHER WORKS

Death and Moonlight Mystery

- Step Into My Web (Book 1)
- Save Me From The Dark (Book 2)

Wilde Ways

- Protecting Piper (Book 1)
- Guarding Gwen (Book 2)
- Before Ben (Book 3)
- The Heart You Break (Book 4)
- Fighting For Her (Book 5)
- Ghost Of A Chance (Book 6)
- Crossing The Line (Book 7)
- Counting On Cole (Book 8)
- Chase After Me (Book 9)
- Say I Do (Book 10)

Dark Sins

- Don't Trust A Killer (Book 1)
- Don't Love A Liar (Book 2)

Lazarus Rising

- Never Let Go (Book One)
- Keep Me Close (Book Two)
- Stay With Me (Book Three)
- Run To Me (Book Four)

- Lie Close To Me (Book Five)
- Hold On Tight (Book Six)
- Lazarus Rising Volume One (Books 1 to 3)
- Lazarus Rising Volume Two (Books 4 to 6)

Dark Obsession Series

- Watch Me (Book 1)
- Want Me (Book 2)
- Need Me (Book 3)
- Beware Of Me (Book 4)
- Only For Me (Books 1 to 4)

Mine Series

- Mine To Take (Book 1)
- Mine To Keep (Book 2)
- Mine To Hold (Book 3)
- Mine To Crave (Book 4)
- Mine To Have (Book 5)
- Mine To Protect (Book 6)
- Mine Box Set Volume 1 (Books 1-3)
- Mine Box Set Volume 2 (Books 4-6)

Bad Things

- The Devil In Disguise (Book 1)
- On The Prowl (Book 2)
- Undead Or Alive (Book 3)
- Broken Angel (Book 4)
- Heart Of Stone (Book 5)
- Tempted By Fate (Book 6)
- Wicked And Wild (Book 7)
- Saint Or Sinner (Book 8)
- Bad Things Volume One (Books 1 to 3)

- Bad Things Volume Two (Books 4 to 6)
- Bad Things Deluxe Box Set (Books 1 to 6)

Bite Series

- Forbidden Bite (Bite Book 1)
- Mating Bite (Bite Book 2)

Blood and Moonlight Series

- Bite The Dust (Book 1)
- Better Off Undead (Book 2)
- Bitter Blood (Book 3)
- Blood and Moonlight (The Complete Series)

Purgatory Series

- The Wolf Within (Book 1)
- Marked By The Vampire (Book 2)
- Charming The Beast (Book 3)
- Deal with the Devil (Book 4)
- The Beasts Inside (Books 1 to 4)

Bound Series

- Bound By Blood (Book 1)
- Bound In Darkness (Book 2)
- Bound In Sin (Book 3)
- Bound By The Night (Book 4)
- Bound in Death (Book 5)
- Forever Bound (Books 1 to 4)

Stand-Alone Romantic Suspense

- Never Gonna Happen
- One Hot Holiday
- Secret Admirer

- First Taste of Darkness
- Sinful Secrets
- Until Death
- Christmas With A Spy